OBLIVION AND OTHER STORIES

OBLIVION
AND OTHER
STORIES

GOPINATH
MOHANTY

Translated from the Odia by

SUDESHNA MOHANTY
SUDHANSU MOHANTY

EBURY
PRESS

An imprint of Penguin Random House

EBURY PRESS

USA | Canada | UK | Ireland | Australia
New Zealand | India | South Africa | China

Ebury Press is part of the Penguin Random House group of companies
whose addresses can be found at global.penguinrandomhouse.com

Published by Penguin Random House India Pvt. Ltd
4th Floor, Capital Tower 1, MG Road,
Gurugram 122 002, Haryana, India

Penguin
Random House
India

First published in Ebury Press by Penguin Random House India in 2023

10 9 8 7 6 5 4 3 2 1

This is a work of fiction. Names, characters, places and incidents are either the
product of the author's imagination or are used fictitiously, and any resemblance
to any actual person, living or dead, events or locales is entirely coincidental.

ISBN 9780143458265

Typeset in Bembo Std by Manipal Technologies Limited, Manipal
Printed at Thomson Press India Ltd, New Delhi

www.penguin.co.in

To the memory of our loving mothers,
Shakuntala Mohanty (Sudeshna's)
and
Premalata Mohanty (Sudhansu's)

A Note on the Usage of 'Orissa' and 'Oriya'

The state of Orissa was renamed Odisha in 2011 by an Act of Parliament. This was considered to be in sync with the authentic pronunciation of the name as spoken in Oriya. Consequently, Oriya, as a cognate derivative and endonym, became Odia in English spelling, again in sync with the way it is pronounced by Oriya people in their mother tongue.

The stories in this book were originally written in Oriya between 1935–36 and 1988. The state was then known as Orissa, which was also spelt so, and the language was spelt as Oriya. As fidelity to this usage when the stories were envisioned and written, we have retained 'Orissa' and 'Oriya'.

Contents

The Way It Happened—This Book   xi

Translators' Note   xix

1. Oblivion   1
2. Dã   15
3. Endless   25
4. Cricket   33
5. The Babu   43
6. Licence   65
7. A Good Samaritan   81
8. The Crow, the Cuckoo   93
9. The Upper Crust   113
10. Paper Boat   121
11. Crows   147
12. Lustre   159
13. Town Bus   171

14. The Heir   179

15. Festival Day   195

16. Just around This Bend   205

17. Despair   213

18. Rebirth   223

19. Chakrapani   235

20. The Foreigner   265

Acknowledgements   275

The Way It Happened—This Book

We did not wish to tread the oft-beaten path—the Preface–Introduction–Stories–Acknowledgement continuum. We wanted to talk turkey and say a few things that couldn't have been said otherwise. An account of how this anthology came together, how one of us took the first baby steps and asked the other to validate, how, through the haze of doubt, it gathered steam, how we came together and, instead of attempting to translate 8–10 stories, decided to put together this anthology of twenty stories. In lieu of a preface, this is our aperitif, our individual stories, before you get to the entrée. Our translation knots, trajectories, fumbles, confessions, frank avowals and averments are here. First Sudhansu, then Sudeshna.

I hadn't read Gopinath Mohanty in Odia before Sudeshna sought my help to translate the stories. I had read two of his novels (*Paraja* and *The Survivor*) and about 8–10 of his stories, but all in English.

A personal note. In school, I studied Odia only for a few years. I wasn't comfortable, even though this is my *matrubhasha*. It was a struggle. In college, the *pitrubhasha* took hold. Over the past half century, I've barely explored Odia writings. I acceded to Sudeshna's request as a tribute to her courage to translate, something I wouldn't have dared, on nudging or under duress. She had done even fewer years of Odia than I had. Even so, we became co-translators, both with a nodding kinship with the source language. She had an advantage: she was armed with an Odia–English dictionary; I had none!

My insignificant translation experience in the 1990s was different: both the stories and the translators were from the same century, largely living in the same space and time. Millennials, the Internet, and the digital age weren't around—the taste for reading was still confined to books held in hand.

Then the world changed. Doubts lurked: Will Gen Z travel back to an unrecognizable past, where tradition was potentate, where changes were God's calling and where mobile devices didn't work? But when we tasted the old tea leaves, they tasted just like the freshly picked ones! Denizens in modern avatars carried stereotypes from the past. The 'Krishna! Krishna! Krishna!' chants had only morphed into '*Jagannathanka jaha barada thiba!*'—It's all Jagannath's Design! Plus ça change had worked its magic.

I waded warily. I'm sceptical about what people in Odisha claim. Most everything is exaggerated. Even a simple matter such as the number of stories Gopinath wrote. Some Odia literary honchos say 'upwards of 200', some others 'more than 300'. A researcher counted 136 stories. We settled closer to the researcher's figure, rounding it out (generously) to 150.

Though contemporaries and simpatico, Sudeshna and I have forked tastes. She's modern, smarter. I'm the 'shy' village yokel. But I die to be me. I find it more meaningful to plough the soil, to furrow deep with my ploughshare and feel the earth, to look up at nimbus clouds and the sky to distil out matters, and to not be swayed by word-of-mouth messaging, social media posts and YouTube hyperboles.

Chugging along, I found the quality of stories uneven; the lack of publishing barriers showed. A famous Odia adage—*Brahma billibileile beda*—signals that the personages' mumbles are God's, their words bespoke Vedic verses! Odisha had no editors helming publishing houses, only printers, like today's digital printers. Lack of editing—revising, refining, rewriting for the readers—loomed. Most first drafts—analogous to Freud's instinctual id—were the last drafts! Critiquing a literary work in Odisha was tantamount to criticizing, not just the work but also the author, risking severance of friendships and social contacts.

The enlightened Odia literati who spearheaded the movement to save the Odia language at the turn of the twentieth century and for a few more decades, battling passionately for the soul of Odia language and culture on the pages of *Utkal Sahitya* and *Mukura* magazines, had evanesced. 'The idea of literature as a marker and agent of the progress of a community which animated the Odia intelligentsia . . . gradually lost its grip over the consciousness of literary critics and the reading public alike,' laments a friend.

As I triaged the stories, another thought bubbled up. Odisha in the mid-twentieth century was a confining world, limiting cross-pollination or cross-fertilization of ideas. Many writers stuck to the formulaic theme of yore. But it had positive spin-offs. As with Mohanty's stories, the dominant motifs of which are the osmosis of rural–urban society. In spare prose, 'Dã' (1935–36), Gopinath's first story, captures a reality—the exploitation of a poor woman by a rich zamindar family in a strident patriarchal setting—that was all too familiar.

Poverty in Odisha ain't pretty, and I daresay the realities of the two boys in 'Paper Boat' still ring true. It's a well-crafted, macabre story. My only regret is that the closure is off-kilter. 'The Crow, the Cuckoo'—emblematic of the DNA of the rich and the poor—brims with potential, but the end gives me pause. How I long for a Chekhovian touch! We whittled parts of many stories, going through one . . . two . . . six . . . seven or more iterations to dissolve the bulge.

Despite its ponderousness, 'Chakrapani' intrepidly captures village life, its seeming immutability, tone-deaf to the outer world, where the comfort of the bubble—despite ceaseless sufferings, diseases, poverty—holds, ensuring no edicts are overridden by future determinations. The wistful pining for life's bounties in Chakrapani's bedimmed moments—'the tall coconut trees, the beautiful face of his loving wife on the wedding night'; even signposting his dismay that Netai Ma's bohu didn't turn up to seek his advice—speaks to man's primordial urges, regardless of age. 'The mind being drawn to the red lips of a woman and those of Lord Krishna cannot be accused of either practising virtue or committing sin,' says Surendra Mohanty, gifted Odia writer and Gopinath's contemporary. 'It is present as much in a libertine as in a saint.'

The stories came together. Saloni Mital, our editor at Penguin Random House India, took them forward, shepherding it at every turn and tweaking them further wherever necessary. We are so grateful to her.

Now over to Sudeshna, to unravel her knots and thoughts.

Sudhansu Mohanty

~

I was a just-retired English teacher with ample time on my hands, looking to hone my translation skills. I had very little Odia, so taking on short stories, I reasoned, would be a good beginning. I chose Gopinath Mohanty, as his persona as a novelist overshadowed his considerably large output of short fiction. A daunting prospect, but the more I toyed with it, the more I fancied it. I was born in Cuttack and had spent my growing-up years there. Even if I didn't read Odia too well, I had an ear for the nuances of my mother tongue, and my cultural compass was tuned to Odisha.

I gingerly got started. And as I progressed, I looked around for validation. That was when I knocked on Sudhansu's door. A family friend, Sudhansu had published several books, including two translated from Odia into English. Sudhansu agreed to check out my work.

One . . . two . . . three . . . and a few more stories . . . translated. Then, one day, I asked Sudhansu if he would care to join me. He generously agreed to this, too. And we became co-translators! Sudhansu is a writer who, to use his own words, 'feels translation shrinks creative spaces and puts lids on them'. Even so, this 'reluctant translator' is the wind behind the sails of this book.

We plunged wholeheartedly into this project even as the world outside was ravaged by Covid. We read almost all of Gopinath Mohanty's short stories, taking care to pick only those that hadn't been translated into English yet. We discussed, we argued, we snipped, we pared. We moved the stories back and forth several times, as we tried to capture the lyricism of Mohanty's Odia and the nuances of his raw, colloquial expressions in a language that would give it a wide readership. The stories became crisper, smoother as we played around with contemporary words, taking care to retain the vernacular flavour. And we exulted as the draft slowly and steadily grew organically from ten to fifteen and finally to twenty stories.

Gopinath Mohanty's short fiction reaches back to the 1930s, spinning tales around everyday lives and ordinary people with whom he shared deep empathy. The milieu may have changed, but the spectrum of unadulterated, earthy human emotions—naive, gritty, undisguised, poignant—portrayed in the stories is timeless.

The prose presented its challenges. Take 'Oblivion', for instance. The story of Sibaram Salura is set against the backdrop of ancient mountains and forests that are 'bathed' in rain. The bath draws attention to the intimate relationship between the mountains and the forests. In parts of Odisha, dousing the bride and groom in water was a part of the wedding ritual. We have called it a 'nuptial bath'.

Onomatopoeia is a regular feature in Gopinath's prose. It abounds in 'Oblivion'. '*Saien hei lorry chutithae*' reads 'the lorry whizzes past as it gathers speed', to recreate the dizzy speed of the lorry. Or consider the story 'Endless', with the *chaein-bhaein-kaein* that Banu, the little boy, strums with a twisted bamboo stick. 'Endless' also records a child's range of emotions on his father's failure to arrive home laden with gifts: chagrin, disappointment and consolation; but it ends on a positive note. 'When Bapa comes home, he'll surely bring new clothes, won't he?'

And 'The Upper Crust'. While poverty pushes women to the oldest profession, starvation could take it afar; it could prompt an old woman to badger her nubile granddaughter to sell herself—to 'earn' and 'feed' the family. This one-off might have defiled the girl's body, not her soul. The next morning, when she catches a rich man's son ogling while she bathed and 'scrubbed' her defilement away, her impudence in spurning the voyeuristic gaze of the rich man's son is bottled in varying thoughts. Gathering her clothes about her, 'she looks up defiantly . . . walks away into the damp hovel—insolent, nonchalant, bristling and unyielding. The rich man's son drops his head to his chest.' The story dignifies poverty, even if it's a case of human dignity lost and restored.

My mother, Shakuntala Mohanty, was the motivating force behind me when I cut my teeth as a translator. Nudging ninety, she delighted in reading both the Odia text and the English translation, and could critique the usage of words. 'Oblivion' is the last story I did with her a little before I lost her. It is to honour her memory that I chose 'Oblivion' as the title story, and Sudhansu readily concurred.

How inscrutable life is! Sudhansu, too, lost his mother while we were working on this book. To Covid. His mother, Premalata Mohanty, smiled indulgently as her youngest child, sitting by her, worked on the stories, lost in what she referred to as his *tapasya*. So this effort, in a way, bookends the passing of our mothers. Odd, even ironic, that the title story 'Oblivion' (from a literal translation) memorializes both our mothers. They would be beaming their blessings at us! It's a poultice for our souls.

It is to the loving memory of our mothers that we dedicate *Oblivion and Other Stories*.

Sudeshna Mohanty

Translators' Note

This is an anthology of twenty short stories by Gopinath Mohanty (1914–91), the doyen of twentieth-century Oriya (now Odia) literature. Many of his novels have been translated into English and published by reputed publishers in India and abroad. But only about twenty of his 150 published stories, like 'Ants', 'The Somersault', 'The Shelter' and 'The Solution', to name a few, have been translated—some multiple times—into English and other European languages. There still isn't a single definitive anthology of his short stories available from any mainstream publisher in India or abroad.

The stories here, written across a half century (from the mid-1930s to the mid-1980s), are a sample of his oeuvre and the variety of his themes. They capture the forgotten others— the tribals, the poor, the dispossessed and the disenfranchised— invisibilized in the feudal landscape of Oriya society of the twentieth century. The banality of ordinary people living on the margins is etched in granular detail and situated in varying settings. The embellished past is not one of nostalgia but a full-toned, layered portrait of the society Mohanty lived in and was intimately acquainted with. Marginalization is the running thread in the stories, manifesting in varying forms—

dispossession, disenfranchisement, social exclusion through class and caste exclusivity, lack of educational avenues and overarching poverty. Together they construct an architecture of a society that resonates with other coeval societies in vast stretches of India. As the storylines pulse around to catch a glimpse of the past, they are enhanced by subtle undertones laden with elegiac, lyrical prose, infused with patois and colloquialism. The collection will help readers recreate the social life of mid-twentieth-century India curated from the everyday life of Oriya society.

'Oblivion' (1941), the title story of this collection, is about the innocence of a young man—the Noble Savage— in the back-of-beyond tribal district of Koraput in Orissa. The oblivion that sets in at the end lends the story its equilibrium. 'Dã' (1935–36), Mohanty's first short story, brings into sharp relief how women, especially the poor, were treated as chattels by feudal zamindars. 'Endless' (1951), a touching story of a child whose disappointment borders on the poignant, is laced with pure innocence, yet the theme of poverty is crushing. 'The Babu' (1951), again, is a subaltern's take—on the moral depravity lurking beneath the Teflon coat of an Indian Babu's dissolute and sham politeness.

'Licence' (1963) works at multiple levels: as a psychoanalytical story, where the past looms into the present seeking personal avengement; as a depiction of the naivety of rural folks in a setting where a man could be killed with impunity; also, as a story about the dominance of policemen over the oppressed tribals. Ditto with 'A Good Samaritan' (1956), which speaks to human psychology—a married man's inner cravings for frivolities and trifles thwarted by a compassionate Samaritan—where the hapless woman holds her own. 'The Crow, the Cuckoo' (1951) portrays the disparity between the rich and the poor, and the ecosystem that binds them. The story speaks of entrenched attitudes. The *cuckoo's deep* attachment to the *crow* articulates the zeitgeist of the time—when, regardless of the treatment meted out by the *crow class*, the *cuckoo* keeps singing the crow's praise. It is a striking contrast to the rich man's son's attitude in 'The Upper Crust' (1967). Here, the storyteller finds his voice and cadence; his words are spliced together in two disparate cultures—the one that merely *exists*, the other that thrives and *lives*—both cohabitating, cheek by jowl.

'Paper Boat' (1941) is a macabre story. In spite of its gruesomely realistic rendering, the story's morbidity is again caused by the desperation of the struggling class, which is shown through its dialectics, its never-say-die spirit, and its depiction of the wretched and the poor.

'Festival Day' (1985) conveys how surreal hopes and illusions are dashed on the harsh bedrock of existential reality roiling in unrelieved poverty. Yet the idealism is poignant, haunting. In 'Just Around This Bend' (1967), the couple's thoughts beneath the surface of reality stir, but the timbre of surface reality in the rickshaw puller's mind doesn't match this. 'The Foreigner' (1963) depicts another group of citizens marginalized during the Indo–China war of 1962: Chinese–Indian nationals—thanks to the xenophobic behaviour of people and society.

In 'Chakrapani' (1956), the vintage Orissa village scenario of the 1940s returns, which is vigorously traditional—immutable, tone-deaf to the outer world of living and being—and admits no change in a poverty-laden villagescape. The story is a masterly metaphor of mental stasis railing against the invasion of ideas deemed external. 'Cricket' (1982), a one-day match, speaks of an alternative universe of happiness wrapped in religious beliefs, untainted by contemporary chic and rage. The social picture is real, as is life—change, age, mutability—and in these discontinuities and gulfs, human life blooms and fades. '*Town Bus*' (1988) is a story of a humdrum couple, but beneath the veil of normality lurks the unspoken craving for the polygynous human traits in the husband's everyday dallies.

As we selected stories, we sometimes battled over which ones to choose. There were two—'Lustre' (1971) and 'Rebirth' (1951)—where our perceptions particularly differed. They were difficult stories to interpret and even more challenging to translate. After much back-and-forth, we decided to retain both: 'Lustre' for the sheer elaboration of imagery and 'Rebirth' for the philosophical content.

~

Translating Gopinath Mohanty's works is a challenge. His prose is blithely colloquial, lyrical and dramatic, and as the Jnanpith Award citation says, 'In Mohanty's hands, the social is lifted to the level of the metaphysical.' But experiencing the process of translation is an altogether different matter. In most sentences, every word, and occasionally even the last word of a sentence, is merged together with the words before and after it, subsuming and radiating meaning that cannot be effectively rendered by a similar word or two in the target language. The hued images, too, are often rich and multidimensional, even concentric; the descriptions are granular and at times prolix; and a single sentence can be continually invested, even impregnated, with layers upon layers of visual and linguistic overtones. Throw in the verve, the ring of the Nativity, and pluck the prevalent Oriya or patois of the milieu described, and the translator is often sucked into an unfathomable pit of being and nothingness, and is left gobsmacked. Add the emotional weight of moping about at times, and megawatt smiley words and dimming wattage at others, and what you get is a smorgasbord of translation knots.

No aspect of life and society seems to escape Mohanty's eye: neither the bare-knuckle politics as luminous in 'Crows' nor the nuanced social disquiet engendered in 'Chakrapani', nor even the tribal innocence and ordinariness of living in 'Oblivion'. There is nothing remotely avant-garde in the tone of these stories, but there are certain predominant themes: the overlaying positivity and the seeking of social justice, a subtle plea for equality, abiding faith in the innate goodness of man and a sense of fairness in normal day-to-day living—especially on the issue of suppression of women. The plebeian, the distressed and the oppressed are all pulled together as ideas to form the core and texture of his stories; they indeed form the warp and woof of his writings.

A word about the tenses in Mohanty's stories. They float in and out, these *tenses*. In many a single paragraph, often the past and present tenses, with their variant participles, merge smoothly and break away, too, just as smoothly. In some, we have hemmed or patted the tenses down to conflate and meld them into one linear tense; yet in others, we have consciously let the *tenses* weave a web of their own.

We would be remiss if we glossed over the lack of copy-editing of the stories in Oriya. Ideas and thoughts drift in and out at times. Though Mohanty was a very meticulous writer with a keen mind and a gimlet eye for micro details and veracity, the lack of editorialization in the original stories is palpable. The prevalent culture of apotheosis in Orissa, which continues even today in its new rubric, Odisha, wouldn't have helped either, given the lack of critiquing to enrich the content. In Mohanty's work, this lack of editing, critiquing or peer reviewing sometimes seems to show. An editor like Maxwell Perkins or Robert Gottlieb would no doubt have done wonders for his work.

Another issue is his prodigious output, which is truly remarkable. But a niggling question creeps in: Did he write prolifically, or did he *overwrite,* meaning, did he write more than he should have for the sake of the quality of his writing? Did the choice of quantity over quality make a difference? Many stories are not quite evenly poised (we dropped them); they overwhelm, weaken and detract. In places, they are slight and abbreviated where some elaboration would have helped; in some others, they are breathless where tightening the narration would have made them crisper, tauter and elegant. The lyrical element, at times, is logorrheic and overwrought. Yet, at the other end, they are sometimes slim and bony, as if bonsaied—the narrative switches, here and there, are rapid and too breakneck for a smooth, seamless transition.

Oriya (Odia) literary criticism still continues to be eulogistic and panegyric—though much of the adulation heaped on Mohanty is immensely well deserved—and a kind of outsized collage of hagiographic outbursts. Also, given the way things were—still are—apotheosized in hidebound feudal Orissa, an inquest into the fetishized bubble of Oriya literature, or any other writing in Oriya, is likely to evoke scepticism. A careful review of such writings exposes many of the hypotheses hewn from the head.

Taking into account Mohanty's language's robust nativity and the colloquialisms he used, we have deviated from the normal translation process. There is no English equivalent to many of the words and expressions used, let alone equivalence in conveying the moods created. As in the case of 'Hauen', we have attempted to match an English approximate to contextualize the thoughts expressed, in the use of 'buck naked', but *they seem to fall flat on the riverbed!* It sounds prosaic, and far from conveying the heady expanse of the river described in the story *'Licence'*. We have, instead— wherever we felt the need for the tone and voice to lilt and ululate—resorted to retaining many of the Oriya originals. So, don't be railroaded by such terms as *Ki lo! Ma lo! Hai lo! Haiho! Chinta, sathi puja, baidi, Saantay, chameli, kadamba, sahada, Bhagabata, deepa, Bou, Jeje, pitha, bohu, Hee! Hee! Hee! Chhua Babu,* etc. Expressions like 'Hau' have a ring of sonority to them, or so we felt, and so we have tried to retain the lilt and resonance of such expressions. They are cognate words in any case, and do not in any way hinder smooth reading and understanding of the meaning and the ideas expressed.

The lyrical, the elegiac, the metaphysical, the social, the political and even the banal lives of ordinary village dwellers are abridged here, too, in this compressed form of storytelling that limits his free-flowing rich expression of thoughts, language and imagery. This collage of short stories he has written across a half century reveals in the reader's mind both the psycho-socio-literary treatment of the critical mass exemplified in the scripting of these stories as well as the way they reflect society as it then existed. Not to forget the quixotic upper-class expressions, like the use of the plural 'us' for 'I' as in 'Chakrapani'—a formulation that may sound bizarre today but which, then, was framed to subsume the hallmarks of seniority, reverence, omnipresence and societal poundage.

For the sake of the relevance of the stories here, perhaps the *Guardian*'s observation is apt: 'Gopinath Mohanty belongs to a generation of Indian writers to whom social commitment is second nature.' Or, as Amitav Ghosh writes in *The Great Derangement*, Gopinath Mohanty is one of those writers 'from whose work neither the aggregate nor the non-human have ever been absent.'

Oblivion

The vast expanse of New Orissa! Roads across the eastern ghat mountains, where signage proclaims 'Orissa Starts Here'. The heart swells with pride. The road stretches ahead, beyond fifty *kos,* ninety-five kilometres to Pattangi, Koraput, Jeypore, Nabarangpur and Jagadalpur.

A huge road, a red road, winding up and down, and over the mountains—four thousand feet, three thousand feet, one thousand feet—it meanders and stretches over into the far beyond.

On the edge of the road, the ubiquitous *Bhima langala* creeper snakes and coils interminably, and drills down to the nether world. From the towering heights of the road, the spurs and ledges of the ancient mountain range are visible, like a set of aged teeth now bared—tremulous, wobbly and shaky. Below, like the waves of the sea, clusters of undulating mountains—some bald, some covered with vegetation. And up above, high on the horizon, the clouds slowly drift by like the poet's many messengers of love.

Sibaram Salura's eyes are fixed on the road ahead as he sits beside the driver of a goods carrier. He is travelling to Vijayanagaram to report to his new job in the railways. It's a good job that pays a salary every month. He whistles occasionally, sometimes blows out rings of smoke from his cigarette and runs his hand through his hair. He looks ahead and reminisces.

He isn't married yet. Negotiations are almost finalized for his marriage to Patnaik's wife's younger sister.

He is a strong young man. Whenever he chances to look at the rear-view mirror of the vehicle, his heart swells with pride. The driver, *heh*! Such a bony, puny man—what strength would he have in his bones?

Just the previous year he had aced the school-leaving certificate examination—without really breaking a sweat.

Chandara, Ramia, Narasingh Rao slogged hard but failed. So, he outran them; he is not wanting in joy, he has not a care in the world and has all the time for enjoyment.

This red road! Many a time he has walked beside this road on his way to school from Jagannath Sagar—soaked to the skin in the rain. Did a little rain daunt him? No way! What did daunt him, though, was the fear of catching malaria.

He has enjoyed life to the hilt. Hordes of girls from the *Paraja* and *Dombo* tribes—their breasts stacked high as mountains, big roses tucked into the hair that's twisted into a crooked bun, their lips bursting with full-throated giggles.

'Hey, girl! Where have you been?'

'*Coolie ku,* earning my daily bread.'

'I had been to your part of the village.'

'We have come over here—to see you.' The voice is inviting, teasing, tantalizing. 'Come!'

Oh, those Paraja girls of Chindari village and of old Koraput! *The Bawdy Street!*

On this road, each day a different rendezvous. The road brings back so many memories! Memories of days, evenings, nights!

The vehicle huffs and puffs as it winds its way up the mountains. This Pattangi is always shrouded in clouds—constantly battered by storms and rain. The pieces of tarpaulin tied on either side of the bus flap in the wind. He's chilled to the bone as the slanting sheets of rain lash and ricochet relentlessly like so many arrows. Rivulets of muddy water eddy around all over the place. The cacophony of the sloshing rain seems to startle even the ancient mountains.

The poor cleaner, dripping wet, lights a *pikka,* a native cigar, and sits huddled in a corner. The driver is single-mindedly focused on the road.

A group of tribal girls passes by. The *topara,* a hat of leaves, on their heads and the *barsati,* a rain protection gear made of leaves woven together, tilted towards the rain. The pounding rain does not bother them. They giggle as if the raindrops are delectable, sensuous quivers—erotically tickling them. The cackling girls quickly turn their gazes upon the vehicle.

Sibaram remembers the chorus sung during the festival of Chaitra. He turns the tune around in his head and hums softly. He begins to babble the ditty and sways to the tune.

Je he mora priyatama, sara satatala bhedi sara
Pahada uhadaru tu aa
Mora hrudayara bhabara dheu upare
Surya udaya belara suneli dheu khelu
Kede sundara tora dui akhi, kete chanchala tora gati
O aphita tora lachhi

Tu aa, tu aa!

'*Come my love, from behind the mountains and pierce me with your arrows,*

Go only after blossoms have bloomed in the tender core of my being.

Let the golden rays of the rising sun dance on the surging waves of the sea of love swelling in my heart!

How beautiful your eyes, how agile your steps, how enticing your still-fastened girdle!

Come hither, come hither, come hither!'

The lorry heaves and ploughs ahead, rumbling as it lumbers along the path. Over the innumerable twists and turns of the rutted mountain terrain, amid the driving rain and the howling wind. Sibaram leans forward, taking in this celestial, nuptial bath of the forests and the hills. Sometimes he looks down the cliff, into the smothering ravines and slopes, where in blotches the deep jungle is set on fire for *podu*, slash-and-burn, cultivation, and the smouldering flames emit transient, intermittent sighs.

Today is 24 June.

Last evening, after the lamps were lit, the moon had risen over the mountains. A sparkling sliver of a moon. A narrow arch. A bright ornament nestled among the dark plaited mountains.

Done with her chores as a coolie, Bhutra Jani's daughter, Olka, had plucked a red rose from the garden of the administrative officer of the court and tucked it into her hair. The *pakhia*, a cloak made of dried leaves woven together, was draped across the shoulders. It hung across her back like the long wings of a bird, and she swayed as she walked. He had met her—much as he had met her every single day for the last seven days—by the bridge, on the slope that led to Ranigadh.

Last evening, after the lamps were lit, Olka had offered herself to him—like a votive offering to the gods. 'It's cold,' she had whistled in a cheerful warble, 'just like a night in the month of Chaitra!'

And then, that night in the club, friends had teased him about the matrimonial alliance that had been offered to him. As they discussed the Patnaik household, there drifted before his eyes the slender form of a slip of a girl. A heart-shaped face, a pair of twinkling eyes. He had heard that she sang well. Sibaram's mind wandered away from the club and wafted into the cloudy, moonlit night looking for a strain of that song.

His friend Jagadish was singing the lines of a Telugu song in a heavy baritone.

And then again in the morning. His sister, Chandra, had come to him smiling, 'Bhai, shall I fetch you some coffee?' Chandra was just like a tendril of the *nirmuli* creeper. Her feet, nimble and quick, never seemed to touch the ground—she was always levitating. Sibaram had playfully pinched her nose and tweaked it. Her eyes were filled with joy even as she squealed through her nose. The even set of teeth, like seeds on a corn cob, dazzled brightly.

Sibaram had hurriedly doused himself in warm water, carefully combed his amla-oiled hair and gone to the house of Hardhona Babu—a clerk in the public works department. Mina, his daughter, was playing the harmonium, Jhotu, her brother, was kicking a football aimlessly around. Sibaram had stepped into Mina's room. Beside her was a plate of fried *kunduri*, ivy gourd, only half-eaten. Sibaram had eaten some himself and had stuffed some into Mina's mouth, forcing her to stop singing. Drawing Mina into his arms, he had planted an oily kiss on her lips.

Mina was like his domesticated pet, like a small flower in his garden, to pluck whenever he pleased.

Everything was beautiful in this exquisite world. Contemplating this bounty filled him with warmth—a warmth that a thousand breezes could not chill, nor water sprayed from a thousand rains extinguish.

Sibaram continues to reminisce. He sings one of Gulzar's numbers on the Chaitra festival.

Hey Beauty, tame sthira aau sundar
Pahadara asumari gachha tumari sundarima pulakiuthe
Harina harinaku singhare khunchamare
Mayura kala pathara upare dena melai natua amba gachha tale
*   nachhe*
Tumara nisa mahula phasara pangu madatu aahuri tana
Amara pahada jholara hathiku bandhi paruthiba
Sathi sapara otarathu aahuri tara jor
Sei jhinkara aara dhanga basare sui dhangi o tui dhangda
(O Beauty, you are still and beautiful,
The innumerable trees in the mountains blossom to
    heighten your charm
The deer nudge each other with their antlers,
The peacock spreads out its tail under the dancing mango tree
Your intoxication is headier than the wine of 'mahula' flowers
It ensnares and tugs like an inebriated elephant
Like the intoxication that enraptures a dhangda and a
    dhangdi in the dhangda settlement.)

The lorry whizzes ahead as it gathers speed. Heavy winds and thundering rain. The red, knobby road cuts its way through the dense forests.

He remembers the vermillion in the parting of her hair. A girlfriend in some distant land. A half-forgotten memory now. She lives with her husband in Rasalkunda. She hasn't forgotten him, though. There was a letter in the morning mail. So much love and affection drip from those crooked, unformed letters. She had written with a lot of care, perhaps sitting very close to her schoolmaster husband. Maybe back to back. Why else should there be scribbled in English at the end of the letter in the same unformed hand, 'Do you still dream of ghosts?' What would the poor schoolmaster- husband have made of it? He would have probably pulled his wife close to him, hugged her lovingly and said, 'How childish you are!' But Sibaram grasped the dream that she was referring to.

Wouldn't her ears have turned red when she wrote those words? Perhaps!

The lorry continues its journey, regardless—jerkily veering to the right and then to the left as it trundles up the knobby, rocky mountain path. On the right, the sharp-hewed face of the mountain rises like a steep wall. On the left in the nether lands, the innumerable mountaintops—some bald-faced, some covered with forests. The grey haze exhaled by the cascading waters envelops everything.

Amid the rainstorm, a lone tribal, a Kondh, clad in a loincloth, tills the lower mountain slopes with a spade. The smoke from the flaming fire of podu cultivation swirls up, like the smoke from an incense stick—mocking the gods in heaven. *Here, come take your mountains and your forests! But I shall not be deterred, I shall not baulk; I shall gather my handful of rice, here. The same handful of rice that you have deprived me of! In these*

*my arms I have the strength—the firepower of thunderbolts. This, my
axe, and this, my fist, and both of which will give me what I want!*

This is how man battles the rules. Destiny mocks man, but
man, too, doesn't baulk from challenging destiny whenever
he can!

In the land of the tigers, step-farming of paddy. Sibaram
surveys the landscape and everywhere he sees the victory of
man over Nature. From above, the gods hurl down thunder,
lightning, rain and storm. He whams diseases and tigers, forests
and hunger, and people crawl like endless lines of ants. Some
lean under a shelter and ride out the trying times. In spite
of everything, man has survived, hasn't he? Mountains have
been blasted to carve out roads. Rocks have been pulverized
to make acres for rice fields. The indomitable spirit of man has
survived.

And then he has his own story to chew on—the story of
his youth, his strength, his happiness. He has got everything
he had wanted—in ample measure. He has opened his heart
and gathered the flowers. If he were to die today, how many
people would mourn him?

*In the abundance of youth, a young man sometimes thinks of
death—mindlessly.*

The lorry covers precipice upon precipice, as Sibaram
soliloquizes. As if he were watching a film. A beautiful film
filled only with laughter, love, affection and the routine rites
of romance—love, a little flirting, a small sulk, a little banter,
the barbed badinage. How the tendrils of love ensnare him!
Which tendril holds him the tightest!

He has received pleasure in plenitude. His is not the
hunger of craving. His is a ledger of happiness only—to record
the loads of pleasure he has received!

The wind has let up slightly. Sibaram crouches, a touch distracted. His mind is blank, his consciousness suffused with images of experiences he has so amply enjoyed.

The Paraja girl with the rose tucked into her hair, the harmonium-playing Mina, his girlfriend far away, and his future wife, the one who sings so mellifluously.

His friend, Narasingh Rao, his sister Chandra, his parents, his pet peacock, his dog, his study room.

The moonlit night, the morning.

The narrow, red jungle road. The pond in Jagannath Sagar.

The temple. The temple bells of the evening.

Everything so meticulously arranged into neat, disparate compartments, so many of them—in the end one melodious experience—the eyes close, the mind filled with happiness.

Memories!

Suddenly Sibaram is shaken out of his reverie. As if the whole world is spinning around his ears. No time to make sense of what is happening.

One moment, he is cocooned in warm, fuzzy daydreams, and the next, he is wide awake, his body racked with pain, tears streaking down his cheeks, his eyes piteous, full of agony, the eyeballs fraught with terror.

Teardrops mingle with his blood. The shadow of death flits across his eyes.

And then something primal—*oblivion!* Beyond and over to a world yonder!

There was a slight furore. Close to Sunki, a lorry had lurched and careened and vaulted down the precipice.

But this news did not create any hubbub in Koraput—nor in Jeypore or Pattangi.

'So many trucks overturn like this! What's the big deal?'

Only a few government officials had gathered there.

Sajet Sahib had hollered, 'The driver too is finished!' His harangue that followed was hollow. 'Else I would've taught the blighter the lesson of his lifetime! I would've booked a case against him under sections 336 and 226.'

The dead Sibaram was lying on the hard rock, his face buried in his arm. As though he were worn out—wearied to death! On the rocks across, a few black-headed geckos, native to the eastern ghats, nodded their heads. It had stopped raining. Some tribal men apprehensively looked on from the distance, ignoring Sajet Sahib's diatribe against the dead driver.

'Three people died.' The small talk had lasted only two minutes. That was all. Life rolled on, as usual.

The world didn't pause.

The news did not reach the village of Chindar, the Paraja girls' village. So many new babus came and left. Those with the ability reached out and grabbed. Those without—didn't. Who cared?

The moon again rose in Chindar village. The guest house was never vacant. Another very senior babu arrived, and with him a woman doctor. One came from the east, the other from the west; they met here and enjoyed each other's company on many a moonlit night. They tried to resuscitate their half-forgotten youth.

In the club, Narasingh Rao sat in grief for an hour. The discussion about Sibaram's death that day had brought some buzz into the club. It had provided the people with a topic—to discuss, to make small talk, to fill in time, and unmoor popular tattle. Offering condolences for the death of someone who is not your own fills people with a fuzzy sense of witnessing events—of a vague, vicarious happiness at not being *that* one. Deep within, the heart resonates, nudging credulity: 'Praise be, I'm alive! Still alive! It's not me; I'm still alive!'

There then rose the zeitgeist of the club—merriment. Someone said, 'Take up the tabla, Narasingh Rao, let's squelch the enveloping blues and lighten the mood.' And then some singing ensued to cocoon the rapturous evening.

It rained a little that evening when Olka was returning from the house of the contractor, Samuel Babu, after collecting her wages. She took shelter in the open veranda of Narsinghachari. The shadows of dusk were gathering around her. Not long after, Tikra Paraja swaggered past, with the unmistakable lurch in his step brought on by a swig of *dhipamada,* the popular country liquor. Olka smiled as Tikra pulled over unbidden, pivoted and swayed towards her singing a tribal song from the *dhangda,* the tribal young men's hut.

Sariaagaru kati kudu sundigaru handa
Alure toki kete resi dinda
Kayeta mana manuli
Kayeta mana sabuli
Come hither, dear girl,
let's test your youth!
The beads around your neck and
the hoops in your lower ears are so you!

Mina was playing the harmonium in the evening. Hardhona Babu came home with the news and called out to his wife. '*Ogo*, dear one, did you hear?'

Mina inched closer to the door and eavesdropped. No sooner had she heard the news than her friends Sakhi and Bejji dropped by. They excitedly greeted each other and sat down to a fun session of laughter and gossip. So much juicy, syrupy gossip to trade and exchange! About this, that and the other—and also a bit about themselves!

A few days later, the girlfriend who lived far away heard the heartrending news as well. She had barely settled down to silently mourn him for a while, when her husband barged in. 'Why are you sitting so still?' he asked, his voice on edge. 'I have three new boys to tutor today. Come, give me something to eat. Quick, I have to leave. And yes, tell me what clothes I have to buy from the market.'

The five deep sighs that escaped her were the only *tarpana* she could offer as an oblation to the departed soul of a relationship that had lasted for half her lifetime.

The news reached the house of his prospective in-laws. The prospective father-in-law, the venerable Sri Chandrabhanu Patnaik, stroked his beard and pronounced like an extremely prescient man, 'Did you hear, Manasi Bou? I had serious doubts from the day I looked at his palm. That unusual sign on one of the high mounts. Early death from a fire accident was indicated. If death from a lorry turning turtle isn't death by fire, what is? A vehicle runs on fire, doesn't it?'

'Yes, whatever God wills . . .' Manasi Bou said. 'You write to Narayana today. Let's try to finalize the alliance with Suryanarayana. Even if he demands a hefty dowry!'

Manasi was in the adjoining room, applying lac dye to her feet, and straining her ears to overhear her parents' conversation. Her heart filled with happiness when she heard this new person mentioned. So, her parents had given up on the cheaper groom. Good!

Sibaram left this world. His name was lost. Nothing unusual in this vast world where so many people are born and where so many people die.

Sibaram died, the moon didn't get any less lustrous, the flowers didn't wilt faster to droop and die, the purling of the jungle stream didn't stop, the full-throated giggles of the Paraja girls didn't come to an end.

The world with its joys and sorrows went on as it always did. Sibaram's place too did not remain vacant.

Only, his father aged—seemingly by twenty years.

And his Bou, a veritable mother Vasundhara, who stoically endures everything, yearns for him—forever. She thinks of him every living moment, day and night—weeping incessantly. And each time she puts a morsel of rice into her mouth, it is laced with warm, salty tears.

Originally titled 'Bismruti', 1941

Dã

*Dã is Gopinath Mohanty's first short story, written in the early
1930s when he was an undergraduate at Ravenshaw College,
Cuttack. It was published in the college's* East Hostel *magazine.
Dã is a sensitive portrayal of the character of a* poili, *a concubine.
In feudal, hidebound Orissa of the early twentieth century, taking
a poili was a common practice among rich, high-caste zamindars.
As heinous as the practice was, it seemed to carry no social stigma
or moral taint. Poilis were abased to chattels in a male-dominated
society; women had no voice in such polygynous practices. The story
raises this nuanced societal issue: how dare Dã, a poili, talk about
Mali, a legitimate member of the family? And how ironic it is that
the roles are reversed: the age-old, haunting tale of Dã—also called
Domi—and Sadei morphs into the frisson of youth in Mali and
Sautia! Mali is Sadei's granddaughter, his widowed daughter-in-
law, MaliBou's daughter, and Sautia is a waif.*

Early dawn.
The dull thud-thud of the pounding of beaten rice in
the fishermen's colony. Dã, the old woman, wakes up with

15

a start. Through the cracks in the walls of her wattle-and-daub house, she sees the darkness slowly dissipating. She looks around the tiny house.

No one around—the empty void! The stillness of early dawn!

Two score years ago, Domi had first stepped into this house. She didn't wake up alone on this bedraggled mat then; her hair hadn't turned grey, her breasts hadn't shrivelled, the eyes hadn't sunk deep, deep enough to hold fistfuls of rice in their creases; she looked desirable, she had fire in her groin and a spring in her step. It felt divine.

On the other side of the door, the scrawny dog thumps its tail on the floor.

'Early in the morning! Out! Out! Out!' the woman shoos the dog away.

Yes, this wizened old woman was a young girl then, the younger daughter of Bholi Behera. Brimming with youth, she would gather leaves in the orchard and groves. But then the chemistry with Sadei Mohanty had caught up, and she had wilfully drifted to this hearth. Sadei Mohanty too had strayed from the straight and narrow path. How long ago was that, how far back? *Aeons!*

That day, so many years ago! Gadei Mohanty had stood guard on the threshold of Bholi Behera's home long before daybreak, a stick in hand. The boy, Sadei, was being wayward—and staying away from home all night, many nights. Must he go astray because he didn't have a mother? Gadei had asked himself this question times without number. But Sadei was clever, canny. While Gadei stood guard outside the front door, Sadei had snuck out through the back.

In the morning, Domi had greeted Gadei with a sly smile and said '*Pranam, Chamukarane!* Greetings, Sir!' and the pandemonium that had ensued! She had the strength in her voice then, the strength in her loins. Gadei had returned home, but charged with the allegation of having skulked about Bholi Behera's garden at night to dig up and steal his colocasia.

Even then, Dã had drifted until she hitched herself to this soil: Sadei Mohanty's homestead, which she considered her own, too. Wasn't she, after all, Sadei's poili?

Ah! The sunken eyes blink at the memory of the romance of those days! The dry lips clasp tight around the two big, yellowed teeth, hiding them from sight as the lips break into a smile—as though it were the last flicker of life on the shadow of death.

'Early in the morning! Out! Out! Out!' She shoos the dog away once again.

Shaking its pointed ears and tucking its tail between its legs, the dog slinks away. What conspicuously remains, however, is the reek of a wet, flea-ridden mongrel.

Dã starts her daily chores. Grunting under the weight of her sixty years, she does the vessels and plasters the floor with a slurry of cow dung and water. She has performed this task every day, but today there is a sadness within her, as if her heart has turned to stone and she is grieving in silence over her memories—those distant memories that now seem a series of dry rendezvous and refuse to peel away.

She is unable to shake it off.

People gossip that Sadei had craftily whisked her away from her family so he would have someone to do the household chores and tend to his ministrations. Years have passed since then. But Dã refuses to accept this. Lies! All lies! If there was even an iota of truth in this, then her whole life is utterly meaningless, a hollow sham.

The room where Sadei Mohanty once slept is now a patch where kitchen greens grow. Dã stoops over it, waters it every day and weeds out the grass. Is she living a memory? Perhaps.

As she scrubs the vessels at the well, Dã thinks to herself: life has been so full of sorrow, her happiness all too brief. She has done loads of household chores, but instead of kind words and tender loving care, all she has received in return is unkind criticism, curses, abuses. In heaps! She has never dressed well. Nor dined well. Those two happy years in the distant past remain tucked away under the weight of the present. And then the hair started to grizzle and turn grey. Her health broke down, her breasts shrank and her eyes sank deeper into their sockets ready to pouch fistfuls of rice.

'Out! Out! Out!' Here, too, the scrawny dog is hungrily begging for a morsel of food.

Each day of the past unfolds itself before her like the pages of a dog-eared book, mouldy and mildewed.

'Hey, Domi! You look very happy today?'

'Who on earth called you Domi? They should've called you *Pemi* or *Premi* the beloved, instead!'

'Wait! Wait! Are you going to seize all the money? Look at this packet! See what I've got for you!'

Domi gazes at the three-pronged date-palm tree leaning towards the ghost-eaten coconut tree down the nether stretch of the yard and daydreams. Memories of her nubile youth tug at the heartstrings of her ancient mind. The utensils slip unbidden from her hands.

A gruff shout breaks the flow of her tender dreams.

'Hey, Dã, you blighted woman! Are you done with the pots and pans?' Dã quickly picks up the dishes, the ones that had slipped from her hands and the rest—a heap of them—and hurries through her chores.

It is Mali Bou, Sadei Mohanty's daughter-in-law, a widow.

As she walks back to the house with the pile of scoured pots and pans, Sana Bou, a close relative of the extended family, opens her front door. Her face is puffy from endless hours of sleep and she is lazily rubbing her eyes. Chewing a stale paan, she exclaims, '*Mala mo!* Oh dear! This is the face I had to see early in the morning!'

'Why? What's wrong with that?'

A commotion ensues. Her berating over, Sana Bou heads to the pond for her bath.

Dã wanders around looking for bits of firewood and some lentils. She has to get something from somewhere. How else will the children survive? Whatever the situation, she's a member of Sadei's family, be it as a wife or a poili—regardless of a Sadei dead or a Sadei alive.

Casting a furtive look at the pond, she tugs at Sana Bou's hedge, all the while saying aloud, 'Look at these accursed cows! The minute one goes for a bath they're at your hedge!'

'Out! Out! Out!' she cries, stacking up the twigs and wattle in front of Mali Bou's kitchen, then squeezes her hand through the gap in the carpenter's hedge and plucks out a green pumpkin.

Morning—day—afternoon. Day after day after day. The days and years are endless, as are her rites of daily chores. But the joy is dead.

Everyone retreats for their post-lunch siesta. Dã sits down to her meal of pakhala, a bowlful of watered rice.

'Hey, Mali Bou, the rice dissolves in the water, there's not a seed here!'

'You want a fine, dainty meal, do you? You've devoured everything, and the rice is unpalatable now, is it?'

The children join in, as if singing a chorus, 'She'll devour! She'll devour everything! Pound her! Pound her!'

'Oh, dear! Oh, dear! What gall! What did you say?'

Hot words are exchanged. Dã gulps down one mouthful of rice and barks out a retort—one retort following each gulp, and on and on it goes. Soon, she has drained the pakhala to its dregs.

Mid-afternoon. Silence everywhere. Dã does the dishes again, as always.

And then suddenly! What's this?

Dã tiptoes forward. What's this that she sees in the wilderness thick with bush and shrub? Isn't that Sautia who lives in their neighbourhood? And who's that girl? Yes, the same striped, torn *gamuchha*, a coarse towel. Isn't it Mali, Mali Bou's daughter? Dã can't help staring, her mind drifting back to those delectable days of her own youth. Amidst the dense creepers and thorny shrubs, she watches, as Mali snuggles up to the pock-marked Sautia. And in Sautia's eyes the same look, so full of yearning—the same unmasked desire, the same naked longing, followed by the same frisson of attraction that she had seen in Sadei's eyes *that* day when she surrendered herself to him—years, and decades ago!

Outside the thicket, in the middle of the path, the leaky *lota*, a metal jug, rolls on—not a drop of water in it.

A few moments later, Mali walks up to the well and asks for water to wash her feet. 'Uff! My stomach hurts!'

'Why did you have to go so deep into the thicket?'

Mali twists her body ever so slightly, coyly indicating that she has to dive far, far and deep, away from the public gaze. She throws Dã a surreptitious sidelong glance, a hint of apprehension on her face—did Dã see her with Sautia?—and then walks away.

'Sana Bou, have you heard this?' In exchange for a bit of paan, Dã gossips about Mali and Sautia. The fervour of youthful passion, the intoxicating, stolen glances, and ironically the age-old story of Sadei and Domi retold now with Mali and Sautia . . . the same youthful awakening—of desire, longing, passion and boundless ecstasy.

Has age effaced her memory? Or is this the revolt of her own frustration? Or is this the manifestation of the secret jealousy that she nurses, the jealousy that the dead feel for the living? Dã doesn't know. Nor does she care to. The sharing and telling of the story are all that mattered to her today—a sort of transference of her vicarious gloating, to make up for the loss of her personal reverberant alchemy.

'Sana Bou, did you get it?' She wants to quickly get everything out there. And she does, without qualms, and without the slightest sliver of hesitation. The helpless striking back at the invulnerable!

On the other side of the eaves, lying on a tattered mattress and pretending to sleep, Gopalia, the tramp, eavesdrops.

The scrawny dog panting on the other side of the threshold, hears the story too.

In an hour, it is as if explosives have been ignited. Wails, abuses, curses, things flung about, thuds and bangs, blows and fisticuffs. Brooms, nails, hands and feet, everything that is within anyone's grasp is used to settle the issue—so surreal is it in its abrasion. How dare a mere poili raise a stink against the acts of a mogul or his progeny!

'Out! Out! Get out!' It wasn't the scrawny dog but Dã who was being shooed away.

They kicked her out with all her belongings—the broken box that she had carefully saved and a bundle of clothes.

Dã wept bitterly as she gathered up her sparse possessions one by one. Under the eaves lay a comb—its teeth broken. This she had brought with her from her parents' home. A shard of antique remembrance cocooned in the sanctuary of her mind.

Pitch dark. The sky is overcast. The trees, near and far, look like clotted clumps of darkness. The narrow embankment beside the river twists and wends its way to the neighbouring village.

Dã leans against her tattered box, hugging the bundle of clothes to her chest. The tears have left a salty taste in the mouth. The old bones are aching from the blows, the body is sore and burning with a high fever.

But her mind is aflame—red-hot and scorching—the humiliation that refuses to go away.

Waste—waste—waste!

This life has been a waste!

God? God is a curse, God is a block of stone, God is this blow, God is this rejection, God is this debasement, God is this pitch darkness.

All this dust!

Dã shudders as she gets up. This is her last plaint against creation and the Creator.

A step forward, and then another and still more.

Images from the past flash across her mind as she walks towards the river. The orchard, gathering leaves—the smiling Sadei, the ecstasy of youthful flesh that had once set her on fire, the banal daily chores, the missing rice seeds, the abuses and curses, Mali and Sautia entwined much as Dã and Sadei once were, decades ago, only the memories hold now—the good, the bad, the ugly and the sad, a whole cocktail of them. They tunnel into her head, they stay, hegemonizing her thoughts and refusing to go away, they shall always remain with her, always within her, in this life or any other . . .

In the two-pronged river a loud splash. Midstream everything disintegrates, melts.

The water of the river surges over the embankment and eats into the soil. It has done so in many places along its path.

Silence all around.

Only the scrawny dog sits on its haunches and beats its tail five times on the ground before emitting a heartrending howl.

'Woa . . . oa . . . oa . . . oa . . .!'

Originally titled 'Dã', 1935–36

Endless

The scorching heat and pouring rain don't deter the children from doing what they do best—play their outdoor games. Through their games, they carry on with their continuous chatter on pertinent issues facing humanity. They may seem insignificant to others since they are children, not adults. But are their views any less significant than those of adults? Their views and thoughts are just like the games they play in the open, amid the heat and dust and fury—innocent, honest, freewheeling, pert.

The mother would often wait for her son at home with eager anticipation. Where has the child disappeared to? '*Haiho*, Pitai, have you seen Banu anywhere?' she would ask him anxiously. Or, 'Yes, go—seek him out, my dear Nimai,' she would urge someone else. 'He'll be playing with Chanduri somewhere, while here the rice has gone bone-dry.'

Banu would then hurl himself into view and charge back home, stomping his feet in ecstasy and delight, using the twisted bamboo stick he carried in his hand as a percussion instrument and willing it to render several musical notes—

chaen-bhaien-kaien—from the walls around him, from the brass lota, water jug, sitting at the doorstep, and from the spotted, lazy dog lying under the eaves. There! Banu has arrived!

He would exult, 'Bou, we will grow into very eminent people!'

'Hear, hear! Just listen to what Banu is saying! All this when he is drenched in sweat and sapped dry from the heat! His body is scorched, his head throbbing.'

Banu would hop around the house like a sparrow for a while. His young head would droop momentarily as if weighed down with serious thoughts. And then he would shout out loud and say buoyantly, 'Bou, we will grow into very eminent people!'

Then he would clasp his mother's neck with both hands to swing around her frame and ask, 'Bou, when will my new clothes arrive?'

'Bapa will get it for Dussehra,' the mother would reply.

'So, how far away is Dussehra?'

His mother would often say that Banu loved to ask the same question over and over again.

His days and nights are lit up in anticipation of the blessed gift. He would see his new, bright, colourful clothes in everything—trees, paddy fields, evening games. He wasn't half as enamoured with the gift as he was with the statement he would make with his new clothes—the honour that it would confer on him. The honour of parading around with Chanduri with his chest puffed up in pride.

Bapa will come home for Puja. He saw his father only a few times every year, maybe just three–four times, but in his little worldview, his father was the embodiment of his dreams. His father worked in a far-off place and doubtless occupied a very high perch in the official hierarchy—because, in Banu's eyes, everything that belonged to him needed to be big, bright and honourable. Then, to top it all, his father wore such an impressive white uniform: a red sash girdled his waist, a second sash was strung over his shoulder, and a third was fastened across his chest like a broad, sacred thread. The thick, round brass epaulette attached to the sash completed his impressive appearance. But why didn't he take it out for public display when he was in the village? Because he isn't a show-off, like Jagu's brother!

Banu kept whispering in Chanduri's ears, 'This time I'll get nice, pretty gifts. And we'll no longer be friends with Jagu.'

Time passed, and Puja with all its accompanying festivity grew closer.

In a distant, faraway place, the poor *chaprasi* too had been looking forward to visiting his small home in a remote village. When he lay in his bed at the end of the day, after getting through his duty and daily chores and cooking himself a frugal pot of rice, he visualized his home—his wife who eagerly awaited his once-in-a-while letter written on a postcard and the five rupees he sent her every month-end. He also saw his little Banu, growing up fast on a diet of rice gruel like the creepers that grow in the wild.

Would the boss grant him leave?

The mesmerizing *sharada*, the autumnal air, wafts in the pleasant, tender whiff of Durga puja and instils an eagerness for more festivities. Here comes the Durga puja, followed by Kumara Punaei and Diwali. The festivals are like the soft, mellow dreams of the less fortunate, that light up their drab, humdrum existence. The Durga pandal will be erected in the next village. There will be an air of festivity with games of pirouetting sticks and swords, and a riot of excitement and happiness.

Puja is fast approaching. Jagu's brother has come home. Jagu has already flaunted all his gifts to his friends. His fan following has now swelled, and whenever he steps out, a gaggle of children invariably trail him. 'Hey, Jagu! Hey, Jagu! give me your mechanized dog,' someone says, 'let me handle it a wee bit and play with it!' Everyone follows him, everyone except Banu, who keeps up his chant, boasting that he too would receive his load of gifts.

'Bou, where are my new clothes?'

As the day progressed, the bearded postman turned up in the village to deliver a letter. Banu ran after him enthusiastically from the outskirts of the village, keeping up a continuous chatter, asking him one question after the other.

Silently, Bou reads the letter.

> The boss didn't let me go. I'll come later. I have bought
> all the gifts, but whom do I send them with? Later, if I get
> leave, I will bring them along with me. Do make all efforts
> to make Banu understand the situation.

'Bou, when will my clothes come? What else will Bapa bring for us?' Banu has an endless number of questions. His mother sighs deeply and sits down with a long face. '*Hau, hau,*' she merely says.

So, he will not come. Whatever little money he had sent home has already been given to the shopkeeper towards repayment of credit. There is nothing left to buy new clothes for the child.

There's a crumb of hope, though. If only Gadei Sahu will let her buy things on credit! Tomorrow, after all, is Puja.

Just as on all the other days, Banu gets up in the morning and sets out to play. Today is Puja. Festivity in so many houses! Just as on all the other days, he absentmindedly calls out cheerily, 'Chanduri, hey, Chanduri!'

It is getting warmer as the day progresses. Children in their brand-new clothes stream out of their houses. The entertainment music fills everyone's minds and hearts. Raghu Badapa, his father's elder brother, comments, 'You, Bana, must you continue wandering about like this layered in dust? Just see how immaculate the others are—'

Suddenly Banu becomes aware of himself. 'Oh yes. It's time for new clothes, another shirt!'

And there at home, his mother has taken out an old shirt that has been freshly washed and is waiting for her son to arrive. Her heart is sinking—what if the boy isn't appeased? She had been to Gadei Sahu in the morning, but he had insulted her and had turned her away.

'Do you think this is a pond that you can dip into and take away whatever you fancy, whenever you fancy? Get lost! Today's Puja and I'm short of clothes for my regular customers, and on top of that . . .'

A loud buzz of romp and stomp is heard, and here comes the raucous Banu.

In one leap he's on his mother's shoulders demanding, 'Bou, give me my new clothes!' All that his mother can offer him is the freshly washed old shirt. 'Here, take this. Your father didn't like the shirt he had bought for you and has returned it. He'll exchange it for another and send a nice shirt for you.'

All hell breaks loose! Banu's anger, his stomps and kicks, his raves and rants, in an almighty tantrum. His mother is trying to console him as he ratchets up his outrage. 'Hau, hau, that's fine. Let others wear theirs, but ours, when it arrives, will be a lot better!' His dreams are shattered. The mind doesn't find any solace in the possibility of patched-up dreams being realized in some distant future. For this is no small fury; it hurts all the more because it is searing; it is as though someone has wrenched out the generosity of his mind and cast it away. In his young mind, the ecstasy of Puja has flipped, his honour has been shattered and he can't pull himself together: how will he be able to face the world now? All his mother's words are of no avail. He rolls on the floor, wailing.

Chemi Bou, Banu's *Badama*, aunt, is on her way to fetch water from the well. She turns around to ask, 'Can't you console the child with some soothing words?'

'You've seen everything for yourself, Apa!' Bana Bou moans haplessly.

Chemi Bou hurriedly gets him a length of fabric which is used to clothe the gods. 'Here, take this; your new clothes,' she says. This to Banu seems a travesty; he contemptuously kicks the cloth aside and maliciously rips the already torn end of Chemi Bou's sari to shreds. His mother grimaces and steals away.

Banu lay down to sleep on an empty stomach, disconcerted, bristling and morose. He doesn't go to the Puja pandal either.

A little while later, his mother returns to find Banu asleep on the floor. The reed mat has been tossed aside; the greasy pillow lies in a crumpled heap under the cobwebs in the loft. His mother notices that Banu's eyelashes still glisten with tears.

Like a thief slipping away into the night, his mother creeps away. Outside, at the Puja pandal, a loud effervescent beat is playing.

In the evening, before nightfall, Banu comes running out of his house on to the village common in a torn vest. He looks around, wide-eyed. In a high-energy tableau, all the children of the village, flaunting their new clothes, march ahead jubilantly. It looks as if this is their celebration. Swaggering ahead of them is the grinning Jagu.

Banu treads cautiously, even surreptitiously. The darkness of his mind burns inside his head like the darkness that envelops the dense thickets on either side of the road.

Who was that walking in the rear, wasn't that Chanduri? Jagu was prattling on. 'When Bhai comes next time, he'll get me a tricycle. And even nicer clothes.'

Banu can hold himself back no longer and calls out, 'Chanduri, hey, Chanduri!' The children in the celebratory tableau look back at him.

'Let's get on with our march,' Jagu promptly instructs those following in his wake, guiding the multitude. 'Let Bana keep calling out. Ignore him! Remember, anyone falling behind will not get his lozenge.'

'That Bana is still wearing his torn clothes,' Sada comments condescendingly.

Madhia quickly adds, 'There is no way we are going to let him join us.'

Chanduri moves ahead with them.

Banu again calls out, loud, 'Hau, don't listen to me. Go ahead, Chanduri—go right ahead!'

Chanduri swivels around to look at him, even as she steps forward. She sees Banu walking away, his back towards them.

Chanduri pivots and comes back running, shouting, 'Banu, Banu!'

Banu will not stop.

She finally catches up with him, clasps him tightly and caresses him lovingly, saying, 'Aren't you willing to be my friend?'

Banu will not utter a word still, but struggles to free himself. Chanduri moves closer to hold him firmly and adds, 'You want to beat me? Fine, punch me.'

The dam broke and Banu begins to sob. At a loss for words, Chanduri merely strokes him consolingly.

The thick, ridge-gourd creeper that spreads luxuriantly across the fence had burst into full bloom.

The new song welcoming the Goddess is blaring away.

Banu slowly raises his face, ventures a smile and says in a voice full of hope, 'When Bapa comes home, he'll surely bring new clothes, won't he? What's that worthless stuff that Jagu is wearing? Mine is going to be many times better than his! Just wait and see!'

Originally titled 'Asaranti', 1951

Cricket

The cricket match is to be played in Cuttack's Barabati Stadium—the Indian team will lock horns with the visiting team from England. Spectators will throng the stadium; thousands of them from far-off places have already paid hefty sums to buy tickets for the match. Many have decided to spend the eve of the match waiting outside the stadium gates, to ensure that they beat the thronging multitude in the morning and get a place to sit. Not that they didn't know that they would have to sit through the day as well—it'll be a long day, indeed; the match will get over only around four-thirty in the afternoon, but that won't deter them from carrying out their strategy. It was a small price to pay anyway.

Kamaladevi lives in this city. For the last few days, she too has been hearing the hubbub that has been created around this match. Everyone at home, the sons and daughters-in-law, daughters and sons-in-law, grandsons and granddaughters have been repeatedly telling her about it. Even her husband—who usually sat quietly in his room, listening to Prabhupada's *kirtans* of 'Hari Krishna Hari Ram' playing from the numerous tapes he has collected and immersing himself in loving devotion to the deity or reading religious texts, and only at times discussing sundry business concerns with his sons—has been talking of this cricket match. But she has dismissed what she has been hearing with a shrug, 'Yes, this is a passing fad—just one of those things!'

Her sons—all five of them—had played cricket during their schooldays. Of them, Jaya and Gobinda were considered talented cricketers. But beyond this, Kamaladevi knows little about the game of cricket. She is neither curious enough to understand the intricacies and nuances of the game nor does she care to know what it means to be a good or bad cricketer. All she knows about this game is that one person holding a polished, wooden plank hits out at a round, wooden object hurled at him from the opposite end of the pitch, whereupon he starts running between one end to the other end of the pitch. She is aware, however, that the game can, at times, be hazardous. That round thing had once hit Gobinda was on the face and had chipped one of his upper teeth. Tears streamed from his eyes—oh, he had been in such excruciating pain!

Yet she has accepted this as the way of the new world. And everyone was riveted to this prevailing craze! What could she do about it? Today cricket has become the opium of the masses—in the children's eyes the cricketers are demigods, so much so that their pictures are pasted on the walls alongside those of film stars. Such has become the craze that the children may not know their own relatives, but they know everything about the cricket players.

Kamaladevi is seventy now. She has a pale, wheatish complexion, a round, plump face and a mop of grey, thinning hair on her head. Neither short nor tall, she has a rotund, heavy build. In her youth she had a shapely figure, but she has put on weight over the years. Later in life, she developed diabetes and arthritis. The body did not exactly shed the extra weight, but the fat shrivelled and the skin sagged; her face is deeply wrinkled in places, while her erstwhile bright pair of eyes have shrunk into their sockets and lost their lustre. But she wasn't troubled by all this. However, what did trouble her was that, despite years of doctors and medication, she continued to feel weak. Arthritis had rendered her knees almost immobile; both hands had become weak and the fingers so badly twisted that she now found it difficult to even carry on with her daily chores without assistance. This was galling to her but, over time, she had overcome her chagrin and had accepted her debility. Helping her in this helpless state of life was the care and nursing that came her way. The two daughters-in-law were always around; also, her married elder daughter visited her often. The three granddaughters, too, were there to help. And the sons and grandsons did their bit.

She would lean on someone's shoulder and hobble to the veranda and sit on a chair. Once there, she would gossip with people, oversee the chores of the house and give advice and instructions. Whenever she wished to, she would even read something that took her fancy, or she would simply listen to the radio. Sometimes she would just sit there in silence; at times she would doze off.

She came from a lower-middle-class, joint family that believed in frugal living and diligence at work. They were content with whatever they had. She had never felt harassed by the pinch of poverty, nor was she envious of those whose lifestyle was better than theirs. A time came when all her siblings and their children did very well in life and prospered. In her lifetime, she too has seen much prosperity. But she didn't quite know how such prosperity had become a reality for them; all she knew was that everything that happens is God's will. Not that her family hadn't encountered lean days and besetting times, but she never wavered from her firm conviction that, 'If we do not wish ill of others, God will always bless us, and everything will eventually work out fine.'

She has been married for fifty years. Her father-in-law owned very little land, yet they made it through the vicissitudes of life. Her husband, Bhajani Babu, had little education to speak of; he worked in a shop in Calcutta selling various knickknacks and managed to live off his own earnings; he needed no support from his father. After living there for a few years, they had moved to Cuttack where they had taken a small house on rent. Bhajani Babu then had started out on his own and immersed himself in his business.

Five years into his newly established enterprise in Cuttack, Bhajani Babu came to be known as a reputed industrialist and businessman of the city. Day by day, his family's prosperity grew: his own large mansion, cars lined up in front of their house, lots of visitors at home and everyone wanting to hobnob with him—all were evidence of their newfound fortune. There had been feasting, he had made large donations and helped others as much as he could—and thus there was a good word for them on everybody's lips. However, Kamaladevi showed no signs of change, neither in her behaviour nor her attitude. She didn't put on airs and was always friendly, sociable and welcoming. A few years later, however, Bhajani Babu's business was upended and the enterprise shut down— the pomp and grandeur evaporated, the cars were sold away;

the uniformed chowkidar was laid off, the crowd outside melted away like birds flying out of an aviary.

The children had grown up by then and were on their own, running their own businesses. The expenses had decreased so there was no dearth of money to run the household. Bhajani Babu had reset his life: he sat around reading religious books and listening to devotional songs from his tape cassettes and rarely emerged from his room.

In spite of the ups and downs of life, the inimitable happy look on Kamaladevi's face—a look that exuded satisfaction and self-assurance—has remained undimmed and undiminished.

Today, the children have gone to watch the match. The cook had woken up early, almost in the middle of the night, to pack lunches for them so that they could enjoy the match without any interruption.

After finishing her daily chores, Kamaladevi came out to sit on a chair in the veranda. It is nine in the morning. The younger daughter-in-law had come over earlier with a transistor, tuned it to the Cuttack All India Radio (AIR) station and placed it on the table before her. The live commentary of the match is on air. The noise made by the spectators and their enthusiastic cheering comes through loud and clear. The English team is batting first. She listens to the radio commentary for some time, but not being able to follow the stream of words, she exclaims out loud, 'Huh! The same news is being repeated over and over again—this man threw the ball, that man hit it, then they're running over to the other end and now this is the score—why make such a song and dance about it? And imagine the big crowd and all their raucous yelling and shouting! Stop it now! Let those who have gone to see the match, enjoy it.'

Pausing, she adds with a sly smile, 'They will pay the price as well; it's such a warm day today, they too will suffer sunburn!'

The daughter-in-law looks at her, her face mirroring dismay. Kamaladevi senses that her words have scorched her daughter-in-law, so she quickly adds, 'Why don't you do it this way—take this transistor to your bedroom, you can listen to it, and you can tell me the news later. Do place the glasses on my nose and lay out today's newspaper here in front of me, so I can browse through it.'

A while later, she could faintly hear the live commentary of the cricket match emanating from beyond the courtyard and piercing through the thick curtains of Bhajani Babu's room.

'The old man's enthusiasm seems no less than the children's, what an age this is!' she chortles. 'Today there's no Hari sankirtan! Instead, it's all cricket sankirtan! Pray, why, then, didn't you rush over to the stadium with the children to enjoy the match?'

Kamaladevi's morning is spent just like every other morning—there's no change in her schedule. With no particular tasks to complete, over the years she had gotten used to marking time, often spending all day sitting in one place— well aware of what activity would follow the other; they had all fallen into a pattern, almost a rhythm.

Like every other day, in the afternoon the elder daughter-in-law feeds her with a spoon. As mothers do, coaxing and cajoling their children while feeding them and narrating stories to distract them, the daughter-in-law says, 'Just one more morsel,' to nourish her some more, as she always does. 'Do you know what the cricket score is, Bou?' she asks. 'The English team has scored two hundred and thirty.'

'Two hundred and thirty!' Kamaladevi repeats the words. In her mind, this is perhaps a big achievement. Not ten or twenty, even fifty or sixty—it's two hundred and thirty—all in one go! What's the meaning and implication of this? She is wise enough to not betray her ignorance in the presence of her two young daughters-in-law. She narrows her eyes and quizzes them cleverly, 'So what then?'

'Well, our team is batting now, and they have scored just about a hundred.'

Kamaladevi seems pleased to hear this news. She smiles and cheerfully exclaims, 'Aha!'

'Tell me, Bou, what's good about it?' the younger daughter-in-law pipes up. 'We're lagging so far behind; half of our players are out; all the top batsmen got out cheaply. Vishwanath isn't playing in today's match. Gavaskar and Vengsarkar have left as well, and the famous Kapil Dev, who alone can hammer out a hundred or a hundred and fifty, left almost immediately after arrival at the crease. He couldn't score even a single run! There's just under two hours left for the match to get over. How then are we to overtake the English total? Let's see what happens!'

Kamaladevi's head suddenly fills with worries. Concerned, she wouldn't even eat any more of her lunch—she says she's done with it. Her mouth is rinsed and wiped clean. Pepped up now, she asks, 'We will win, won't we?'

The two daughters-in-law remain silent, exchanging knowing glances.

Kamaladevi suddenly brims with positive energy, 'We won't lose, we will prevail!' she declaims. 'We have to win. *Oh, Ma Budhi Mangala!*' She closes her eyes, presses her forehead to the table and whispers a silent prayer, 'Dear Mother, you always hear my prayers; this too is for you to fulfil! Please let us triumph. If we win, I'll offer you a dark-coloured sari and dark-coloured bangles. Heed my entreaty and let us win!' Her eyes, when she raises her head, are moist. 'Won't we win?' she was interrogating herself. 'Of course we will, we shall! Go fetch the radio, let's listen to what's going on now.'

'Come, Bou, let's go to the bedroom. You can lie down on the bed and listen.'

'No, I'd rather sit here, listening to what's happening.'

The radio spews out fast and furious updates of the match. She doesn't understand cricket, nor does she care enough to understand it, but she recognizes that India will *have to* win the match. None of her kith and kin nor anyone she knows, is playing in this match. But as she listens to the rapid-fire description of the match's progress—the enthusiasm, the deafening noise and the crackling shouts have conspired to create a consciousness of profound significance in her mind—and she visualizes with bated breath the trial of strength between *Us* on one side and *Them* on the other; sometimes the *Us* melds her universe into one—her husband, her children, her relatives, her own people, her acquaintances and expands to embrace the whole of India which, although she hasn't travelled or experienced the 'whole', she holds dear to her heart like her own loving village, sometimes like her mother—and *Them*, the *Outsiders*, embodying those unknown, rapacious invaders or sometimes the smartly bedecked, cap-wearing sahibs, those nasty reprobates who once ruled this hapless country.

Without appreciating the game, she only remembers that the *Outsiders* had scored two hundred and thirty and her ears are keened to how much we, the *Us*, have already got and how much we still need. From time to time, in her anxiety she calls out *'Ma, Ma*, give us some more, some more. *Ma*, take us to victory!' The cold air of anxiety nips at her and her heart pounds heavily in apprehension. If at times it is, 'That's the way to go!' the next time is, 'Yes, yes, do it that way!' She feels as though she has entered the field and is running around the players encouraging every one of them with her words: '*Arey!* Don't give up, don't be intimidated, keep trying hard, you just keep pushing!'

When the radio commentator says the shadows are lengthening and the game will get over in less than half an hour, the two daughters-in-law seated on either side of her exchange tense glances, sighing deeply. Kamaladevi looks at their faces and her heart races once more. She remains seated with her head bent, but she is no longer listening to the radio. Her head drops into her two arthritic palms as she hums silently in her head—*Ma, Ma, Ma, Ma!*

The excitement builds to a crescendo and the crowd goes berserk. The two daughters-in-law jump out of their chairs almost in unison and start shouting and doing a victory jig, 'We have won! We have won! Our score is now two hundred and thirty-one!' Bhajani Babu too starts rhapsodizing in ecstasy from the threshold of his distant bedroom, 'Have you heard? Have you heard? We've won, yes, we have!'

Kamaladevi's face crinkles into a wide beam of exhilaration and fulfilment.

'Of course, we had to win!' she says, squinting through narrowed eyes. 'Didn't I pray to Budhi Mangala!'

Originally titled 'Cricket', 1982

The Babu

The Babu has arrived.

Standing under the coconut tree behind the guest house, Bhagi, the peon, shouted 'Chowkidar! Chowkidar!'

A short distance away was the chowkidar's house. Hanging out her wet sari as a curtain in front of the house, Nikhi, the chowkidar's daughter, said, '*Ba*, they are calling out to you. Can't you hear?'

Hata was crushing pot in the palm of his hand. He drawled, 'Who?'

Nikhi burst into laughter. 'That foolish moustachioed fellow! Who else but that one-eyed man? His boss is a perfect gentleman, though!'

Glaring menacingly at his daughter, Hata said, 'There's an axe in the corner, beware!'

Nikhi's face fell. She plonked herself on the floor. Tears trickled down her cheeks. 'What offence have I committed?' she asked plaintively.

'Chowkidar!'

Hata mumbled, 'You poor, motherless child! What do I know? I suggest you leave now—you go to your uncle's house; stay there for a couple of days. They are calling for me, I have to answer their summons. I'd much rather you didn't stay here for even a minute longer.'

He rushed out of the house with a bucket and a rope for drawing water from the well. Bhagi was still hollering. The chowkidar saluted Bhagi, then went around to the front of the house and prostrated himself before the Babu, who was loitering on the veranda, a lit cigarette between his lips. Fair, slim and tall, he could easily pass off as a twenty-five-year-old, even though he was ten years older. A round, bright face, large, dreamy eyes. White shirt and white trousers. Socks and a gleaming pair of shoes.

'You made us wait!' he said. A calm, soft voice; the words clearly enunciated.

'I came as soon as I could, Huzoor!' He hurried to open the door and, carrying the luggage inside, busied himself in making the Babu comfortable.

A two-room guesthouse. A disused road roller, in which people said snakes nested, blocked the view from the front veranda. A hedge of lush trees and groves—coconut and mango—marked off the compound in the front; the backyard was even larger with some more groves along with some space for a kitchen garden.

Outside the compound lay a big settlement where the city and the village merged. Concrete buildings beside thatched houses and paddy fields: an ice factory and a husking paddle; trucks, motor cars and bullock carts jostled with each other. If you walked a quarter mile further, you could catch glimpses of the Chilika Lake.

The Babu leaned back on the armchair, puffed at his cigarette and gazed outside. It was around ten in the morning. There was a well in the compound, and women came to draw water from it. A few stray dogs loitered around. The chowkidar's cow, tethered with a long rope, grazed contentedly. The chowkidar's chickens scurried about. The squirrels squeaked as they frolicked around the coconut tree. The Babu, accustomed to the urban ambience, appeared to be soaking in this verdant, calm environment.

Hata gave him sidelong glances as he went about his chores. He felt too diffident to look him in the face. He told himself that the Babu had to be from a well-established family. People held him in high esteem. As soon as he arrived, people flocked to see him. He had heard that Babu had immense *pabar*. Many a time he has voiced his woes to the Babu—the salary that he gets isn't enough, couldn't he help Hata get a raise of at least ten rupees? When the Babu was around, non-vegetarian food was cooked twice daily—fish, chicken, eggs couldn't be dispensed with! Tea, well, by the hour—not just for the Babu, but for all those who came calling on him. Even when he came for half a day, there was a generous tip of one rupee when he left! Must be rich—to the manor born. Such a dapper gentleman! Only when one is well-fed, well-cared for, free of worries and lives a life of comfort can one look as good as him! Not a hair out of place! He smiled pleasantly and nodded his head when he was spoken to: a man of immense patience, and so full of compassion. Hata often eavesdropped when the Babu conversed with others. The Babu always spoke of dharma, justice and morality. His words were measured; Hata didn't have the intelligence to understand all that he said. But he had the common sense to appreciate that what the Babu said carried gravitas. An ordinary person would not speak this way. And the piles of books with glittering covers that surrounded him! Books written in *Engeelisi*! Two of them rested on the wide arms of the armchair, and another book and a few newspapers were piled up on the table beside him. He was indeed a Big Babu!

And the peon who came along with him? A veritable storehouse of vices! A one-eyed man with a scabrous and pockmarked face that resembled a ruffian's, he shocked people with his profane swearing. What utterly scared Hata was his roving eye. When he caught sight of Nikhi, his eyes lit up with a lascivious glint. He guffawed lecherously. He stalked her. He longed to talk to her.

The peon's fingers itched to pluck a cucumber from the loft or a brinjal from Hata's garden. Yes, he cooked well. The aroma of the dishes he whipped up pervaded the surroundings. That became a potential threat. It enticed Nikhi and she wanted to go to the kitchen. He was adept at getting things done as fast as possible. Either by cajoling or by threatening people. Whatever it took. He had won the Babu over completely. And liked to gossip about him. Of the elite circles he moves in. Of Delhi, Calcutta, Madras and many other big cities; of sprawling houses and skyscrapers. He speaks of big vehicles, sophisticated vehicles—vehicles with delicate mechanisms which are not brought to Chilika, as the saline sea breeze would damage them. And he speaks of money, thousands upon thousands, even lakhs and crores of rupees. Money and *pabar*! All too scary for Hata.

The day began with the usual bustle. People arrived. The Babu set out for Chilika and returned in the evening. A gathering of many distinguished people on the front veranda

in the evening. Hata knew all of them. He had borrowed
money from one, rice from the other. Top businessmen,
big agriculturists, high priests, village honchos. All very
distinguished men in Hata's eyes. If all these men kowtowed
to the Babu, the Babu must indeed be very eminent!

Come eventide, all of them congregated around the Babu.
As Hata brought in the chairs he would eavesdrop on their
conversation. The Babu would talk of such idealistic things.
Wearing a sparkling white dhoti and kurta in the evenings,
the light from the petromax would reflect off his fair forehead.
What he says is so true!

'There is no morality these days. Where does one find
character today?' And Hata remembered so many untoward
incidents happening in the village. So many people crawling all
over the village, looking for a livelihood. This village once was
so pure, pristine and uncorrupted! Everything was destroyed
when people came in from outside.

'No brahmacharya!' Hata thought he was talking of Brahma.
He knew what that was; it brought to mind the austerities of a
Brahmin, sandalwood marks on the forehead, fasting, raw rice
and rituals. And there sat the Acharya, the Brahmin, did he
adopt an iota of all that? No, he traded in fish and dried fish. Of
course, Hata owed him five rupees—so what?

'See how addiction to alcohol is spreading.' True. If you
stepped into some settlements now, your heart would flutter;
you could smell alcohol from miles away! Most people drank
these days. It isn't good. Hata himself imbibes alcohol once in
a while. But to consume it every day!

'And hoarding! Were there any hoarders earlier? Never!'
And now, Hata looked around and thought wistfully, the
hoarders are sitting right here.

'People do not believe in God any more. Such a pity! All the pillars of society are crumbling. The future is engulfed in darkness.' All of them nodded their heads vigorously and agreed with what the Babu had said.

'In such a situation, the meek shall stumble and fall, the poor will be that much more oppressed. And discontentment will spread wider. This will affect everyone. All of you must take responsibility for the poor.'

Oh, these were not mere words; it was ambrosia dripping from the Babu's lips! Hata stood spellbound. Babu is so concerned for the poor. Would the others listen to him? Would they act as avowed? Would they take responsibility for the poor? A hundred-odd rupees and he would land a decent groom for Nikhi and get her married! Would these honchos shoulder their responsibility and, indeed, give? He would try to seek out a philanthropist among this lot after the Babu left.

Shatrusala Babu sat at the edge of the group. A big dealer in dried fish. Hata went over to him and spoke to him in a low voice. Shatrusala Babu knew him ever since he was a little boy and was familiar with his woes. He nodded his head sympathetically.

'Hey! Why are you standing around doing nothing? Come, grind the spices for me.' The peon whispered in his ear. Hata followed him. The Babu was about to talk about Bhishma's bed of arrows.

As soon as they were out of earshot, Bhagi said, 'Skin the chickens first. And another thing, why is your house so quiet? Isn't your daughter around?'

'She's visiting her uncle, Bhagi,' Hata said.

'Were she around, she would have enjoyed the chicken curry.'

'She doesn't eat chicken. Her stomach aches when she does.'

'Stomachaches, eh? You should have brought her to the Babu. You won't find a person who knows medicines better than he. *Himpathy*—just one dose would cure her! I too was suffering like that. The Babu set it right for me.'

'Hau, the next time he comes, I'll take my daughter to him.'

'Such a chowkidar is a real boon indeed! You have been given a house. It should be full of people. But it is empty. If there were people around, they would have been of help to run errands.'

Hata suddenly lost his temper. 'If you want anything done, ask me. I am the employee, I am paid, and you can make me do whatever you want. What business do you have with other members of my family? Ask me to do the chores; if I don't do them, take me to task.'

'You are overstepping your limits,' Bhagi threatened. 'A stoned rat thinks no end of itself!'

Hata stood up and glared at Bhagi. 'Don't provoke me, chaprasi babu. Those red eyes and belligerence will not keep me down! You are stoned, not I!'

'What did you say?' Bhagi screamed. 'Say it again and you'll know who you're talking to!'

'I've said what I had to say. Know this, your threats just won't work, you windbag!'

'Look! Don't blame me if I raise my hand!'

'Don't forget, I may do quite the same. Don't blame me either!'

Bhagi was taken aback, cowed by the acerbity of Hata's reply. 'Hey! Why are you losing your temper? Don't you value your job?'

'I value it as long as I have it. If I lose it, I won't care how much I value it! I can make three to four rupees a day by carrying loads.' Off went Hata to his house, bringing closure to the issue. The world is so strange! A Babu, a veritable god, and with him, this demon of a peon. He wanted to take a few drags of the pot before going back, but he could hear the Babu calling out to him. He runs back. The petromax lamp needed to be pumped.

'Are you making your evening meal?' the Babu asked. 'Join us for your meal today; I don't let people cook in separate kitchens when I am around. Else, cook for us all in your kitchen and we will be your guests!'

Everybody applauded what the Babu had said. Hata's anger dissipated. He thought to himself, 'I have seen so many people, but no one has ever volunteered to be my guest.'

Shyly he muttered, 'Huzoor, could I be so honoured?'

'The honour would be all mine!' the Babu declared, beaming at him. And then turning to the congregation, he said, 'A couplet from Tamil poetry comes to my mind.' Everyone looked at him, bemused. What was he saying? Oriya gentlemen knew English, Hindi, Bangla, some also knew Telugu. But this gentleman had read Tamil, even Tamil poetry. The Babu looked at their startled faces and quoted a couplet in Tamil.

Yaadhum oore yaavarum kelir
theedhum nanrum piran thara vaara

Translating it into Oriya, he said, 'The universe is my home as every man is my family. This is what I believe.'

The dried-fish dealer, Acharya, waxed eloquent, '*Vasudhaiva Kutumbakam.* So, the same philosophy is envisaged in Tamil too? Yes, why not?'

'Merely uttering these words won't do,' the Babu counselled. 'One must match one's action with one's words. We are put on this earth for just a short while, and unfortunately, we waste it in jealousy and bickering, and notions of thine and mine. What's wrong with everybody eating from one kitchen?'

'Who practises this, Sir?' Shatrusala Babu asked. 'These days the father and the son have separate kitchens even as they live under one roof.'

'That's very sad indeed! Awful! Morality is crumbling everywhere. Love, camaraderie, compassion, generosity don't exist anymore. No one trusts anyone any more. Only cut-throat rivalry pervades!'

'That is the way of the world,' Gendu Jena piped up.

'You can't absolve yourself of your responsibility by saying that. You should find a solution. Why do people not connect with one another? Why this incessant rat race and one-upmanship? If one overcomes this desire to exploit another, you will see people living in harmony like brothers. When one meets someone, he should ask himself, how can I help him? If everyone were to adopt this principle, we would have the kingdom of God on earth!'

The Acharya was far from convinced. 'This is Kaliyuga. Who thinks like this or acts like this in this accursed age?'

'Why bother about what others do?' The Babu was interrogating the assemblage. 'There has to be a beginning. If you get started, others will follow. Why don't we start a collection drive? Let's build a corpus to which all of you can donate. The money can be used to help people in need in this locality. When you help each other through difficult times, you will establish a deep connection with them. You will work to the best of your ability and be an example at all times. And everyone in this locality will have a high degree of integrity which will be reflected in their behaviour.' Still waxing eloquent, he carried on with his peroration, 'The scriptures will be read in every household, and what is verbalized in them will be followed. This is true sadhana. Things will not change overnight, but if we were to make a beginning, things will gradually change for the better. So many people do so many things to make the world a better place; why don't you people, too, embark on bringing about this change?'

It was as if everyone was aglow with joy and enthusiasm. Excited murmurs rose among them.

Sapani Chhualsingh was moved. 'Let us formally kick-start this project. We'll fix a date. An inauguration function will be arranged. We will choose a prominent person as the chief guest. And we'll give it the publicity it deserves.'

'Let's herald this with a community lunch,' Raghu Behera added. 'And an entertainment programme with *pala* and *dasakathia*, the popular folk ballads.'

Panu Mukhi too chipped in, 'And speeches? The Headmaster will definitely speak; we will find many more skilled orators. But it will become the function of functions if we get speakers from outside. They would talk about ethics, the scriptures, character, morality and such things.'

'That would be nice indeed!' Acharya exclaimed. 'Let there be an exhibition also. And sports, games, wrestling, flat races. And film shows at night to entertain. People would attend in droves.'

'People would love it if we had a lottery,' added Shatrusala. 'And we would be able to raise money for the cause.'

Over the cacophony of voices, Hata noticed that the Babu was sitting quietly, looking low and dejected. And then the Babu exclaimed, 'All things begin with an idealistic goal in mind, and then it takes a turn that swiftly moves it in the opposite direction.'

The chatter stopped. Something was amiss somewhere. They looked at one another, puzzled.

The Babu continued, 'Publicity is the enemy of any moral or spiritual enterprise.'

Gendu Jena said, 'Very true! Everything must be done quietly, without fuss.'

The Babu responded, 'First let the project get rolling. It will publicize itself.'

'Exactly!' Gendu Jena picked up on the Babu's words. 'We are just wasting time on empty talk. Let's get going. I love the idea.'

'But there is a rider,' Acharya said, looking at the Babu. 'You should be our chair.'

Many others joined him in insisting on this condition.

'I don't want to hold any office. But I will keep coming back here and I will stay involved in the project. Look upon me as one of you.' With folded hands, the Babu added, 'Always consider me your *sevak*!'

The environment was charged with excitement.

Standing up, with folded hands, Gendu Jena beseeched, 'Sir, we are your servitors. Such noble thoughts and such inspiring words! With your blessings, we should be able to achieve something remarkable.'

Hata left, his heart swelling with pride, wondering, 'Is the Babu a man or a god?'

Gendu Jena had grown cautious now, but he had given his word. He was rich and influential, but when Hata brought to mind the stories that he had heard about his nefarious activities he felt the blood drain from his face. Such was the power of dharma, he mused, the devil in disguise could pass off as a saint.

Maybe they would help him get Nikhi married; the marriage wouldn't get stalled for lack of funds. As his hopes soared, he thought that maybe he had found a means of improving the quality of his life. He knew that he was a slave to pot but wondered if he could give up the addiction. The Babu's presence made him feel ashamed of this habit.

Bhagi interrupted his thoughts. Placing a conciliatory hand on his shoulder, he whispered in his ears, 'You never lose your temper with me, why are you angry today? I was only joking, and you got so upset? Come, come, skin the chickens and grind the . . .'

Hata's anger had evaporated long ago. Stumbling ahead of him, he mumbled, 'Why would anyone be angry with you?'

As he ground the ingredients for the chicken curry on the grinding stone, he thought of the Babu. He had found in him an extraordinary personality. The Lord had reposed in him all good qualities. Hata planned to unburden himself to him. The Babu would understand his travails; he would empathize with his woes. When should he do so? Not today, maybe tomorrow morning, when the Babu was alone.

Dinner was done. He cheerfully rushed through all the chores that Bhagi dumped on him. After all, he was doing all this for that godlike gentleman. He didn't mind at all. He had, of his own volition, enslaved himself to this man. He considered it a privilege. All he wanted was to stay close to him. The Babu came out of the room and sat silently on the chair in the veranda. Bhagi was nowhere around. Crouching in the darkness, unobserved by the Babu, Hata gazed at him and the nimbus around his head from a distance. He thought this was the right time to confide in the Babu. He cleared his throat.

'Who's there?' the Babu asked.

'It's me, Hata, Huzoor!' replied Hata.

'It's late. Go to bed. You've served me throughout the day. I don't need anything now.'

'Huzoor, I can lie down here—on this veranda. How can I leave Huzoor unattended?'

The Babu said, 'No! No! That's not necessary—that's completely uncalled for.'

'Oh, no, no, no, Huzoor! That's not how it's done. When you refuse my services, it hurts!'

'Leave!' the Babu said, his voice a touch stern. 'I would sleep better knowing that you are comfortably resting in your house. You have so many chores to attend to in the morning!'

Hata left, very reluctantly—and hesitantly. His respect, gratitude and love for the Babu had swelled manifold. This Babu had visited a couple of times earlier. How could he have been so blind to his virtues? How wrong had he been to think that the Babu was just like any other man? The Babu was sitting in a posture that reminded him of a sadhu about to start meditating. He had met sadhus, had turned to them when he had lost a cow or had been in dire need of money or whenever he felt upset or desperate. He had listened to them and felt calm and reassured upon return. He thought that on this pitch-dark night, sitting all by himself on the veranda, the Babu too was probably focusing his thoughts on something, but he was not merely a man of pointless words—he was a man of action. So, he would be wondering about how people in the world would benefit; how the poor and the needy would live a life of dignity; and how strife in the world would wane.

Hata tossed and turned in bed. Mosquitoes swarmed around him every day; they did so today as well, but that was not what kept him awake. He was mulling over what the Babu had said, and many new ideas were taking shape in his mind. Why didn't more such noble people emerge from this locality? Earlier, so many sages had been born here, their graves bore testimony to their existence. And he was thinking, this great idea which he had sown in the minds of the people, if it were actually implemented, how much it would help the poor. Love and affection were also withering away. Earlier, you got help if you asked for it—now rarely. No one would offer you so much as a paan even if you were sitting together for a long while. Scheming, deceit, falsehood—on the upswing. Of course, there was still a handful of people who were above all this, who trod the path of piety, but he didn't think that any one of them could hold a candle to the Babu. They were ordinary, puny men; not one of them had the Babu's looks, his ideas, his wealth or his capability. They were all good for nothing.

Hata drifted off to sleep while dreaming of a life of happiness. And woke up with the crowing of the cock. He headed towards the Babu's chambers to bask in his presence. This time of the day was called the Brahma moment. In another hour, another day would break. If he was lucky, he would begin his day with a glimpse of the Babu's benevolent face and work out the visions of his life's possibilities. The Babu would be having his morning cup of tea. Hata would unburden himself to him. The responsibility of getting his daughter married gnawed at him—as soon as that was sorted, he would be at peace. This neighbourhood teemed with loafers; if someone defamed her, there would be a scandal and all would be lost. He would say, 'Huzoor! Living in fear is like living in hell. If actually a kingdom of God were to come about with Huzoor's initiative, couldn't it start alleviating one poor man's fears? There were so many moneylenders—couldn't each contribute a little to help a poor man?'

Huzoor would smile and say, 'Yes!'

Holding up a lantern that cast a dim light, he first went around the guesthouse. He had sometimes come here at this early hour to gather coconuts from the tree in the compound. And then he climbed on to the veranda. He stood by the window of the Babu's bedroom. The door and window shutters were tightly shut. 'Let him sleep soundly. May God bless him!' he thought to himself. He could hear strange sounds emanating from the room, sounds that abated for a while and then resumed, repeatedly. He cursed the rats. Too many of them. The squeaking, squealing, squawking and gurgling sounds would wake the Babu. For an instant, all was quiet. Then again, some rattling, some scuttling and then a thud. That was the last straw! The rats had succeeded in waking the Babu, and perhaps the poor dear had fallen off the bed!

A few moments passed. The door opened. Stoking up the wick of the lantern, he stepped forward, eager to serve his godly master. But, but . . . but . . . what does he see? The silhouette of a woman passed before his eyes and then the real form emerged from the room. Behind her, the Babu.

It was as though lightning had struck Hata. He couldn't believe his eyes. Still, in the debris of confusion, his eyes and ears burned with rage. He held the lantern aloft. It didn't take him long to recognize Rupali, the tart, who had been around here for about a year. She lived in a hut along the wayside by the liquor shop. Sometimes she worked as a labourer, but everyone knew her for what she was. Shocked, Rupali tried to duck and slide back. But there was no getting away. Hata, now adrenalized and more daring, moved forward heroically. The Babu was trembling, a deathly pallor on his face. Still shaking from the shock of being surprised by Hata at this early hour, he grasped Hata's hand instinctively. But Hata would have none of it and he shook his hand free instantly. The Babu stood before him, hands folded in supplication, a beseeching look on his face. Hata spat out loud, 'Shame on you!' By the time he turned around, Rupali had already made a quick getaway.

Hata turned away in shock and shame. What has the world come to!

He could hear the sound of doors being unlatched. The Babu had been holding a torch when he came out. He held out two ten-rupee notes to him. Hata grabbed it, but without any gratitude. His head was in a whirl.

The Babu regained a bit of his customary poise when Hata took the money. He called out, 'Hata!' His voice was still trembling.

Hata went to the door.

'Don't tell anyone,' the Babu said. It was not a command.

Hata did not reply.

The Babu repeated emphatically, 'Don't forget.'

Hata remained silent. The Babu's fall from grace had left him shellshocked.

The Babu mistook Hata's silence for consent. He ventured an explanation for his peccadillo, 'We are but small men, you know. No one is a god. Even if a man reads the *Puranas* every day, he can't suppress his basic animal instincts, can he? He has to relieve himself when he feels the urge.'

The argument could be true, but it held no appeal for Hata Mallik, whose mind was moulded upon the ancient values of India. Although he himself may have many faults and vices, he expected that the person he idolized would be exemplary, not only in his words but in deeds too. He could be well-born, intelligent and educated, but beyond all that, if he lacked the ethical touchstones and did something that was immoral or illegal, Hata could well be intimidated by his status, but Hata could not respect him.

There was no reason to be afraid of this Babu. In Hata's eyes, he was despicable, vile.

'You didn't say anything. Will you comply with my request? My honour, the respect . . .'

Hata grumbled. 'Such vulgar, shameless deeds will not be tolerated in this guesthouse. Be warned!'

The Babu hung his head, turned around and retreated into the house. And then there were the sounds of boxes being slammed shut. After a while, the Babu called out in a more formal and distant tone, his voice a rich, gravelly baritone. 'Chowkidar! Wake up my peon! Fetch the register! I'm leaving. I have a train to catch.'

Hata made his way to the peon's chambers and shook him awake. Rubbing his eyes sleepily, Bhagi said, 'What did you say? He's leaving? Where is he heading off to? Which train? He didn't so much as whisper anything to me about his departure. We were to stay here for another couple of days.

Listen, aren't we going to Satapada tomorrow? You woke me up even before daybreak!' he complained.

Hata had already left. He was busy checking to see if all the supplies that had been issued to the Babu and Bhagi had been replenished. His faith in these people had dropped to the lowest ebb—the shards of his shattered faith lay strewn all around. Bhagi wasn't the only low and vile man!

Bhagi came up and whispered in his ear, 'Won't you carry our luggage for us? Arey, Babu will tip you.'

Hata stood stock-still, his back to Bhagi.

They eventually left. Babu strode ahead in front, and Bhagi followed him with the luggage. The Babu walked erect, his chin up and head held high, a serious expression gracing his face, a cigarette on his lips. All the dignity of his office that he could muster contrived in bestowing upon him an air of gravitas and blanketing him with a velvet cloak.

As soon as the duo had left, Hata's excitement also died down. He felt enervated—an inexplicable sense of defeat and sadness spread over him. He flopped down on the veranda. The darkness of the night was thinning. Light so fresh and bracing! Flocks of birds from the Chilika flew overhead. The world seemed to come back to life.

He was thinking about himself. He was a mere chowkidar; all sorts of people would come to the guesthouse, stay for a while—and depart. He would remain where he always was—tending, serving, observing—everything. He has met many people, from all walks of life, from various places. People high and low, young and old, rich and not so rich, but . . . but . . . has he ever met an ideal man?

But did that mean that the world would not change, would refuse to change? And people would keep on beating cymbals and praying for a better world while vices swirled about maddeningly, growing and billowing every living day? Jealousy, envy, violence, falsehood, deceit? Each one tilling the soil to enhance his own personal wealth, and not a word or deed of comfort for someone who fell by the wayside.

The day had not broken yet. He could hear the chants of sankirtan in the distance. Hata sensed a new lease of life pulsing through him. He went up to the gate. The troupe had come right up to the guest house. Around fifteen to twenty people, many of whom were here the previous night. Freshly bathed, *tilaks* on their forehead and garlands around their neck, they exuded happiness. Standing inside the compound of the guesthouse they sang their songs. The potbellied Shatrusala and Gendu Jena raised their arms over their heads and did a vigorous dance.

Then the sankirtan ended. 'Hata, isn't anybody in?' Acharya asked.

'Why? All of us are here. Who else are you looking for?' Hata's reply was pat.

'I meant, where's the Babu? We were to kick-start our association today.'

Hata was perversely elated. Masking his enormous let-down feeling and disillusionment and trying to get on with life, he said, 'If all the people of the village got together, the association would definitely take off. There will be no hurdles. Has anything been done already? Or do we start with this sankirtan?'

'Lots of things have been done, Hatia,' Shatrusala said. 'We were up until late into the night yesterday. From here, we went to the temple of the goddess to continue with our discussions. We have resolved several issues including fish breeding, many age-old land disputes and other vexatious litigations. All boundaries are dissolved, and no factions are left to fracture the village. Today we will look at the problems of the poor and needy. But where is the Babu?'

'The outsider, who had flown in yesterday, flew out this morning. He isn't one of us,' Hata taunted, his words acerbic. 'Something got into him and he got into a train and bolted before daybreak. Let him go, let him be. Anyway, he isn't one of us, is he?'

Faces fell—everyone's! The shock was overwhelming. After the long silence that seemed to spread across the gathering, Gendu Jena was finally able to interject. '*Bah!* He was speaking of such lofty things last evening, so strident and buoyant he was, so encouraging, and he left without saying so much as a goodbye!'

Hata remembered what he had once heard a sage say. 'A parrot may take the name of Ram, but that doesn't mean he understood what he was saying! There are some people who are just like that—given to shooting the breeze! They are born to preach, not to practise what they preach. When he gets back here again, he will again preach to us the idealism that he preached last evening. But does that mean we shall not practise it ourselves?'

'True! Very true!' Gendu Jena added for good measure. 'We have resolved, with the goddess as our witness, to do certain things. It's our job to do so. Must we expect someone else to do it for us? Come, come, let's go to the temple and decide what is to be done next.'

The sankirtan had started again, building up into a crescendo. The crowd left, one by one. Hata stood there motionless, speechless, sunk fathoms deep in his private thoughts, wondering which Babu would be visiting today!

Originally titled 'Babu', 1956

Licence

The river, two miles across as the crow flies, is wide open in its expanse and flows buck naked. In the far distance is a row of undulating, bleached forms fleetingly visible in the faint shadowy light of the sun before the flimsy fog mimicking the contrail of a passing aircraft gobbles it up. They seem like matted bamboo doors in the sky, these mountains—at times bulging out, at times leaning back to disappear behind the clouds.

In the monsoon the surging waters in the river make it resemble the sea. But now, the riverbed is dotted with dry islands of sand.

Adikanda feels the river breeze on his face as he stands at the edge of the stone embankment, gazing out at the vast openness of the river. The nip in the air gives him a foretaste of the cold winter months that lie ahead.

Adikanda is like an old, tiled house in dire need of repair. Sunken in, twisted, the mud on the walls washed away in streaks—yet unbroken. A dark, wide furrowed forehead, the hair on his head like a blighted bush, grey and blunt. A high nose tilted slightly to the left, wide and high cheekbones, protruding bushy eyebrows that hood a pair of deep-set eyes. A chin like a spade, the cheeks hollow over toothless gums. An unusually broad face, but only the size remains, everything else has flattened and hollowed out.

The shoulders droop. Once upon a time, they were broad. On either side of those shoulders, he could effortlessly swing two clubs made of sheesham wood, each weighing a tonne. But that was a long time ago. Many were the stories that were passed around then testifying to the strength and courage of this tall, awe-inspiring reserve havildar, Adikanda Biswal. He had deliberately sported a thick moustache; his friends had nicknamed him the Brave One of Bisalapada and his moustache had earned the epithet of the Bisalapada Stache. Many people tried to grow a similar moustache. People spoke about his exploits with reverence. Would Nalla Sahib have successfully dealt with the revolt of the Kondhs in the north had Biswal not been with him? And when that other sahib had run into the rampaging congregation of the Melia tribe in Baliguda, it was Biswal who had saved the day. And in the ghats of Mala in Mayurbhanj, when it rained arrows, but for Biswal's prowess, all would've been lost.

Stories were not only told about his feats with people, they included tales of his exploits with animals too. Legend had it that the credit for killing the countless tigers which the numerous sahibs claimed as their trophies, the myriad photographs they clicked with the dead tigers and the prizes they professed to have won—actually belonged to Biswal. *The sepoy did the deed, the sardar stole the fame indeed!* Apparently, Biswal summoned tigers by clapping at them. The man and beast looked at each other, eyeball to eyeball. The tiger snorted, Biswal twirled his moustache. The tiger snarled, Biswal guffawed. The tiger growled, Biswal pulled the trigger. And then the tiger was freed from its tiger incarnation!

Those were the stories that went around. And stories about his ravenous appetite. Sometimes he devoured an entire goat, sometimes he wolfed down five seers of rice laced with some salt. A long banana leaf would be laid out in front of him and piled on it a mountain of rice from one end of the leaf to the other, looking like a ridge in a furrowed field. It would be gone in the blink of an eye.

And no one remembers that story—of his braggadocio. When he stood with his chest puffed out in pride, twirling his moustache as a statement of his greatness and his power over others. That was a mistake, he had quietly admitted.

He has shaved off the moustache now. Diabetes has shrunk the body. Arthritis and haematuria too have taken their toll. He had been bedridden for some time and had only just returned from the jaws of death. He looks at his reflection in the still waters of the village pond and in the mirror—just a withered, wizened face on which droops a thick, chalky-white moustache. He himself had sent for Binodia, the barber. Now all that remains is a stubble, nothing more. The old rifle always stands erect beside him, the butt resting on his right foot. An age-old habit, otherwise it would be soiled. He runs his hands gently over it and slowly lifts it up and, out of habit, places it on his shoulder. How heavy it is! He sighs deeply. Like Arjuna struggling to lift the divine Gandiva bow after he had lost his unique skill, Adikanda Biswal too thinks about the past with melancholic nostalgia, 'Those were the days . . .!' he dankly reminisces moving the rifle from one shoulder to the other. How blissfully oblivious the body is to its parts when young and healthy, and how even a tiny bruise or an itch in the finger when old and frail, chivvies into the mind—much like a pesky eye infection seeking attention!

His head reels. He moves back a couple of steps from the edge of the embankment. And then he brings the rifle down and stands holding it like a walking stick. So many people had sought it; he could have sold it for good money. His wife, his sons, his well-wishers had kept drilling it into him, 'You are senselessly hanging on to it—when you've no money to buy even bullets. On top of that, year after year you have to carry it to the town and renew the licence—what a chore! You would do well to sell it off.'

But he has always responded with an unequivocal 'No!'

The rifle rests against the wall over his bed. He would occasionally scrub it clean. He would open it, hold up the barrel to the light to confirm it was sparkling clean and then reassemble it.

The old man has four sons—Nanda, Gopala, Gobinda and Hari. Nanda and Gopala have themselves experienced some of the stories told about their father's uncanny hunting skills. Gobinda carries faint memories of the hides of tigers, deer and bears. Hari has none.

Nanda grew up to become a fitter, Gopala a compounder, while Gobinda and Hari turned out to be tillers of the soil. The old man didn't recommend his job to any of them. None of them had to handle a rifle.

The grandchildren arrived. Not surprisingly, they've been familiar with the rifle ever since they started crawling. They've been chastised and spanked by their fathers or other adults in the household for fiddling with it. They've heard stories associated with the rifle. Some of them know all the animals

by name—tigers, gayals, sambars, deer, bears, wildfowl—
although they haven't seen any of them. Some among them
haven't even seen a bullet. But they all know Adikanda, the
skilled shikari. They superimpose the qualities of a daring,
gun-toting hunter on to this, his aging visage.

Hari's older son, Bulu, a chubby, fidgety six-year-old, was
very dear to the old man's heart. Sometimes, when alone, Bulu
imagined the old man running across the field, rifle in hand,
hunting animals. With shoulders slouched over the rifle, arms
and legs slender as twigs and a twisted, angry face, he points
the rifle at the cattle and goats grazing in the field, and there
they collapse to the ground, their limbs flailing and writhing
in pain. Then stiffness sets in and Bulu, who fancies himself
as the old man's disciple, excitedly picks up a whip and runs
across the field, yelling. And then, he runs seeking out his
grandfather and implores, 'Jeje, Grandfather, tell me a tale of
a tiger hunt!'

Adikanda's thoughts are far from tiger-hunting when he
stands on the bank of the river. He gave up hunting years ago,
even before he retired from his job. The rifle hasn't been fired
since. Sometimes he even contemplated selling it off, but the
very idea filled him with a gnawing sense of losing himself. As
though nothing remained! His head droops over his chest and
he wanders about like a mechanized, hand-wound toy.

'Arey, Bhai Saab!'

He lifts his head to look up. Another old man with a
rifle. Yakub Mian. Bent from the waist, a long, white, flowing
beard and the eyes, a shrouded grey. As he grabbed Adikanda's
hand and pulled him towards the veranda, he said, 'It's been
a long time since we met, Bhai Saab. How have you been?'

This is Yakub Mian. He too was a havildar, both very trustworthy—they had become friends. They had been together for so many nights, so many days, through so much wilderness and so many forests. The grip of Yakub Mian's palm pressed on his own brought back many a memory. Adikanda felt stronger. People with rifles who had come from afar crowded the office—some old, some young.

They moved away from the crowd just as they would in the depths of the jungle when they wanted to consult each other in private. The long-bearded face raised itself to take a close look at Adikanda's narrow, sliced-off face. It lit up with happiness, just as some house or a tree or a field sometimes glows momentarily in the dusk. The lustre of the face was reflected in Adikanda's. He was speechless. Yes, this was Yakub in the flesh.

The same veiled question that his eyes would ask in the days of yore, 'Tell me, Bhai Saab, what fresh entertainment do you want today? Your wish is my command!' In those days, off-duty hours were devoted to rollicking fun. The duty too wasn't demanding. Stand to attention with your chest puffed out, your head held high, the rifle by your side and obey orders. When they asked you to catch someone, you did; when asked to thrash someone, you did; when asked to march, you marched; and when asked to run, you ran. You didn't have to think. Eat well, exercise hard, keep yourself strong and ready—that was all. When at leisure, you set up a machan, a raised platform or a hunting blind, or tracked animals: you hunted, and you exploited any means available to enjoy yourself. You lived without fear, inhibitions or any sense of modesty.

'Yakub!' Adikanda gushes.

'Yes, Badabhai! It's a big day for me today—me meeting you here! *Khuda mehrbaan*, praise God!'

'So glad to be alive! This means a lot to me—seeing you!'

'Why wouldn't you be alive, Bhai Saab! You don't look a day older than before! Feels like I met you only yesterday!'

'Alas! What remains now?'

'Everything! I'm just a little bent at the waist—a bad back muscle strain. But I'm still young at heart. Still your devoted disciple! What tactics haven't I learnt from you!' Yakub shrieks in laughter.

Adikanda's insides warm as he catches Yakub's drift. He smiles impishly at the memory and says instead, 'Tell me. I hope all's well with you?'

'So far so good,' Yakub says. 'I'm true to what I learnt from you, Bhai Saab. What was it that you said?

Compromise on everything, but never compromise on what your heart tells you. Always follow your heart. Death is the end of life, so why shouldn't life be lived to the fullest!

Didn't you always say that?'

'Yes, I did.'

'You never were an average person, so why should you talk like one? I always remember you, my guru. My sardar! I talk about you to everyone I know—friends, relatives, grandsons, granddaughters—even to the plants and the leaves! I keep telling them, "Arey, you guys are a petty, quarrelsome lot—but you live in fear, your heart trembles at the slightest twitch and glitch. You ought to have met Havildar Biswal— he succeeded in covering up so many things, and no one could even touch a hair on his head." I wanted to have another *nikaah* and remarry; I cited your principle and told myself, "My heart desires another nikaah and what the heart desires shouldn't be denied!" I had three, I brought one more. No more dreams now!'

'So, to the three, you added yet another queen! Now you've got four, Yakub?'

Yakub laughs. 'That's right. But then the other three are shrews. This one's tame. Tell me, Bhai Saab, what could I have done? Those older wives don't listen to me any more. But this one, she waits upon me, she massages my feet and my waist for hours on end, without complaining. The poor thing has no family, she was skin and bone when she came. She has filled out nicely now and has become plump. She takes good care of me; I have no worries now.'

Adikanda is pleasantly surprised. He gulps a couple of times before saying, 'Good! Good! So, you're fine, Yakub!'

'Yes! Yes! I'm just practising what you preached. You said live well, have fun, to hell with the rest of the world! That's exactly how I've lived my life. Unconcerned and unfazed about what others did or what happened to them. I live for myself; I do things that take my fancy, I live my life. See, I used to take a two-anna worth of opium, now I've upgraded it to a four-anna worth. Toddy for eight annas, the boy home-delivers. Chicken is cooked at home six to seven times a month. I used to shoot doves every day with my gun; it doesn't happen any more, now that I'm bent at the waist. But I still go fishing with fishing rods and baits. Twelve grandchildren to amuse me, if one asks me to make him a kite, the other wants some wood to be whittled. Life goes on, Bhai Saab, it really does! *Khuda mehrbaan!* Well, you're still youthful. Tell me, what do you shoot with your rifle?'

Adikanda laughs out loud. He says, 'Those days are long gone, my friend. I'm an old man now. Now it's only telling beads.'

Yakub gives him a piercing look, examining him from head to toe, as if ascertaining whether this man is the same Adikanda Biswal whom he always idolized. Rolling his eyes, he says with wonder in his voice, 'What do you say? You don't shoot any more?'

'Not at all.'

'Astonishing, Bhai Saab! How do you go about life then? In those days, no matter how stressful the day was, you would always come back with a deer at night. You drove away the tigers. And all you had to do was snap your fingers and the *haradachadeis,* those little partridges, would drop like berries raining from the trees—four or five at one go. We didn't know a better marksman than you! You'd follow the sound of wildfowl rustling in the bushes and show off your prowess by downing them with balls! Unbelievable!'

'Gone are those days, Yakub! I'm just not inclined towards marksmanship. As I said, it's only telling beads and chanting the name of Krishna that gives me peace now. I've enjoyed sensuous pleasures all my life. Isn't it time to realize the Supreme Being now? Otherwise what will happen to me when I die, Yakub? Won't I be reborn as a swine?'

'*Tobah!* Tobah! Tobah! God forbid!' exclaims Yakub. Bemused, he paces up and down. 'What's all this? Who knows whether there is rebirth? Even if there is, how would you be reborn as an animal? But why do you think so?'

With a dry laugh, Adikanda says, 'I do think like that. Today I'm not like I was then. Those habits, too, are dead. Honestly, Yakub, I get a lot of solace out of telling beads and chanting the name of the Lord. I pray to the creator. In my prayers, I seek deliverance.'

Yakub twists his head from one side to the other. All this felt very odd. As if his friend Adikanda Biswal has betrayed him, and he finds it hard to believe that he has been betrayed.

Coming closer to Adikanda, he whispers, 'And?'

'*Uuhoon!*'

'*Sharaab?*'

'Uuhoon!'

'Ganja?'

'Uuhoon!'

'Opium?'

'Uuhoon!'

'Chicken?'

'Uuhoon! Your inquest will yield nothing, Yakub Mian. This man is different. He desires nothing but a few tulsi leaves and some holy water. People in the village will testify to it. He had to venture out today to attend to this business of the rifle, otherwise he doesn't step out of the village. He has surrendered himself to God, everything is His will.'

Yakub retorts, 'So you've ended up as an ascetic, Bhai Saab. You didn't do well.' He continues excitedly. 'You remember those halcyon days, Bhai Saab? Once you sat down to a meal, you'd finish half a goat. And two bottles of liquor was never enough. Always youthful! A liver stronger than iron. The go-to man of the bosses. The youngsters' guru and their role model. Your mere presence dispersed the enemies. Sans fear, sans panic, sans worry when something went wrong. Nothing flustered you. And the merrymaking and rejoicing! How we blindly followed you and hung on to your every word!'

Adikanda is feeling uneasy. 'Forget it,' he says quietly. 'Those are tales of a bygone era. I have no memory of those times now. Tell me more about yourself.'

'What do I say? You're one in a million. This asceticism doesn't suit you. Remember those days of revelry, Bhai Saab! The dense forest. The tiny village next to it . . . Remember?'

'We've walked through so many sal forests, Yakub.'

'Wait a while,' Yakub continues. 'Champa! Yes, that's her name. Can we ever forget the Champa tale? What a spooky, dark night it was! I was scared someone would descend on us. Even the odd light in any shack was clearly visible.'

'Tell me, Yakub, whatever had to happen, happened,' Adikanda tries to feint and philosophize. 'What came of it eventually?'

Yakub laughs a hearty, full-throated laughter.

Adikanda stands still, thunderstruck.

Yakub's name is called out. 'Yakub Hussein!'

'My turn has come,' Yakub says. 'Let me go. We'll catch up when I get back. It seems like it all happened yesterday. Honestly, you are nonpareil! There's none second to you. I think of you often. Your visage appears in my mind's eye and I tell myself, I'm not me, I am him! And then all fear evaporates and I don't give a damn!' He leaves.

Stupefied, Adikanda stands there stock-still.

He's looking back at the past.

This is not the first time. Earlier too, he had looked back. But then, looking back on the past had meant a nostalgic regret for the loss of his physical strength. And the strength was bound up with some blind, wild orgies which he had indulged in when he was intoxicated with the warm flush of young blood. He considered the world his oyster. He made mountains out of molehills, glared menacingly, twirled his moustache—he was the veritable tiger. He's here.

He has distanced himself from those tales long ago, and has gradually forgotten them. The wild days have been lost in the past; he doesn't remember if they were even real. In the course of time, the blood has turned cold, the tautness of every pore has given way to flaccidity, and he has calmed down. Earlier he would speak in a loud roar, but his voice has become softer, he speaks at a normal decibel. His stomping and flinging of objects have also disappeared. His children come up to him and speak to him. His wife doesn't sulk or weep anymore. He has come to appreciate his wife's intelligence and qualities; he listens to her; in later years, he did what his children wanted him to do, and lived the way they wanted him to live. It's been some time since he has asked for something or insisted on something being done.

But now everything has turned topsy-turvy. That man whom he had long forgotten because he was mortally terrified of him, that illiterate, irrational, cruel, masked man of the *jatras,* folk theatre, stood before him, the mask off his face. He, the Adikanda Biswal of yore, fills him with dread—his tales have not died, they are still alive.

He feels as if he were crumbling beneath the weight of his dilemma. His heart is churned and kneaded. Then becalmed. He stares unblinking—what is this that he sees before him? Encircling clouds as the sun sets. The waters of the Chilika lap the shores. And floating towards him are the many maimed and mutilated corpses.

His skin prickles with goosebumps. Someone is whispering in his ears and warning him, 'They are coming to settle scores.'

He closes his eyes, but the image still haunts him. Now he sees the sal forest. Here, close by, is the familiar village—you can see the thatched roofs and gables. A narrow path. Beside it, the dam into which water trickles and accumulates. With a pot tucked under her arm, a woman slowly approaches. This is she—Champa.

That is how he had met her the first time.

Then he got to know her intimately. Just like he knows the back of his hand. But that came later.

The scene changes. It's twilight. A shadow startles him. Bounding like an animal. Holding something in his hand. His ears are flushed. 'Where're you, you bastard!' Before him, 'a short, puny man holding up an axe. 'Where'll you end up, now that I have found you? D'you think you can scare me because you brandish a rifle? Don't you know whose woman she is?'

He kicks the man on his knees and the man falls flat on the ground. All his attention is focused on the hand holding the axe. He doesn't know what happened next. All he can hear is a discordant, muffled rumble that rises in his throat like the screech of an ape. Adikanda takes his hand away from the body and moves aside. In the blink of an eye the job is done. And the flailing and writhing body has become still.

A quaking hand rested on his shoulder. He looked up. Yakub was trembling like a leaf. Adikanda tugged at his arm and pointed to the corpse. They lifted it up. A solitary light glowed in the village. It appeared as though someone was walking towards them holding a lantern. They hadn't paused. The lantern hadn't stopped. There hadn't been any problems. A little ahead of them a mound, beyond it a cliff and then a sheer drop of 500 feet down into a deep chasm. They had tossed the corpse over the mound and into the chasm. A dull thud. Like an animal plunging into the darkness.

Yakub and he held hands as they walked back together. Yakub took out a thick bamboo pipe with a knotted base and a loop on top. Adikanda put it to his lips and tilted it.

And then he shouldered the rifle and set off, his boots crunching. In the darkness, the narrow path unfolded itself. He climbed over the mounds and walked the lowlands. The watchmen of the fields blew horns and beat drums atop their platforms. He heard them all. A tiger roared in the distance. On another mountain, an elephant trumpeted. He heard that as well.

In the morning, he reached another camp where a sahib was stationed. Adikanda told him about a man-eating tiger he had located. He knew about the territory of three such tigers. The sahib immediately set out on a hunt. The two of them walked through the forest for two days. They killed a large tiger. The sahib gave him twenty rupees and a used sweater as a reward. Then seven days passed in carrying out official chores. He returned to his old house. Yakub was still around.

In the dark of night, Champa came to him and told him of her loss. Wrists bereft of bangles. Sorrow writ large on her face. It was from her that Adikanda heard that some eight days ago her husband had lost his way in the dark. He died by slipping off the precipice into the chasm below. Piteously, Champa shed silent tears. 'He cared so much for me,' she said amid her tears. 'But God alone knows what came over him that day. He came home in the afternoon, fuming, totally berserk. He was crazy, hopping mad and on the warpath. I left the house in fear. And then this! Maybe something possessed him that day. He had never raised his voice at me. Who knows what happened that day!'

'Must have been drunk,' said Adikanda. But even in death, it is her husband who has been victorious.

Adikanda stood, a tad aloof, his head bowed. Champa was drying her eyes with the end of her sari. 'Champa, there's an emergency,' he said. 'I've got to rush over now, immediately. The call of duty.'

He had left that day. He had moved to many more places, many more assignments—he never had met Champa again. So much of the past had jostled and shoved to hide itself in the dark caverns of his mind. Whenever the heart burned and pinched, time the great healer had caressed it and taken the pain away. It had even turned the truth into an untruth. He remembers it no more. Therefore, it did not happen!

Why, then, can he not overcome this delusion? Who is this before him? Yes, it is that man! He is advancing towards him with an axe held high! And Champa is following him.

Suddenly, Adikanda hoists the rifle on to his shoulders and swaggers forward. Darkness in front of him. The crunching of his boots follows him. He has to . . . go away! As fast as he can! Fast . . .

A hubbub ensues. People prop up their rifles and peer over the edge of the embankment. Some people have climbed down the steps and are crowding at the bottom. An accident has happened. An old man, who had come to renew the licence of his rifle, had accidentally slipped off the embankment and fallen on the rocks below. His tongue protrudes out. He is dead. The rifle lies a short distance away.

A little while ago, that man was Adikanda Biswal.

'There, move away from the brink of the embankment! Move out!' two policemen shout from the bottom, waving their batons.

Originally titled 'Licence', 1963

A Good Samaritan

Kokila was a warder at the prison.

The male warders were in awe of Kokila's temper.

She has walked on the smouldering fires of life for thirty years and is now in her thirty-first year.

When the young veterinarian, Sushobhan, came to see a house on a spring afternoon, he knew very little about Kokila. He considered himself lucky to have found a house he could rent. Two houses adjoin each other—a single house, in a manner of speaking, with a wall in the middle mercilessly splitting it into two separate uniform halves. On each side a five-hand-wide veranda is enclosed by a wooden grille. A one-room house. A four-hand-wide courtyard. A tiny storeroom. The kitchen—a small, thatched enclosure on the other side of the courtyard. The door opens into a small, narrow backyard. Some sixty feet down, through the undergrowth, an area enclosed by a half-raised brick wall serves as the toilet. Beyond it is a fence, and past the fence a wilderness of *kiya*, screw pine, flowers. A well in the centre of the two courtyards. A wall above the well, so half a well is on either side. A gaping crack in the wall. The house is at the edge of the settlement; the road stretches over and beyond.

Sushobhan can hear the roar of the sea even as the cold sea breeze sweeps into the house, heightening his sense of excitement. In the reddish glow of the setting sun, the dappled play of light and shadow around the tall trees makes it look like a maze. The flocks of birds returning to their nests from the nearby casuarinas and kiya forests creates a pandemonium.

Changing into trousers and a shirt, Sushobhan steps outside. He's the pillar of strength for his family. The husband of a petted, pampered mother of four, the brother of a crippled sister—whose large, lustrous eyes present so many unspoken requests—the cherished mainstay of doting, aged parents.

But *that* Sushobhan has stepped over the threshold to fly out into the vast unknown.

Leaving another behind! A huge, beefy lump, with broad shoulders, heavy thighs and calves. She has no ties but craves them. She has no friends, but she yearns for friendship. Stark loneliness within and without. Her ears are pricked up, her eyes sharp and her skin taut.

Sushobhan shuts the front door. Taking off his office clothes, he stands in the courtyard in his underpants, facing the crack in the wall. He can hear the sound of a woman sweeping the floor on the other side as she softly hums a tune. Through the crack in the wall, he catches a glimpse of her—strong, fleshy and glisteningly dark.

A new desire surges in Sushobhan, there is a catch in his breath. And through the crack in the wall, he sees a pair of eyes—large as a buffalo's—deep, melancholic and vacant. The two pairs of eyes speak to each other—silently—exchanging their unspoken tangles of thoughts from across the crack.

The rutting sambar of the spring has just arrived in the jungle. He has no friends or acquaintances; he is destitute. The sambar's eyes ricochet off the buffalo's eyes without sinking in. The buffalo's eyes say she is huge but disconsolate, rugged but cold. Sushobhan's desire does not wane, however. *Aren't women meant for men's pleasure!* The unspoken thoughts. He moves a step forward. His frenzied hot breath scalds his upper lip. Suddenly the eyes on the other side look away.

Sushobhan moves away from the crack, and like a caged animal lumbers from one end of the courtyard to the other. He wants to put on his clothes again. But when he puts them on, he changes his mind. The front door is closed, the courtyard feels like a cave, and the emptiness is overwhelming. He quickly opens the front door and stands on the veranda, looking out. He exhales long, intermittent sighs and unconsciously stares outside, seemingly searching for something.

The evening is slowly spreading across. An unusual glow suffuses everything outside. A narrow path winds its way across the front of the house. An occasional passer-by walks past, sometimes a lone cyclist. Everything is new and unfamiliar for Sushobhan. Yet within this unexpectedness, he cannot find what he's seeking. An unrealized, whimsical dream from the past! Sushobhan is now trying to mould that dream into a reality. *Women for men's pleasure—designed, moulded, made for them!*

In the village, as a child, he had a playmate, Koki—the neighbour's daughter. Eight-year-old Koki and twelve-year-old Sushobhan, then called Dhadi. The affectionate attachment between the two was phenomenal. Koki was like a lump of clay in Sushobhan's hands—to be kneaded, to be moulded, to be tossed about, to be gathered. She didn't object; instead she willingly acquiesced to whatever she was asked to do. Those days Koki's life revolved around Dhadi, forever moving around him—she merely returned home to eat and sleep; she was verily Dhadi's shadow. She'd sit gazing at him, obeying his commands and gladly putting up with his dominance.

And then Koki grew up. She was bashful in Sushobhan's presence, and before he knew it, she was married. In the humdrum existence of day-to-day living, Sushobhan had never even bothered to find out where she had buried herself or what turn her life had taken.

When Koki was eight or nine years old, on evenings such as these, the two of them would often disappear. Lost in a world of their own making—on the banks of a river, or in the precincts of the old brick temple near the cremation ground, or amid the ruins of an ancient temple on the other side of the village—their own world of solitude wrapped within the real world where there was no space for anyone else, not even their parents.

Dhadi grew up to become Sushobhan. As his life progressed, he dealt with duties, promotions and other standard sentiments of life, and the usual rude, prickly exchanges. He married; his family grew. But at times, he was restless. He wanted to break free from the accepted norms of living, seeking release from his humdrum existence by making off with someone and living an unfettered, aimless life—a life indeterminate and indefinable. His desires—garbed in familiar experiences, morph into the unfamiliar—take wing in his imagination and he summons them. Amid the randomness of his imaginings, at times it's an astral world of earthen substance. Sometimes it takes the form of an imagined animal, and at other times it's a mere mortal being.

As he peers into the thick, dark orchard, Sushobhan longs for a body—an entity; his desire is to shape this form, and to accomplish an event with this form—that would satisfy his long-elusive raptures. As the battle of acceptance-rejection or agreement-disagreement rages on, all he wants is a simple consent, enabling him to fetishize his fantasy. With that form he could sway into the deep jungles, fly in the skies. At this moment, as the night is falling and the chatter of birds slowly dying, that form would be drawn into this house and the door slammed shut.

His thoughts are pierced by a soft voice from the other side of the veranda, 'Babu, when will your family come?'

Sushobhan is startled. Then Kokila appears on the other side of the veranda. 'You've rented this house,' she says, 'and when will you fetch your wife? And children?'

Kokila's voice has a touch of quiet intimacy, but Sushobhan thought that her looks were overwhelming. She has a round face and towers a foot above him; in girth, she is, if not twice, at least one-and-a-half times his size. She seems an enlarged human form carved out of a block of black stone.

Without waiting for a reply, Kokila walks up to the veranda and sits down beside him. 'I am your neighbour,' she announces and continues, 'I was a warder in the jail. I had a difference of opinion with some people, and now I am on leave. I heard that somebody had taken this house for rent. And then I saw you here today. It's a nice house. When your family arrives, it'll become a home. What's a house with a lone inmate? When will the children come? What do you do for a living?' The words came out in a torrent.

Sushobhan answers her while masking his surprise as best as he could. He hasn't yet decided when the children would arrive, but Kokila's proximity seems to have helped him make up his mind. Yes, the children would come. He has a couple of holidays coming up shortly, he would go and get them. Then he tells Kokila a few things about himself.

'At this time in the evenings, thugs and sluts frequent this part of the city,' Kokila tells him. 'It's the outskirts—secluded, full of groves, a perfect place for their rendezvous! But you have nothing to fear. I've smacked these notorious characters, boxed their ears and have all of them under complete control. They quake in fear when my name is mentioned.'

'Hey! Who goes there?' Kokila calls out, as she notices a movement in the shadows. In a quaking voice, a woman answers from the thicket, 'It's only me, Kokila Apa! Me, Mali.'

'Who are you stalking, girl?'

'Why should I stalk anyone? Am I a tigress or a vixen? I was intending to buy two naya paisa's worth of *badi*, the sun-dried Oriya lentil dumplings.'

'Then why aren't you using the road?' Kokila demands. 'Why are you creeping through the grove? Haven't I told you not to set foot in the city in the evening? Leave the place instantly, will you!'

Mali quietly retreats without so much as opening her mouth to assert her constitutionally guaranteed, fundamental right to walk anywhere she pleased. Her voice, full of supplication, comes from the darkness, 'Don't get angry, Kokila Apa, I'm leaving.'

Sushobhan is amazed as he takes in the conversation. A while later, in the distance a child's wail rents the air, followed by voices berating the child and beating him. 'Wait here, Babu. Let me go over and check with that Dhanu, the carpenter. It's a mere child, Babu, tell me does he know the difference between right and wrong? If he does something wrong, Dhanu starts beating him black and blue. I warned him this very morning, but he just isn't prepared to listen. When you hear a child crying so piteously, how can you bear it? How *can* you swallow your morsel of rice?' Shouting out loud—Hey! Hey! Hey—Kokila hurries away.

Sushobhan is intensely aware of a sense of awe for Kokila creeping up on him.

Without any further ado, he heads back to the house of the friend he was staying with.

Four days later, around eight in the morning, when Sushobhan moves into the house with his family and his belongings, he notices Kokila massaging oil on a child. Six or seven children, wearing different kinds of clothes that speak of their different social backgrounds, surround her.

'Oh, so you've come!' Kokila happily greets him but makes no effort to get up.

In the bright light of day, Sushobhan sees the form of Kokila and turns his face away. Big built and solid, a full body radiating youth and vitality, pitch black as night, vermillion in the parting of her hair. She wears the frank, nonchalant look of a familiar, simple person from the neighbourhood. But once you've seen her, you wouldn't want to carry her around in your mind. Kokila isn't the woman of his dreams. He feels no emotion for her, no dreams of pleasuring himself, and neither does she whet his curiosity to know more about her. But in his polyamorous mind, he'd like to take whatever comes—*if not a stand-in star, at least a dummy!*

But her name has become a jingle in his own home. He hears Kokila's name any number of times as soon as he returns from the office. *Kokila had dropped by several times; Kokila has built the chuli, the earthen fireplace; Kokila has found a part-time gig maid for them; Kokila has arranged a milkman to supply milk daily; Kokila has provided them with brooms; Kokila had brought over a grinding stone and a* paniki, *the traditional vegetable cutter, from her own house.* The litany is endless.

Sushobhan's wife and his four children—two sons and two daughters—have terrible colds. *Kokila has provided them with barks and flowers from the locality, instructed them to boil the bark in water and drink it, and eat the dry roasted flowers—her home remedy for the cold. The hairstyle that Sulochana wears is also Kokila's handiwork. Kokila has fetched a barber to give seven-year-old Tutu, the eldest child, a haircut. Kokila has given Munu, the younger one a bath and has baby-sat the twins, Moosi and Tiki, through the afternoon.* The children have grown fond of her—what with biscuits, lozenges, flowers and many such things that she has showered them with. There are many more stories—like taking care of her own child, Kokila has even wiped Moosi's bottom after she had defecated.

As the days go by, he gathers more information about Kokila. She treats all the children in the locality as if they were her own. When someone's mother goes out to work, Kokila gladly takes over the care of the child. If somebody's child isn't well, Kokila's anxiety knows no bounds. She prays unstintingly for the child's recovery, follows the traditional practice of *manasika* to make a solemn pledge and anoints the idol of Lord Mahadev with water while asking Him to answer her prayers;

she fasts on *ekadasis* for the well-being of all the children; abstains from non-vegetarian food on Mondays: eats pure vegetarian food in the month of *Kartik*, and yet would never ask anyone for any favours. In the mornings and evenings, she would gather all the children around her and arbitrate their quarrels; if she reprimanded one child, she would cajole another. Often, eve-teasers would come to her door and make passes at her; at times she would lose patience, shout at them and they would scuttle away. Kokila lived alone, she didn't have children of her own, she was married but separated from her husband who was a morphine addict. He visited her once in a while, took whatever money she had and left.

All this mention of Kokila made Sushobhan feel as if she lived in his house, not in hers. But Kokila would never drop by when he was at home. *Repelled! His secret longings, dreams and fantasies read—bared and trashed in her head! Huh!*

Sitting on his veranda, Sushobhan observes Kokila going about her chores with a stout, equanimous face, as though she carried the entire burden of living on her shoulders and needed no other help. It is only when she sees a child that her face lights up with a smile. She picks up the child, wipes her nose and carries her in her arms, crooning softly to her as she walks.

When occasionally Sushobhan runs into her in the marketplace or in the streets, Kokila betrays no glimmer of recognition or of having met him before.

In his room at the veterinary hospital one day, Sushobhan is startled to realize that he has doodled the picture of a woman with a child standing next to her. He has given the figure of the woman the head of a buffalo. A little below is a wide plateau, and on it are two mountain caves and two mountain ranges. The primal form of a child beside the primal form of a woman!

Uncanny! As he thinks of Kokila, he recalls how Kokila had occupied his thoughts, dreams and fantasies while he lived alone.

The mind flits about randomly. If Kokila had a son, how huge would he be?! His delight was dashed by randomness. He releases a deep sigh. Unbeknownst, in his head, he juxtaposes Kokila and Sulochana, and in alternating images compares them: Sulochana diminutive but wide across like a mridangam; Kokila huge, a veritable wrestler.

Kokila's affection for the children in the neighbourhood, her devotion to them, the small sacrifices she makes for them or the example she made of herself do not come to his mind. He remembers instead the raunchy men who sometimes crowd outside Kokila's house, who gossip and laugh at her before she chastises them and drives them away. Sushobhan tears up the paper into bits and throws it away.

In time, however, Sushobhan has purged himself of his obsession for Kokila as soon as he has freed himself of his inner thoughts about her.

He has heard the name Kokila spoken so often in his household that it has started to cloy.

Then one day, when he returns from the office, he hears Kokila wailing loudly. Neighbours crowd outside her house. The pitch of her wails is directly proportional to the size of her body. Piqued, Sushobhan says, 'What a racket, this!'

Wiping away her tears, Sulochana enters the house. She is followed by the wailing children. 'Kokila's husband has passed away.'

'Kokila's husband?'

'Yes, he lived in the village, a morphine addict. He squandered away everything. He came to Kokila every month and took money from her. The last time he came, Kokila couldn't give him anything; she herself doesn't get a salary—how could she? This morning she heard of his sudden death. He had been laid up with fever for the last few days—that's all.'

'Good riddance!' he says airily. 'A thorn in the flesh!'

With her eyes spewing fire, Sulochana cuts in, 'What did you say? The poor woman has been widowed and you say "good riddance"?!'

Sulochana's scalded look and scathing words seem to have forced Sushobhan to acknowledge Kokila for what she is, the quintessential woman—the woman as a nurturer. He lowers his gaze. *Women for men's pleasuring—designed, moulded, made for them! The long-elusive raptures in his mind! Sambar and buffalo!*

When he returns from work the next day, he learns that Kokila has left.

'Such a kind Samaritan has left the town today,' Sulochana commiserates. 'The poor woman cried profusely when she left with her belongings for her in-laws' place in the village.'

Sushobhan doesn't say a word.

'When her husband was alive, she couldn't perform her duties as a daughter-in-law. Now, after the death of her husband, she is called upon to be the dutiful daughter-in-law. You see, her mother-in-law is alive. And she's blind.'

A good Samaritan indeed.

Originally titled 'Kokila', 1956

The Crow, the Cuckoo

A telegram has come—he is very sick.

He's very sick and in the hospital. Many eminent doctors are attending to him round the clock. A tussle seems to have ensued between the doctors and Yama—who, ultimately, is going to prevail?

Whoever emerges from Babu's house says so. Two cars have swiftly dashed away, horns blaring: Bhima Babu has driven off ahead, as has Rama Babu. A host of prominent people from the village rushed over to Babu's doorstep to express their solidarity and to give moral support. There are words of shock and empathy on everyone's lips—*ah, uh, chu chu*—as people, worried to their bones, rush in and out of the house, weaving their way through the crush of people milling around. What a mad rush!

By now the sun has started to dip. The sky is an eerie shade of smoky brass.

Pahala Ma is leaning against a coconut tree. She's been tying dry coconut fronds in bunches, and many such bunches still lie in front of her. One arm is wrapped around the coconut

tree while the other hangs limply by her side. The end of the
sari that goes over her head has a gaping hole in it. At the
back of her head, a clump of frizzy hair sticks out awkwardly
through the hole.

Pahala Ma's sunken eyes bulge out of their sockets and are
riveted on the doorstep of the Babu's house. She has been in a
stupor. *A telegram has come. He's very sick.*

Who are these people who are all so concerned about the
illness? How are they related to him? Orphaned as a child,
he has no family to call his own. Here in this village live his
father's relatives—well-known, famous, much-respected: who
doesn't know zamindar Gobardhan Babu's mansion? In this
wealthy household, unmoored, uncared for, neglected, he had
grown into an adult. He would take this path on his way to
school in filthy, torn clothes, his satchel tucked under his arm,
dispirited and his head hung low. Who could say from his
appearance that he was the scion of a rich zamindar's family?

Then, Pahala Ma went by her name—Nepuri. Theirs was
a wattle-and-daub shack at the end of the village. Ba and Bou
were around. Ba had epileptic seizures almost every day, and
he was unable to go out to work. Bou worked and ran the
household; Nepuri too helped the family, grazing the cattle
in the fields and gathering cow dung wherever she found it.
She was like a young calf, prancing about in front of their hut.

Nepuri would be hiding behind the luxuriant bottle gourd
and pumpkin creepers in the forest of *kaniara,* oleander, trees.
She would teasingly call out to him. 'Oh, Babu! Has the teacher
caned you today?' Her mother would be irate, flashing her a
piercing look that said don't tease him. But Nepuri would go
on, regardless. 'Oh, Babu! What have you learnt today?' He
didn't mind her teasing and fussing. Somehow, in some way

and for no reason in particular, he had come to love this shack at the village's edge, where the village ended and the ingress and egress to and from the village ensued. For one who offered a poker face to the world, he was in his element here, laughing uproariously, climbing the guava trees to scout for guavas and letting himself loose. It was very bracing. 'Oh, Babu,' Nepuri would start playfully, 'let me run. Chase me, catch me if you can! If you catch me, I'll give you the kaniara flowers I've gathered, I promise. You can enjoy the nectar.'

Here in this house, he was loved by all: she, her Ba and her Bou. Poor Ba would be sitting on the veranda, his legs stretched out in front of him, the protuberant varicose veins conspicuous on his bloated belly. He would be smearing all kinds of smelly oils over himself. His eyes would light up when he saw him arrive, and he would call out joyously to the little master whom he addressed most lovingly and endearingly as Chhua Babu, 'You've come, Chhua Babu! Nepuri, now go get that bunch of guavas.' He would ramble on beatifically. 'Sit down, Chhua Babu. Today I'll tell you the story of the elephant menace in Keonjhar. You'll love it—it speaks of the same kind of bravery I was telling you about the other day.' Ba had lived in the forests of Keonjhar; he once worked there. Nepuri didn't remember anything of Keonjhar. In his treasure chest of stories were locked tales of tigers, wolves and elephants. Every time he saw Chhua Babu, he would forget the pain caused by arthritis and the tales of adventure would spill out.

Bou would often lament about Chhua Babu's fate and cluck with pity. 'Aha! Such an adorable child! What a family he hails from, and what suffering he has to endure! All because, poor boy, he's motherless!'

A telegram has come—he's seriously ill.

Pahala Ma exhales a deep sigh of despair, gathers up the bunch of coconut fronds she had tied together and walks to her house. One by one the memories of her childhood days float before her eyes. Copious tears stream from her eyes.

Who's connected to whom in this world? Why do floodgates open to drench people's cheeks? Where's this distinguished person, Sitanath Babu—and where's she, this frail widow, Pahala Ma! In people's telling, no one can boast of a house like Sitanath Babu's in the entire town. The cars and vehicles that are lined up in front of his house choke the traffic on the road; all the influential people of the country visit him. His wife addresses public meetings. His daughters sing and dance in various forums. His foreign-educated sons lord over people in Rengama and Howrah. Sitanath Babu is rich and famous and has left the mark of his personality in every field—literature, politics, the arts. He's omniscient, omnipresent, omnipotent. The mere mention of his name is enough to make the enemy flinch.

Once upon a time, this Sitanath Babu was Chhua Babu, and Pahala Ma was Nepuri.

The flow of tears doesn't stop. Yes, he did his schooling here. Then he moved to the town and clawed his way through college on a scholarship.

He would arrive in the scorching afternoons. With a book in hand, he would roam around the grove and his feet would involuntarily take him to Nepuri's shack whenever he came to the village. He would lovingly start teasing. 'Hey, Nepuri, how fast you're growing up!'

And, as she pounded the tail end of the rice-husking paddle with her feet, Nepuri Bou would reply, 'You're telling me that, Chhua Babu, these nubile girls grow up devilishly fast! I don't know what destiny has in store for her, and where I'll be able to settle her.' Nepuri had grown into a tall, reed-thin, gawky girl, with a shock of frizzy hair on her head. Only her complexion and the two large eyes shone bright.

Chhua Babu was again back in the village after a number of years. This time he had really grown up; he looked different with a moustache sprouting on his upper lip. The financial condition of Pahala Ma's family was a little better than before. As always, the young man humorously called out, 'Nepuri, hey Nepuri! Where're you?' Nepuri was standing behind the door, the end of the sari demurely covering her head. She came out, cast a glance at him for a moment and then quickly retreated into the house without so much as a word. Her mother had to call her out, '*Ki lo*! Who're you trying to hide from? This is none other than our Chhua Babu!'

Nepuri responded heroically. 'Oh, no. D'you think I'm fighting shy of him! No way!'

With downcast eyes, she had said haltingly, 'So you *did* think of us! Now that you've grown up, why'd you care to remember us?' She rattled off a whole lot of her whinges. But is this what she had wanted to say? He gaped at her in astonishment.

This rangy Nepuri was no more the gawky girl of the past; her body had filled out and she had blossomed like a willowy tree full of boughs and leaves, and heavily laden with flowers. That day they could not talk for long. But he would return again and again, almost every afternoon, and leave only when dusk was falling. Gradually, the childhood friendship of the past had changed into a new, mature relationship. So much to talk about, so much to laugh over, so much to share and exchange—beside the hedge of kaniara flowers, under the guava tree, up close behind the hut and inside the hut too. The two chatted nineteen to the dozen, taking in each other's tales, with neither of them able to decipher the meaning of the other person's words. Just standing side by side was enough, as one of them spoke the other approvingly listened and smiled generously.

'Chhua Babu,' Bou said one day, 'What're you worth and what are we? Nepuri has grown up and, God willing, come next spring you will be bonded in wedlock. You're such a decent boy. How much love and affection you have showered on Nepuri! As if she were your uterine sister!' She paused awhile to hold back the overwhelming emotion engulfing her and added, 'People in this envious village are unable to reconcile themselves to our well-being. They'll pour worms on fresh flowers. Sania Ma and Madhei Jethi are spreading rumours everywhere. People will gossip and defame us.' She broke down.

'Remember this, Mausi,' he began, quick in his response, 'I may have been born in this village, but I don't belong here. There's no one here who I can call my own, neither am I beholden to anyone. Why should I be afraid of speaking my mind? You too put in hard work and live off the sweat of your brow. No one showers favours on you that you'd be wary of losing. Remember this, Mausi, you need to listen to those who feed you, no one else! What does it matter what people say or do? Get this, Mausi, I'm going to do whatever takes my fancy without heeding the words of others.'

Nepuri quietly slunk away, pretending that she hadn't heard anything of the conversation. The evening was approaching and the *rangani*, four o'clock flowers, had bloomed. Chhua

Babu had continued, 'Whatever I *will*, I shall *do*. What's there in it, after all? Yes, what's there?'

Nepuri's body prickled with goosebumps. With her left index finger over her lips she had stood unselfconsciously, looking at the vast sky overhead. How red the sky was, how beautiful!

'Nepuri, I'm leaving.' Nepuri couldn't hear this. Or so she pretended.

The words drifted in from afar. 'Nepuri lo—'

She looked out this time. Dusk was falling, and in the distance, he had started to walk away.

He had asked Bou to not be afraid. So, she hasn't been intimidated. The day he left he had told her, 'Nepuri, I had said to you earlier that I would be leaving today. So, tell me, what are you planning to give me?'

In the afternoon, Nepuri had strung some kaniara flowers together. So, without any ado, she put the string of flowers around his neck and said, 'Today I'll give you just this. Won't you come back again? Will you just walk off like that?'

He took Nepuri's hands in his and his eyes held hers in thrall for a long while. 'Nepuri, you gave me this! Good!' he had finally said.

Why were his eyes brimming with tears? Did he know that he wouldn't return? Under his breath he muttered, '*Hau!*' and walked away. Nepuri cried like a child—with a passion she had never felt before. Much later, Bou came in and commented, '*Ki lo*! It's been dark for an hour, and you haven't yet lit the wicks!'

Months and years passed as Nepuri waited for him to return. He was always in her thoughts. '*Alo*, unfortunate one!' Bou had once said, 'Just your luck that your father is an epileptic. I am a daily wage-earner. Tell me, who's going to look after you? If only you had a brother!' Rubbing her wet eyes with the filthy end of her sari, she had said, 'I had given birth to so many, where've they all disappeared! If only they were alive, wouldn't they be looking after me today?'

'Bou, do you think I don't have a brother!' Nepuri had retorted. 'Do you think brothers are only those who are born to the same mother? Isn't Chhua Babu like a brother to me?'

Nepuri would've liked to say a lot more, but Bou cut her short with her fiery, acerbic words, 'Aren't you ashamed of yourself, you shameless girl? Huh! Chhua Babu is indeed this girl's brother!'

Her voice had become a taunt. 'I'm in the virtual dead end of life, slogging my tail off, we aren't able to manage three square meals a day, we don't even know if we'll be able to put a new thatch on our hut this year. And who do you think Chhua Babu is? He comes from a rich, zamindar household; he may come to us and be like one of us, but this is only up until the time he grows wings; and then he'll wing out of sight. Alo, why do you keep muttering that boy's name repeatedly? Is he ever going to care for us and look after our family?'

She was breathless in her rant and kept going to let Nepuri live the reality which they were in. 'Yes, in villages we address elders by various terms—Mausi, Peesi—but tell me, how will the son of the rich ever become your brother! When will you ever acquire the common sense and the smarts, and how on earth are you going to set up your own little home? My dear, know this: the rich people are cut from very exclusive cloth, while we poor ones are a pathetic, miserable lot! If you keep addressing them as Bhai and keep following them around, they'll only get you to slog more and burden you with even more drudgery; there'll be no end to it, and there'll be no spinning out from this reality; and one fine day they'll throw you out in a pulp and you'll be the laughing stock of your kinsmen and neighbours. If only I had my boys! They would have built a house for us somehow or the other—why would I have been fated to live this way? Oh my God!' Bou lamented.

Nepuri had remained silent.

Later, they heard that Chhua Babu had left for foreign lands. In the meantime, Nepuri got married into a very poor family. She soon had a son, Pahala. But her happiness was short-lived. Pahala and his father were taken away by cholera shortly thereafter. Here, at her parents' house, her father had passed away, and her Bou lived alone. So, she came back to her natal home.

Sometime later, she heard that Chhua Babu had returned from abroad, put down roots in the town and had grown into an esteemed personage, earning heaps of money. Denizens of his affluent village household, who until then had never given much thought to his existence or cared for him in his younger years, were full of praises for him now. Every mouth in the zamindar's family now spewed out the incessant chant—our Situ, our Situ, our brother, our uncle, our relative. Well, why not, you would ask, isn't that nice? You damn Parsua! Get out of my sight, Parsua! And then it morphed into Babu Parsuram! He married into a pedigreed family—a car as a dowry and an educated girl as a bride. A house was built for him, a zamindari was purchased, money and wealth flowed in limitless amounts and the loans were repaid. He was blessed with sons and daughters.

He moved in elite circles. It was rumoured in his home village that the government was repeatedly requesting him to take up a position of authority, but he wasn't quite willing to accept. On the strength of his name and honour, his relatives intimidated people to get things done for themselves. No one dared challenge them. How true was that saying, 'Kichaka's muscle power validates Virat's kingship!' After a long time, the zamindar Gobardhan Babu's family stood out among the rich families of the neighbouring villages, and they now strutted about with heads held high. The people bowed their heads before them. Situ Babu comes from this illustrious pedigree, people said. No matter what they thought, did they have any other option but to endorse his greatness?

Yes, he's that boy—yes, that boy—the one Nepuri's family once called Chhua Babu.

A fever ravaged Nepuri Bou as she lay crumpled on the torn, old mat. There was no money at home to pay for a doctor, Nepuri was alone—Nepuri alias Pahala Ma. Her situation had only gotten more dire. Just one stomach to feed, but she often went hungry. Yet she survived. From time to time, she got news about Sitanath Babu. He didn't come to the village any more; he got no respite from his daily schedule. His wife is a city girl; the children too have been brought up in the city, so how can they come and live in the village?

Pahala Ma has weathered so many years, so much untold misery and suffering—and so much indignity over the years. Today she's just skin and bone, but memories are hard to bury, and they resurface time and again, to scorch and torment her. He had crooned, 'I'll do whatever takes my fancy. Whatever I *will*, I shall *do*. What's in it, after all?'

Where's he now, where's his will? Is it true that people who go places forget their origins? Bou was old, but hers was the voice of experience. Her words, although harsh, now seemed true. Pahala Ma awaited his visit with anxious, beseeching eyes, much like a beggar's waiting for alms. Wouldn't he ever come? Just one more time? She had thought of him so many times, so often before her wedding—and so often even after that. When at her in-laws' place she carried Pahala inside her, she was so full of tender feelings that she kept thinking about him. And in the days before Ba died, even when her Bou was dying, how often had they remembered their Chhua Babu, and how often their dreams of seeing Chhua Babu one more time had remained a pipe dream! It rankles inside her—men can be so stone-hearted! At times, she gets on the offensive and wants to heap curses: well, these wealthy people—let their wealthy souls stash away their wealth in their chests! Such deceitful liars and fabulists! Would it cost them anything to come and exchange a few words with people they once knew?

She is enraged but then her mind clams up. Huh! Who's this rich man at whom she hurls her imprecations? The world is an inscrutable place. She senses his shadow on her doorstep. In her ears is the familiar ring of his voice, 'Nepuri lo, alo Nepuri!' Her vacant mind pines for him, and she winds up roiling in those memories.

She did not remarry and start a new household. When asked, she would say, 'Won't a curry that's burnt taste awful? My mind refuses to think of those matters.' Truly this is how the years have flowed past, much like water! And her hair had started greying in sections. Encased in the depths of the earth, buried beneath fathoms of water, the dragonfly had remained hidden in its casket—but today! Why does it drone again?

A telegram has come. He's unwell. There's no hope that he will survive.

Her teardrops spill from her eyes like berries from the *barakoli* tree. With a bunch of coconut fronds in her hands, Pahala Ma walks back home.

'Nepuri is crying!' old Sania Ma exclaims.

'Poor hapless woman, she has no family around,' Madhei Jethi added. 'She lost her son, her husband, her parents; her mind is a piteous tub of anguish. She has probably remembered something—and is weeping now. How can she deny her fate!'

Nepuri sleeps on an empty stomach. She sees him in a dream around dawn. His face has shrunk and his eyes are brimming with tears. It is as though he is beseeching her, 'Nepuri, lo! I'm about to leave this world. Won't you come to see me?

'Nepuri, lo! Everyone seems busy in their own worlds. They keep telling me that I'm theirs; but, in reality, no one has been mine—ever! Everybody is looking out for his own interests. All they ever wanted was my money. They neither know nor care for me. Nepuri, lo! I have no father, no mother, no one I can call mine, my own. And the one who truly could have been mine, I foolishly did not care to claim!' He had cried inconsolably and then walked out of the room. Nepuri now remembers seeing that string of kaniara, the flowers now dry, still around his neck. She wakes up with a start. Tears stream from her eyes. The door is wide open. The crisp morning breeze wafts in, and the day is breaking.

Her tears continue to flow. 'Oh, almighty!' Nepuri begins, 'listen to the entreaties of this accursed soul, let him be around until I get to him. Cure him, *dharma debata*, heal his body! Oh, God! He truly is like my own brother.'

Secreted away in a small tin box stuffed into a larger broken one, were two coins—a rupee coin and a twenty-five-paisa coin—tucked away for aeons. She had never tried to use these coins hidden in this box even when she was hungry. But today, the situation is different. This is the only resource she has and she is determined to use it to go to the town. For go she will. Her skin prickles with goosebumps whenever she recalls the dream. But whom does she have to confide in? What will the people of the village say when they hear this? She doesn't know the town; she's never been there, so how does she navigate her way to the hospital in the Big Town? And then she remembered, there is Dhadia, the village boy who studies in the town, and he'll be going into the town today.

So, early in the morning, she goes to the boy's house. To coax and cajole him into agreeing to help her. 'Dhada! My precious darling,' she begins. 'You know the hospital in the town well, don't you? Won't you take me there?'

'My dear Nani, you're so anxious to go!' Dhadia replies. 'But tell me, will you be able to walk the five *kos,* nine-and-half miles, to get there? Do you have the strength in your spindly legs?'

'Huh!' Pahala Ma snorts, dismissively, 'Five kos, huh! If required, I can even do ten kos! You'll see for yourself today.'

In no time, they are on their way to the town.

'Why did she go?' Sania Ma is curious to know.

'So many of the poor are on their way there,' Madhia Jethi is quick with her response. 'Well, so many people are heading there, so she has to do so as well. The Babu might give her a rupee or two out of pity and it'll see her through for a few more days.'

Sania Ma pulls a face. 'What a joke! As if people were just waiting there to give away money! Strange how one man's doom is the other man's fortune!'

By the time they have traversed the five-kos distance, it is noon. She is gasping, exhausted and drained by the heat. Dhadia takes pity on the old woman. 'Nani, come, have something to eat at this place.' But Pahala Ma is in no mood to pause. 'No, Dhada! If you are hungry, go ahead. But be quick, we had better hurry up.'

Pahala Ma is petrified by the town—so many people and so many vehicles all around! She tightly clutches the pleats of Dhadia's dhoti at his waist as she walks along.

'Nani, let go of my dhoti!' Dhadia keeps telling her. 'People are laughing at us!'

'No, no, let's quickly get to the hospital,' Pahala Ma eggs him on instead. She is thrilled to have come this far on her mission.

So, this is the hospital! So many buildings here, where would he be? The moment Dhadia inquires after Sitanath Babu, people point to where he is. There is a steady flow of people in that direction, assorted people in a variety of clothes. On that side of the building, there is a huge number of cars and rickshaws huddled together, as though some significant meeting was being held nearby.

'Nani, let's hurry,' says Dhadia quickening his pace. Pahala Ma's heart is thumping loudly.

Halfway down the road, Pahala Ma hesitantly says, 'Dhada, you didn't ask about his condition, did you? Is he okay?'

'Hau, Nani, we'll inquire a few steps down the road.' Pahala Ma walks with a doleful face. Gentrified people, who speak in an alien tongue—*gaat, maat, shus, mieow*—crowd around the entrance. Pahala Ma can make little of their conversation. There stands a uniformed and turbaned gentleman who looks like a country yokel but sports a thick moustache that instils fear. Dhadia finds out from him that the entire mob gathered there is the crème de la crème of the town—educated, rich and powerful. Well, who doesn't know Sitanath Babu? Hence this crowd. People from every household are coming to see him. What will others say if they don't come to him now? What will Sitanath Babu himself think about them when he recovers?

'Well, this or that person didn't bother to visit me! Well, we'll see, let's figure it out!' Therein lies the heart of the matter—the reason for this rush.

Everyone wanted a piece of Sitanath Babu's hands or feet as though it were a pie. His hands and the feet hurt and had gotten swollen with the constant ministering of the day-long throng of visitors—someone touching his hand, someone at his feet, someone tugging at his toes, someone massaging the palm, and yet someone else—who couldn't touch any part of Sitanath Babu's body amid the crush of people caressing the hands of some other person crowding around the bed. The cries, the compassionate words of sympathy of the sixty-odd people there in the room!

Finally, the doctor had to issue an order, 'Whoever comes here, let him stand beyond the door, let him look from there; if he needs to enter the room, it can only be with my permission.'

Pahala Ma takes in all the conversations in a daze, her mouth agape. Oh dear, what kind of a place is this! What sense can a woman make out of it? Her hopes have completely evaporated; will she really be able to see him? All these comings and goings of people who are crowding here are charades, Pahala Ma thought to herself, this is mere masquerade to telegraph their concern to the world. Aren't they the agents of Yama, disguised in whatever garb they are in!

The truth is not that difficult to find: who is there with genuine sympathy? She's feeling more and more distraught as she recalls the dream of the early morning. 'Nepuri, lo, all they're after is my money. They neither know me, nor care about me.' Sobs rise and slam her; she feels neither hunger nor thirst. Chhua Babu is asleep in that room and there is no way for anyone to reach him, and there are so many people around in the room, and so many restrictions.

'Oh, God! How I hope and pray he recovers; no one is seeking his money, only please let him recover from this illness.'

Pahala Ma stands there overwrought, leaning against a pillar for more than an hour, her head drooping in defeat. The crowd seemed to thin out and a lady who seems to be in charge walks out of the room.

Dhadia is getting impatient by the minute. He walks over to her and says, 'We've come from Babu's village. Can we please go in and see him?' The lady peers at Pahala Ma's crestfallen face, pauses, thinks awhile and then waves them in. 'Come in, but please do stay quiet.'

Pahala Ma steps in with much trepidation. Sitanath Babu is asleep with his eyes open. A grizzly stubble on his chin, his body so shrivelled that he is reduced to a bag of bones, so closely plastered to the bed that it is nearly impossible to distinguish the body from the bedclothes. Yet, he is Sitanath Babu, no other! Even before she walks into the room, copious tears are streaming from her eyes.

But she is startled the minute lays eyes on him. Her tears stop abruptly. Who's this? Is this the Chhua Babu she knew so well? Where's that demeanour—the look that she has held close to her heart for so many years? She can't discern even a scintilla of that expression on this face that lay before her eyes. Instinctively she had started comparing this visage with the memory of the face she carried in her head—this face and that face—and she could see not even the faintest resemblance between the two. A horrifying moment! Stupefied, she can cry no more, she can do nothing but stare at this faceless face, her mind shattered into fragments of isolated thoughts—the past memory rushing by as the present reality scoops in to splice the two—and all hopes of drawing close to her imagined moment are nixed. Despite the depth of her emotion and feeling, Sitanath Babu doesn't even condescend to cast a look at her. That felt like an unmitigable jab at her already bleeding heart.

After a while, she seemed to have gotten out of the shock and steadies herself.

Dhadia interrupts her reverie, 'Nani, shouldn't we be leaving?' Pahala Ma releases a deep sigh. She takes one long, last look at the surreal human form lying on the bed and drags herself out of the room.

Outside, the crowd has swelled and mills about as before. She trudges out of the hospital, clutching the pleats of Dhadia's dhoti.

Two hours later, at the dharmshala, tired and drained, she lies down to rest. Out of the blue, she hears a bustle outside. There are drumbeats, a procession and a crowd of people.

Dhadia runs back to her. 'Nani, have you heard?' he squeaks. 'Sitanath Babu is dead, lo. See, they're carrying him away to the cremation ground.'

Confused, Pahala Ma rushes out to look at the procession. She lunges towards the cortege, but Dhadia grabs her hand and sits her down. 'Have you lost your mind, Nani? Where are you running off to? You'll get lost in the crowd, and where will I go looking for you?'

The procession marches forward. Pahala Ma beats her head, crying loudly—her make-believe world has been upended.

Dhadia is trying his best to console her. 'Why're you so upset, Nani? The man's dead, let the people who're alive live. Tell me, who he is to us? Let the rich mourn the passing of this rich man. Has he ever given you a pie so delicious that you beat your heart and wail? Who's he to you, after all?'

What reply could Pahala Ma give to that question? Fighting back her tears, she tries to gather her thoughts and fortify her mind. 'Come Dhada, let's go back to the village,' she says mournfully.

'Right now? Do your legs have the strength to carry you back?' Dhadia is apprehensive. 'Think of the distance to plod back home!'

'No, Dhada, let's get back. We saw him! What more is there to hold us here?'

The distance to trudge back!

The legs ache, the knees wobble and the mind is a vast black hole. She empties herself in this town of all that she has bottled up for all these years. She feels an all-consuming hollowness within her heart. She is a helpless, destitute woman; it feels as if the big town is mocking her for her naiveté and ridiculing her simplicity—why did you have to rush this far? For whose sake did you undertake this journey? Who's he to you? Serves you right!

Her head reels, she feels vertiginous, her vision blurs.

'Careful, Nani,' Dhadia says.

Originally titled 'Kau Koeli', 1951

The Upper Crust

The Big City.

On the terrace of the three-storey building, the rich man's son stretches himself on the armchair. He straightens the collar of his shirt over his warm clothes.

Filtering through the fog at the end of the day, the cold lashes at him and makes him shiver. With fingers adorned with multiple rings, he stuffs a cigarette into the corner of his mouth. The smoke curls out lazily from his lips.

The Big City.

Bricks, stone, dark smoke. A multitude of people throng the streets. The noise of the steady stream of vehicles is deafening.

The rich man's son looks on with irritation. In the distance, the grey fog snakes its way up and over the splendid buildings like plumes of smoke. The golden light from the setting sun streaks it with rays of gold.

So many buildings! Some pretty, some not so pretty; some old, some new. A jungle of concrete, a forest of people. But each is separate, discrete.

The son gets up. He lights another cigarette and strolls over to the other end of the terrace. He waves the newspaper multiple times and holds it before him.

In the distance, on another terrace, a young girl holds a book on her lap and is *reading* it, her mouth agape, eyes focused ahead. The book answers the newspaper every time it is waved on this terrace.

From time to time, the slender arms climb up the air, as if swaying in the breeze, and each time she bends coquettishly, the neckline of her sleeveless blouse plunges a bit deeper.

The boy has watched this game play out every day. He has imagined so many things, dreamt so many dreams with this unknown, young girl. Today he feels annoyed, he is petulant. He turns his face away.

On another terrace, this girl in a green sari, her face caked with powder, paces up and down as she does every day. The same enticing come-hither look in her coquettish eyes.

The boy is back in the armchair. Today he feels lonely in this Big City—the senseless urgency of this urban sprawl, the harsh reality; the flirtatious young girls—so coarse, so rude, so lifeless.

The boy sits and contemplates. He buttons up his coat. He looks upwards and cogitates. He looks at the vast expanse above and below him and ruminates. His heart cries out for novelty—for trendiness. Not for him the shameless attempt at camouflage—of powdered cheeks and chapped, lipstick-smeared lips.

The boy is fidgety and gets up again. He walks over to the banister, bends over and looks down from the terrace of the three-storey building.

Old houses, a slum that houses the poor—filthy, hapless, bare.

He cranes his neck to look down—the lit cigarette stuck between his fingers—at the naked squalor below. Where distressed cries rent the air for the want of succour that can be provided for with as little as the cost of one cigarette. Where three mouthfuls of betel spit squares three morsels of food in hungry mouths.

Irked by the cloying tawdriness of splendour surrounding him, the boy is indulging in a soup of bizarre, fanciful imaginings. He continues to stare. His mind flits about, racing from one site to another.

His eyes rest on a patch in the courtyard where rays of light from the setting sun play hide-and-seek betwixt the crevices of the tall buildings.

The jet-black hair is neatly plaited, the fullness of youth on the face marred by the dark shadow of poverty. In the room, beside the small courtyard, he can see a pair of legs walking. In that room, a bit of a sari peeping out from under a tattered blanket, the tip of a broom sweeping the floor.

The boy can no longer hold back the surge of raw desire that is rising within him. He continues to ogle. His chest heaves. The feral instincts are in full swing. In the fading light, and amid sinking hopes, the girl rests her hand on her cheek, lost in thought. In the front room, the walking blanket straightens up. An old woman stands at the door.

The old woman berates her. The girl looks at her with her big, limpid eyes. And then she weeps, drying her eyes with the end of her dirty sari. Unconvinced and torn.

It gets dark. The boy looks straight ahead. Big City! As though it has turned garrulous in the darkness. The fog is interspersed with streaks of electric lights.

Night. A winter night in the Big City.

Below—

Where the mocking, tortured, ominous darkness hegemonize the meaninglessness of wasted lives.

Where the epicurean city's sound of music, radio and entertainment mock the heartrending cries of unsatiated hunger.

Below—

Where the long-winded, rambling speeches of corpulent politicians cannot provide even two morsels of rice.

Where the hundreds of thousands of epistemological theories expounded in universities cannot quell the flame of hunger burning in empty stomachs.

Where vehicles whizz past, spewing out dusty germs of disease and pestilence, but do not pause.

There below—

Two people in the still darkness. The young girl weeps and hangs her head. The old woman coaxes, cajoles and, at times, coughs, straining her frail frame from her continuous chatter.

'Poverty and arrogance!'

'I've spoken to you through all these days, I've spoken to you through all these nights, I've whispered it into your ears so many times! You still cling to your pride. While we are starving to death, while all of us are shivering in the cold!'

'Despite!'

'He came to you time and time again, and each time he's gone back sore and disappointed. You snarled at him, barked at him and drove him away. And at a time when we are dying of starvation! How long will he grovel at your feet despite your red eyes, your barks, your snarls? Let us die of starvation! Do you care? You keep clutching on to your pride, your hubris! Tuck your virtues into the folds of your sari and keep holding on to it as if it's your whole life! In our deaths, your pride shall flourish and swell!

'Your looks, your youth—tell me, who nurtured it?' She asks the young girl. 'Whose care nourished your burgeoning youth? Ask who? And now when we are consumed by hunger and thirst, you don't even spare us a sidelong glance. You throw away fortunes when they come knocking. You swoon over your good name, your chastity—you think your purity, honour, dignity and personal preferences are more valuable than our *mere* survival, don't you?'

The old woman hasn't exhausted herself. 'My dear, who's hustling and damning you? Who'll ever come to fill a poor man's house? Have you seen anyone in a poor, hungry family clinging on to pride and righteousness as tenaciously and as senselessly as you do? You lose nothing and, in exchange, we get to fill our starving and famished stomachs! But you obsess over your righteousness, your purity; know this—if only we live through today, can we think of another morrow.

'Why has the almighty kept me alive to suffer this harsh life of starvation and indignity? Even a prostitute who toils in jail gets a few morsels of food.' The old woman groans through rasping coughs. The young girl drowns herself in tears.

After a while—
Someone is at the door. The crusty old woman comes to the young girl again. She cajoles her, caresses her and then steps up to open the door. She quickly retreats into one corner of the house and disappears under the tattered blanket. Only a dry cough occasionally interrupts.

The girl stands transfixed. Unmoved. She scrubs her face and then bursts into tears. The fog of the cold, dark night combines with the icy numbness she feels within, and she trembles like a leaf in the storm.

He—

Two strong, muscular arms hold her in a vice-like grip as a bruising chest forces itself on her—seemingly wanting to crush her into pulp. The sharp, prickly stubble pierces her cheeks, her face and her nose, as if it were so many nettles. In the raging storm, she has no time to think. Every sense of right and wrong has been upended within her—coiled, spooled, disarrayed, thrown out, trashed—as if they mattered little.

The next morning—
The boy sits on the terrace basking in the tender rays of the rising sun, enjoying his cup of tea amid the flowerpots. He grimaces at the squalid settlement below him. He smokes a cigarette and looks at the city slowly revealing itself as the fog lifts.

And then he walks up to the edge of the terrace, cranes his neck and peeps down.

The girl he saw last evening is bathing. She is scrubbing herself with a coarse piece of cloth as she shivers in the cold—as if she wants to scrub away the dirt and dust of a million years, scrub away her poverty, scrub away the dark stains of frustration and the prickly scars of her bitter experience.

The boy bends down to peer below. He forgets to button his coat as desire grips him.

The sheer, raw, carnal excitement of naked flesh. Wet clothes. Droplets of water. Bare, gorgeous bosom. Fulsome youth and pulchritude. The deafening, piercing lure of a young body! Unbraided hair. All drenched in the pleasant hue of the morning sun. The horny call of raw desire!

Suddenly, the girl looks up. Her face turns red. She hastily arranges her clothes and covers herself. The flaming, ravenous, exploitative eyes of the rich over the nubile shapeliness of the poor. It unsettles her. She might have lost her all to a labourer the night before, but like a fierce animal springing into action, she wants to shield herself from the voyeuristic gaze of the rich young man. She looks up defiantly, fervently seeking transcendence from the humiliating defilement of the night before and wanting to consign it to the dung heap of her memory. Still dripping in her wet clothes, she walks away into the damp hovel—insolent, nonchalant, bristling and unyielding.

The rich man's son drops his head to his chest, the priapic arousal snuffed out. He moves away from the edge of the terrace and turns back. He sticks a cigarette into his mouth in utter disappointment and frustration but forgets to light a match. The mind is elsewhere, flitting through the scenes it has created to ingratiate the senses, and contemplates the moves he must make to fantasize, explore, regain equipoise and luxuriate. Resignedly, he looks at the other terrace where the girl from the tall building is languidly touching up her lips after her cup of tea.

The Big City has picked up its tempo. A motley crowd of people rampages across the streets.

Originally titled 'Uparatali', 1967

Paper Boat

Run-run-run fast, run flat out! It'll vanish or sink into the river, or someone else may grab it, and damn! All this frantic running shall come to naught. It's foolish to air counsel while running in this frenzied manner; others have gone ahead of him and he's way behind. Ella is jolted out of his foolishness and runs as fast as he can. The rain pelts down hard and loud. The road is flanked on either side by small, recently electrified stalls. As he runs past them, they sparkle like a garland. He can hear, in the distance, the clanging of the gongs as the evening prayers commence in the Jagannath temple. The gongs goad him to run even faster.

What's this on his path? Oh! That familiar swarthy, pitch-black bull. Indifferent to all the blows rained on his back, the bull nonchalantly strolls towards the shops, cranes his neck and munches on the vegetables and grains stocked there. And the shopkeeper's eyeballs rise to the middle of his forehead as he frantically tries to shoo the bull away with his deafening screams and screeches. Ella loves this sight. He has now reached the end of the settlement—here, there are no more shops.

As he skirts around the bull and the bullock cart to sprint towards the river, five others spring out from behind the bushes. They're Doms, an ethnic community.

They too are running in the same direction. Ella Reli hears the refrain ringing in his head—run–run–run fast. Run as fast as you can! He feels the cool breeze on his face and can hear the gurgling sound of the surging river. The river flows at its own pace, the deep waters murmuring, but the murmur is not just a sound, it's a language! Ella Reli slows down. Ah! The dark waters that stretch far beyond! The clouds heighten the darkness of the approaching dusk. The lights twinkle from the shop windows across the river. Up into the distance, both sides of the river are deserted—only the eerie river ripples along.

Suddenly, he realizes that many people have already overtaken him. They'll find it first, gather it to themselves: what, then, will be left for him? Abruptly, from one side of the road, a ray of light from a flashlight flashes on his face, and someone asks, 'Ella, is that you?' He recognizes the voice of police Singamu Reli. Singamu is not a real policeman—that's just a title prefixed to his name. Both boys are of the same age—Singamu twenty-three, Ella twenty-one—and both come from the same Reli community. They have the same mode of livelihood—felling trees in the deep forest to sell wood; gathering mahula and tamarind to sell in the market; earning daily wages as coolies or finding work as labourers in the rice mills and brick kilns of the city. Ella is short and stout, Singamu, tall and slender. Singamu clasps Ella's shoulder with his bony hand. 'Why are you running in the dark?' he asks. 'Don't you have a light with you?'

'Light?'

'What else? Do you think this job's as easy as picking up tamarind pods? See how heavy the darkness is in this pounding rain! Are your eyes fitted with a pair of flashlights to locate things in this murkiness?'

Ella laughs. 'When you picked up this torchlight and walked away, how many lights were tied around your groin . . .' Ella knows Singamu's dark secrets.

'Shh!' hushes Singamu, 'Shh! If someone overhears you, we'll be in trouble. Here, have a bidi. Well, you are loping ahead so bravely, but if anyone spots you, be ready to leap into the waters. I hope you've had something to eat. Or did you have a swig of something stronger?'

'Oh, I forgot that!'

'Well done!' Singamu's sarcasm is telling. 'You may float like a fish in the water—who knows for how long!—if you haven't put out the fire in your belly you may well end up like the person you're seeking. Listen, let's take a quick swig. Just a short distance ahead—there, in the garden shed of Bhima Das's house, the Saoras, an ethnic group of people, of Nuaguda, would be selling it. Come, let's take a chance . . .' They turn the bend.

In the distance they can see some moving torches, and Ella's head once again resonates with the call to run. He grabs Singamu's arm and starts running. 'You're smart, Singamu,' he says, 'but this craving for alcohol will be your undoing, you dipso! You're just like that Jaggu, the *nahaka*, the astrologer, so smart that he can pull the wool over the eyes of any rich businessman, but such a slave to his addiction that he hardly is out of one problem than he finds himself knee-deep in another and gets kicked around by the very people he had duped. Run-run-run, otherwise go back home to your bed and sleep tight.'

'Say it, say it, else at Gurubari's house . . .'

'Did I say that?'

'You don't have to say it, I get it. Today Gurubari won't spare anyone a glance. The lame moneylender's elder son has come. Didn't you notice the imposing red car cruising around the town today?'

'Run, Singamu, run! Your gossiping will distract you from the job at hand. You and your incessant chatter!'

Darkness spreads over the river, the forms are barely discernible. The screech and bursts of rain have increased. Then the display of intermittent volleys of thunder and lightning illuminates the entire landscape in flashes. The glowing torches ahead are lost from sight. People from the Reli community, Dom community, the boatmen community and strong men from so many other communities have all faced off head to head, and those behind them are catching up fast. Ella feels the exhaustion now.

'Wait, Singamu, let me relieve myself.'

Singamu laughs. 'You do realize now the magnitude of what you've taken on, don't you? Say that you can't run any more, why're you making excuses? Well, sit down. Let me light another bidi.'

Ella dilly-dallies awhile. Singamu stands there, puffing hard at his bidi. Ella comes over to him. 'Let's walk for a while,' Singamu says. 'We can run later.'

The river stretching over and beyond looks like a stream of gold amid these whorls of darkness. No, not gold. Ella rolls this covetous idea in his head and concludes that it is a living, pulsating entity; it isn't merely a river, but some evolved, sublime energy disguised as a river. Many mountain streams from far away flow into it and then they move forward in a ceremonial procession. Where does it go, where does it disappear, flowing as it has from time immemorial! A momentary sparkle overhead lights up the fields, the groves and the solitary settlement at the mouth of the river. The bank is inundated, not on this side but on the other. Ella and Singamu have left the bathing ghats far behind.

Freeing himself from Ella's grip, Singamu asks, 'What do you say, friend? Should we go back?'

'Let's go back . . . but who knows, we may find it . . .'

'Are you running to find it?' Singamu teases.

When Ella talks about finding it, his eyes sparkle in the darkness. Singamu can't see that look, and neither can he see the way Ella licks his lips greedily, running his tongue from one side to the other. What Ella is witnessing is not back-breaking labour. He sees instead the mansions of the moneylender and the businessman, and he imagines a world of repose and abundance behind those doors. A place where one can feast to one's heart's content! Where one can wear a variety of splendid clothes! Who knows what the future had in store for him! Would he ever have a house of his own? Not a mansion, but at least a tiled house that he could call home! Where he would be free from the nagging of his cantankerous old grandmother who has always found fault with him, berated him and threatened to complain to the police if he teamed up with Singamu and broke the law!

'He was poor, he was a labourer,' the old, crotchety woman would say, 'but your father was such an honest man! The moneylender trusted him with the keys to his godowns.'

Uff! The moneylender and his father's honesty! Ella has heard the story many times. He doesn't remember anything about his father. He has left nothing behind and has been gone far too long. From the stories he has heard, it appears as though his father was born to live and die tending to this horde of moneylenders. Where are the people before whom he had genuflected all his life when he, Ella, his son, battles hunger and oppression? His mother is a shrew but works hard in the rain and storm. She carries whatever she gathered in the forests—be it oranges or custard apples or vegetables—in a load on her head and sells them on the streets. She used to carry loads of bricks when she worked on road-building sites, but now her health has failed; she is a bag of bones and has no strength to do such work. Sharp-tongued, tight-fisted, she wouldn't spare a penny but is always ready to snatch away whatever Ella earns. Ella remembers all this as he walks. And he burns with jealousy. He is jealous of all those who are rich and respectable. Ever since his childhood he has always grudged them their wealth, he has always felt insulted by them. And here, on this secluded bank of the swelling river, amid the gathering darkness, while he is chasing something that might transform his life, it is this covetousness that has turned sharper and venomous and is pouring out of his eyes.

Singamu asks, 'What's it that you have set out to get?'

'The river's eating into the embankment on the far side,' Ella replies, and anguishes. 'There's an embankment on this side, too, but the river doesn't seem to notice it. Would it be as execrable if it were to inundate this side as well? The people here—they have so much, but they have no largesse; how does their wealth matter to us? Think, what don't these people do . . .?'

'Black marketeering, corruption, profiteering . . . the rich get richer; we rot in hunger and die in starvation.'

'Everyone dances to their own tune,' Ella grinds his teeth in rage. 'We have no one to stand up for us. Even when we're innocent, our houses are ransacked and we're rounded up, but raise just one murmur against them and you have everyone standing up for them . . .'

'And under the guise of respectability and honour, they indulge in every despicable activity,' Singamu says, adding his own despair. 'And all the fields and lands and orchards you see, everything belongs to them . . . One could go on and on.'

'Come on, double up,' Ella urges. 'Everyone has overtaken us.'

'What's the hurry?' Singamu asks. 'Keep talking like this. It's good to hear you talk. What you're saying is the absolute truth. If they didn't exist, today you wouldn't be running so breathlessly! Because that *one person* owns so much wealth!'

Ella slows down when the words 'one person' fall on his ears. His skin prickles all over with goosebumps.

Hearing the calls of 'ho!' as people set out on the search, he too had joined them in a trance. Since that moment he has thought of the many things he would get, a large number of things, but he hasn't given the person a thought. Through swollen lips he stammers, 'Why mention the person? Whoever goes . . . well, is gone.'

Singamu quips sarcastically, 'Who knows whether they go or remain? We are two to their one. Like a *Dongria Kondh* landing on the back of a buffalo in a herd in one quick leap, we, too, will jump on it. But that'll come later. Let's find it first. Where *is* it?'

It seems like it was somewhere close by. The battery in Singamu's torchlight is running low and slowly dying.

Sometimes it flares up like the flickering embers of a dying flame blown into.

Suddenly, Singamu asks, 'Aren't you afraid of ghosts?'

As a streak of lightning flashes, a sudden smile, Ella catches a glimpse of Singamu's face. He laughs.

Singamu's face looks bizarre as he continues, 'Ghosts are everywhere. They look just like us. They're no different. Don't ghosts take human forms?'

The precipitous riverbank, the darkness of the groves and the waves bubbling over in the lonely river. Ella's palm sweats in Singamu's grip. As if reading his mind, Singamu says, 'I've broken open chests. Pried open locks. I've walked around in the dark and done what I had to do. I'm always living, *re,* in flesh and blood. I'm not a ghost. I'm talking about *her.* So many people have gone ahead of us, looking for her. What if here, just here, she comes charging at us, corners us and asks, "Where are you two off to?" Will you be able to talk back to her and tell her that when she, the moneylender's wife, was alive, she didn't part with so much as a speck of dirt from her body, so what difference did it make now?'

'You'll always talk like this . . .'

'You're scared, aren't you? And rightly so. You're going to snatch the jewellery off her. She would deck herself up with ornaments, looking like the moneylender's veritable treasure chest—her greed for gold was boundless. Any money that came in, she converted into gold to wrap herself in. They didn't go out to relieve themselves at night. Instead, they extended their bedrooms on to the drain that ran alongside their house. And made a round opening on the floor which was covered with a plank and the mattress went right over the plank. So, none was any the wiser. Just the pigs let loose to cleanse the swamp under the bed. Clean and hunky-dory outside; who would peer under the bed to look at the filth and muck beneath? A polished, bright, sparkling exterior, burying all the misconduct, injustice and festering sin inside.'

'That's why I say, the water's inundating the settlement on the other side of the river where the poor and the downtrodden live—the *haadis,* the *paanas* and the *paikas*; there are no fields there nor any standing crops; if their houses are washed away, they take shelter under a tree, they don't have the means to build another house. Oh, river! Why is your focus so skewed—do spare a glance at this side, too! Let all sins be washed away, and let this sand again be purged clean . . .'

'Is that all you can talk about . . .' Singamu retorts. 'You still haven't answered my question. You see, the moneylender's wife was a woman who lusted for gold. So many people are running to snatch the gold from her—will she take it lying down? Imagine if her ghost arrives. And creates a pandemonium? Tell me, what then?'

Ella Reli suddenly turns thoughtful. Many a time, in daylight, he has swum across the river and has also fished in these waters. And he has looked at this shore from the opposite bank. It looked like the entire town was huddled around the river. The clusters of orchards, the coconut trees, the white, double-storey, concrete houses, the temple of Lord Jagannath, the church and beside it the countless temples devoted to various goddesses tucked amid the big trees. Beyond that, over the mound, are visible the many settlements. And fringing these settlements and giving them a rustic charm are the many spreading tamarind trees. Despite his familiarity with these environs, he could easily lose his way here, where live Hira, Moti, Kajal. And here, too, lives Lalita.

That upper track winds up into a path covered with bushy wilderness. They often take this path when they go to collect firewood. Where he would meet—them, and the others. There's no food at home. So what? They don't live in double-storey, concrete structures, those mansions enclosed by the chest-high iron grilles. So what if they don't live in such gilded cages! So what if they have nothing! What they do *have,* instead, are lean, sinewy bodies, the supple muscles coiling around like a snake and not an ounce of extra flab. Both men and women live by hard labour; they do not have to conserve anything for the morrow. Tomorrow will be a new day, it will have to be faced and it'll play out according to the whispers of their open, unrestrained minds.

They work together as a group and share their joys and sorrows as they bundle firewood with their strong, bony hands. Between bouts of work, they rest awhile in the shade on the clean, flat rocks by the stream. They enjoy a few moments of camaraderie, and then shake themselves free to go about their chores.

As Ella Reli casually looks back on his life and reminisces, he stumbles on a truth: man, indeed, glorifies his surroundings with his presence. People teeming around the river make it beautiful: someone crossing it with a load on his head, someone rubbing down his livestock on the banks and yet someone else bathing on the ghats. Even those who throw modesty and inhibitions to the wind and squat on either side of the sandy path leading to the river, they, too, add to its charm. Without people what is a riverbank, what is a forest! He has seen it too—the deserted riverbank, where the river seems to weep at the desolation. A lone crane loiters, a *gendi,* spot-billed duck, buries its face in its feathers and preens itself in solitude. Of what use is all this if man didn't grace it? *Man*— it is his presence, his acts, his living—who glorifies Nature!

Suddenly, he grasps Singamu's hand. The urgency of the gesture startles Singamu. 'Are you scared? Really? Why?'

'Don't speak to me of courage, Singamu! I know how intrepid you are! Why should I be scared? Fear, too, is a luxury enjoyed by the rich. Those who have something to lose are scared. We're ghosts from birth, so what terror can ever strike us? Come, let's hurry up!'

'Let's go back home,' Singamu affirms. 'It's all futile. See, those torches are moving back towards us. What else is this but a wild-goose chase? What would they find on a night like this? With such strong currents in the river.'

In front of them, a piece of the embankment gives way. They can hear the sound of the splashing waves. The river seems to have again started to mutter. 'We don't need to run any more,' Singamu says. 'See, they are all heading back. And this river sweeps away everything, washes away everything!' There's a sudden flurry of firebolts. Then, in a trice, they see something resembling a huge tree and in a moment, it is swiftly swept away.

They stand stock-still. Both seem drained at the same time. And both of them have the same idea in their heads— this river.

It flows and it flows. Everything seems to merge into the yesterdays. The yesterdays too, evanesce into the approaching tomorrows, and then everything seems to pick itself up to mingle with the darkness. Police Singamu Reli finally says what has always been on his mind.

'Aha! Poor Srinivasu's mother! How old do you think she was? Maybe forty or thereabouts. Srinivasu is her eldest child, and he'd be either your age or mine. Isn't it so, Ella?'

'I can't say how old he is. A plump, big-built person, he looks much older than us. Also, he's the father of two, and we aren't even married yet.'

'Yes, she welcomed a daughter-in-law, she welcomed a grandson. She would have enjoyed it so much more if she hadn't died all of a sudden. When she went to the ghat to have her bath this morning as she did every day, would she have ever imagined that she would slip and fall into the river?'

'Come, give me a bidi,' says Ella, stretching out his hand. 'She paid for the sins of Sadu, the moneylender. The high rates of interest that he charged! If you farmed his land, he would negotiate in such a way that there was hardly anything left for the farmer after he'd had his share. Selling with a small measure and buying with a large one! Huh! He has sunk so many people—extorting and gouging them financially! And how ironic that fate should exact poetic justice by sinking his wife in the river!'

Singamu wouldn't agree with Ella. 'Look, is he the only sinner? He stands nowhere when compared to the loan sharks. What do they not do! It's not that, *re*. It's destiny. And when one's time is up, Yama comes a-calling.'

'The woman left, and the gold followed,' Ella chimes in with his thoughts. 'She was layered with gold from the head to the waist. Had she not been weighed down by the gold, do you think she would've drowned? The sheer load of gold! If we could lay our hands on it, we would become rich overnight. She's gone now. When alive she never lifted a finger to help anyone in need. If only we could receive something from her in her death . . . her posthumous munificence . . . her blissful quietus!'

'And on receiving the bounty,' Singamu is quick to interject, 'we sprout horns and strut about! Money goes, as do people. Nothing remains, my dear Ella.'

'That too is true. Ugh! It has again begun to drizzle, Singamu.'

'Wait, let these people pass. Let's hide behind the tree. They may recognize us.'

The search party, some with lit torches and some without, was returning. They have been unable to find the corpse, but they haven't given up hope. They will look a little more, perhaps they will look in the morning. The haze from the torches gives the river a surreal look.

They plaster themselves to the trunk of the tree, Ella Reli peering from one side and Singamu Reli from the other. Under the red glow of the dancing torches a clump of familiar men, men who live in this town. It is just that they aren't men right now, but some other beings. So aroused were they by the avarice that has possessed them that it drips through their every pore, they surge forward. Nothing before them, nothing behind them, just a patch of moving red light that illuminates them in the darkness.

Here you can identify Nallu, the *paika* of the peasant-militia community. A tall man, a reputed swimmer. The same man who risked his life to save the lives of four people in the floods this year. His frizzy hair is plastered to his face. In the glow of the light, his hollow, bony face looks like that of a wolf. With him is Dama, the scavenger. A puny, bony man, a loincloth swathing his legs, a lit torch in his hands. He appears the most enthusiastic. Nine more people; together, they all add up to eleven. Bringing up the rear is Nokka, the supervisor, dressed in white, a pen tucked into the front pocket of his shirt, a cane in his hand. He holds his head down, seemingly a little aloof, but walks with a bounce—he too has joined the chase in the hope that, when the corpse is found and people scramble to grab and pull and snatch her ornaments, he would make a weasel move and tactfully claim a share.

All of them leave. The two boys hiding behind the tree exhale a deep sigh of relief. 'It's impossible to imagine what would happen if all of them were to find the corpse at the same time!' Ella says. 'In the scuffle that would ensue, as each one snatched and grabbed, one or two of them will probably be trampled to death. The number of gold ornaments on her would weigh up to more than a seer. All of them are so intoxicated they'd scratch and bite to get a share!'

'It seems like the flames of a funeral pyre are glowing on their faces!' Singamu exclaims. 'The woman is dead. She drowned and her funeral pyre shall burn like this! On the faces of living men! Anyway, what'd you say—one seer of gold? Have you added it up? So much at the waist, so much on her neck, so much on her hands, so much in the ears and nose—and silver on her feet. Was it Sadu, the moneylender, or did you overhear someone else say it?'

'Maybe the moneylender mentioned it,' Ella says. 'I don't remember hearing anything else. Let's get back now.'

'Let's keep our eyes open,' Singamu is alert. 'Look beside the embankment. There's still some battery power left in our torchlight.'

'She was tight-fisted, not in the least bit generous, but she was a gentle soul,' Ella's words are empathetic. 'She had to fit into the ethos of the family she was married into. Had she been generous, wouldn't her husband and son have made mincemeat of her?'

'Quiet!' Singamu whispers. 'Let's make one last attempt. If we don't find it now, we will have to go back empty-handed. Look, the sky is so overcast, if it starts pouring, we won't be able to distinguish the land from the water.'

They are like two shadows walking beside the embankment. The procession of burning torches has long since passed, but some of its fire remains in their heads. All the excitement that surrounded them converged at one point and trickled down in droplets—gold, a seer of gold, more gold. It wasn't just the gold; it was also the conflation of the lust and focus of the many people who had marched ahead of them. Involuntarily, there surges from within them a desire to do something daring and audacious, to vindicate the boundless frustrations of their lives by engaging in this sepulchral hunt.

As they walk with measured steps on the muddy bank, every pore of their being is awake, their eyes alert and sharp, and locus-focused on the path lit up by the feeble ray of light from the flashlight and the occasional flickers of lightning—scanning the riverbank for the corpse of a woman who is in no way related to them. They know nothing about her attributes as a person; when alive, she was someone's mother, someone's wife, a housewife, someone's friend and someone's enemy—tied by so many strings to so many pegs. She was respected and loved. In the temporal space and consciousness of her living, there was no fear of the dead, there was no fear of ghosts nor abhorrence of corpses.

But from the get-go, Ella and Singamu have abjured the natural human state of living. They have nothing to hold on to or cherish. If you find anything, eat; if not, stay hungry. When you find something, you first look at it to see if it could be useful to you. As naked, half-naked children growing up in the cloying underbelly of the well-known town—dirty, damp, overcrowded—they had to face life on their own, foraging in the garbage bins outside swanky shops, and salvaging a half-rotten guava here or a half-eaten banana there. When there was an epidemic, everyone got free drinks in the village square. Right from the beginning they accepted the truth—that one has to find his own happiness and snatch whatever comes one's way. And not think too much about life—that would only give one an aching head.

The Reli settlement is next to the Harijan settlement, and the nearby settlements of the hapless destitute. On the other side of the town is the thatched hut where films are screened. Next to it, in that patch of land into which flows all the sewage of the town, is the Khamata settlement. Strips of tattered tarpaulin held up by dilapidated posts and shacks with thatched roofs are punctuated with a few one- or two-roomed shanties—otherwise everything is decrepit and filthy. A little ahead, a rice mill, a brick kiln, stacks of bricks and potholes in all shapes and sizes.

These settlements have provided the towns and cities with so many labourers. Many have moved out to different towns, some hawking their wares on the streets and some keeping watch over the orchards. Some virtuous men, some vile, but no one cares. Every man for himself is the law of the land. The respectable people of the town keep away from this area. Not a nice place, they say. The police come here to break up brawls, to keep an eye on things and to look for clues when there is a theft. At times, there are searches and arrests. When the respectable people of the town flaunt their status by building concrete, single- or double-storey houses with scant regard for the sentiments of the people living in these settlements, there is a sense of inscrutable jaw-dropping stupefaction—seemingly the preserve of the poor and the indigent.

Growing up in this part of the town, Singamu, too, has thought about his life. On the other side, in front, is the double-storey house of Raghav Murthy. People said his money was measured in a *goyni*, used to measure paddy! Such was the bounty he had made from lawsuits against the sharecroppers on taking over the lands that Naau, the goldsmith, had a story to relate: in just six months, he had a ten-layered, gold chain weighing twenty *bharis*, with 'Sharecropping' embossed on it as a memorial to the lawsuits he had won. Jaggu Naik was the farmers' counsel and Raghav Murthy represented the landlords. Jaggu was unsparing in foul-mouthing Raghav when the case was before the court. Yet, when Jaggu Naik had a case slammed on him, it was Raghav Murthy who represented him. 'Raghav Murthy is such a gentleman,' people said, 'he would go out of his way to defend an enemy if the enemy asked for protection.' The farmers screamed, 'This is betrayal! Let the evil eye afflict you! We'll get our own back!'

Further, there's the huge, concrete structure of Pattanayak. The owner of the cinema theatre, who owned vast swathes of land. So many houses! Carts loaded with bags of paddy gather here in front of his house. There were several houses too, both big and small, tightly packed together. Shop owners, businessmen, lawyers, doctors, senior officers, all lived as they pleased. You rarely caught a glimpse of the people living in these houses. What you saw were the houses standing in front of you, a testimony to the upper class of society. Here festivities still happen, the sound of drums is heard, the sound of celebrations rend the air when a child is born and the whole town is invited to partake of the feasting that follows.

Yes, the whole town and sometimes the people living in this part of the town. They are made to sit in two rows flanking the street. Certainly, the street is swept and sprinkled with water, but as they wait, the dust gently settles back on the leaf plates in front of them even before the food arrives. Squeaking, screeching they arrive in noisy waves—the children and the aged, the men and the women, some holding an empty tin container, some a bark from a tree. Unkempt hair, ragged clothes, threadbare, coarse towels locally called gamuchha, loincloths—they come wearing their everyday clothes. Emaciated, skin and bones, ulcers on their cheeks, sores on their backs and some faces looking like flowers that have withered and died even before blooming. All the fresh, clean clothes, the healthy bodies and the blossomed flowers, the beauty and the stability reflected in happy faces, are from the other side. All the delightful rules and calm restraint can be felt only by those whose hunger is satiated and is not a constant gnawing pain.

He has seen it all. So many friends with whom he had shared his joys and sorrows— where have they all disappeared? Many of the houses have been obliterated too. Epidemics strike—fever, cholera, smallpox and many such dreadful diseases—and right in front of one's eyes, an entire household is wiped out and a house falls vacant. Again, some more are pushed out of the fringe of respectable society, like the garbage of an unfeeling town, and here they come to begin a fresh life. People died; people left. When they lived here, they were driven by the onerous responsibility of feeding the family without owning a patch of land to till—in a world that demanded you pay for everything you needed.

Singamu understands what is good and what is bad, but what he understands even better is that it's easier to plunder under cover of darkness than it is to put in hours of back-breaking labour to rightfully earn a handful of rice. When he is drunk, his mind wanders. What does he gain by walking on the path of righteousness? Bathing thrice a day, eternally blabbering the truth, standing a respectful ten feet away while waiting at the door of the privileged for a chance to air his woes? An ultimate refusal of help, he has to return empty-handed after having snarls and insults hurled at him. He doesn't have the inclination to ignite within him the dying flames of honesty lurking behind his tattered clothes.

But there's one certainty in Singamu's mind. That diseases are inevitable. They can afflict anybody. Just like one of them did Lalita. Or the police would take you away. Just like they took away the criminal Husuna, the bootlegger Magata and the petty thief Nakhia. The circumstance you are in twists and breaks you, just as it has broken so many others. Embrace the danger, grab the opportunity and seize all the chances you get before inevitability strikes. A missed opportunity doesn't come back. Who knows what would happen when you try to reclaim it later: you wouldn't have the time, the strength and maybe not even the breath of life itself!

Look at what happened to his friend Narua. His mother was roasting a piece of dried fish for him, his sister was laying out a meal of watered rice when Narua saw a pigeon trapped on top of the electric pole and heroically climbed up the pole to save it. However, the next minute he himself had dropped dead. The incident has stayed in Singamu's memory like lines etched in stone. Narua was such a close friend! He doesn't even honour his dreams with his presence any longer. When he thinks of Narua in his waking moments, he recollects the startled look on his face just before he was gone. And in his passing, it was like he had told you that ghosts and other supernatural forces are mere fabrications. What was real was this—the raw, living flesh. That and the experiences you have had in life. Police Singamu Reli has deeply imbibed this belief from Narua and lives by it. He hasn't heeded the beliefs of the elders and has deliberately sniffed at a flower even after seeing the insect in it.

He knows that the police are after him. His name is on the wanted list. Like scores of others. Not all of them will be rounded up. In his horoscope that no one cared enough to write, it would probably have been stated that Saturn is unfavourably placed and looks at him with a baleful eye. He doesn't pretend that the eye of the police is the eye of Saturn. With a haughty tilt of his head, he scoffs everything and looks at everything with suspicion and mockery. This mask that he wears makes people call him a shameless, obstreperous rogue. The big businessmen go to the police and ask them to fix him. He thinks that all this glorifies him; he's so famous that people remember him and mention him.

Ella is yet to measure up to Singamu's level, but closely follows in his footsteps and tries to match his speed. He has accompanied Singamu on his nocturnal forages and has courted danger. When there was a fire in the Mala community last *Baishakha*, and people were scurrying about, it was Singamu who had rushed into the raging, suffocating flames and rescued the one-eyed grandmother of the beggar, Malla, from her house that was fast getting engulfed in flames. Balancing himself on the sloping, tiled roof of the storehouse of the moneylender he had sardonically beckoned to the flames, 'Come, come here!' all the while hurling vulgar insults and mechanically stretching out his hand to pick up the buckets upon buckets of water that were being handed to him to douse the raging fire. That lone shadow ran fearlessly along the line of fire. A respectable person watching him would have probably excitedly remarked to the man standing next to him, 'The boy is so fearless!' A hue and cry was raised about how the fire happened, but not even a whisper about the heroism of Singamu. Not that he cared.

The two of them continue to walk beside the swollen river that flows in the dark. So many people they knew had lived like animals and left the world like the roll of the river. Despite the bravado, sadness creeps into their minds, as if the desire was ebbing. Then the mind wakes up and the thought disappears just the way it had come. The persona changes. The mind is obsessed over one thought—the thought that drives their footsteps, that the gold must be found; the person is of no consequence. It is the gold that man has wasted himself away searching for. They have to find what they are looking for; they have to go in search of it.

Maybe it's the weight of the stifled sorrow of their lives that cries out to free itself. They continue walking, agility and caution marking their steps. The night smiles indulgently at the two ants floundering on their way. The dying, reddish glow from the torch momentarily casts a dull light.

Two specks of light glow from their *bidis* as two heads crane and twist around, fervently searching for something.

At one spot, Singamu grasps Ella's arm with one hand and points at something with the other. In the water, in a crevice beside the riverbank, by the clump of date palms, something appears to have lodged itself. A pack of jackals eye it and wait patiently under the banyan tree. He flashes his light on the pack. Immediately, clusters of small, round cinders sparkle and the specks of red move. The grey, indistinct shapes can be clearly discerned—small jackals, big ones, the bulky males, the slim ones, some on their haunches, some standing, even some stretching themselves like dogs, with their front legs stretched out in front and their backs arched like a bow. A flutter of wings accompanied by squawking and screeching takes over. The light picks up the forms of vultures perched on the branches of the banyan tree. Singamu and Ella Reli stiffen, their minds alert.

Singamu Reli moves forward and flashes the light on the date-palm cluster. He can see a heap of something; it sways softly as the waters lap against it, seven or eight feet away from the bank on the vacant land that is submerged in waist-deep water. He goes closer. He can faintly distinguish its form. Something lies spreadeagled there, buoyed by some force beneath it. A pale form that doesn't have a stitch of clothing on it. On the far side, wrapped with dark moss and lichens, lies a round object, half-submerged in the water; on this end, clumped together, are three piles of big, fat lumps flanked on either side by two round, thick, white pillars as though protruding from the bloated heaps and arching into the water.

Singamu's mind goes back to the round, white electricity pole that Narua had climbed when he lost his life.

The realization of death flits back and rests briefly on his face. He stands in an unnatural stance, looking on tauntingly; behind him stands Ella Reli, his cheek resting on Singamu's shoulder, just below his ear. In the dying light of the flashlight, it looks like the bloated corpse of a calf—this naked, female form wrapped in loose strands of hair, undulating slowly as the waves lap against it. Intermittent flickers of lightning illuminate the huddled forms of vultures craning their snake-like necks.

The two boys are possessed by the same idea: if you look hard enough you will find gold. Gold! Gold! Something that they have lusted after but never found! It would come to them! Lumps of it! Heaps of it! Like a flat, starving, bloodsucking flea that bloats up when it feasts on blood, their bodies become taut from head to foot, and a strange quivering possesses them. They wade through the water and rush towards the corpse like they weren't men, but animals. In their eagerness to reach the corpse, they step into a pothole underwater. Their feet slip and they fall on the corpse, one on top of the other. Wrapped in slimy, cloying wetness, cold and soft—it burns wherever it touches the skin—Ella Reli experiences the feel of dead flesh on living flesh. He recoils and stands up; he sees Singamu holding on to the corpse and tugging at it. He too tugs. Their mouths fill with saliva, too gross to be swallowed; they pull and drag as the corpse floats closer to the bank like a swan swimming in the waters.

The vultures on the trees let out an eerie screech. Singamu runs his flashlight's beam over the body. Neck. Arms. Waist. All bare. Nothing, nothing—anywhere. Where's the gold? The gold! Only a few rings on the fingers and toes, some brass, some silver. They push back the hair from the face to look at the nose and the ears—no gold there either. A plain, round face, the mouth open in a twisted grin, the nose, cheeks, the round shut eyes, the eyelashes, all horribly swollen. It has taken on a new look, lumps of swollen flesh that look like tumours, over which trickle streams of water.

Devoid of gold. Devoid of silver. Devoid of life.

Ella suddenly realizes that this is a corpse. His wet body shudders. His teeth chatter. The excitement suddenly abates and tears trickle down from the corners of his eyes. The feet turn cold. Flashing his flashlight one last time, Singamu looks at Ella and the corpse at their feet. Grabbing Ella's hand, he says, 'Run for your life, Ella! If anyone finds us here, they'll say that we've made good our escape with the gold. They'll cudgel us to death, re, run, let's run away . . .' Taking giant strides, leaping and jumping, they leave.

On the left is the dark brimming river. The cold slivers of rain pierce them like needles. Ella Reli's mind drifts back to the feel of the corpse, and he recalls its cloying stickiness. Waves of horror and revulsion sweep over him at the memory of that uncanny experience, and he suddenly realizes that there's a sanctity about this: his living body, the limits it can take, with the limits clearly defined.

And Ella Reli sees that the path he's running on has ended.

There, the settlement is right in front of him, the haze from the fires in the settlement filtering through the rain, making it glow like daylight. The steamy light diffuses and comes right up to him. He looks at the pelting rain with a heightened consciousness. He feels its tender touch on his eyes, on his neck and behind his ears. The rain touches his mouth and drips over his body. This blessed water washes away the layer of dirt that cakes over him. And he takes deep breaths of relief. Like a starved, greedy beggar, he bares his chest to lap up the moist air and feels an immense sense of solace. He drowsily opens his eyes to realize that what he craves is the company of people.

In front of him lies the crowded settlement, packed to the brim with living people. Being one of them is all that matters, nothing else does.

He slows his pace and wrings the water out of his hair and body with his fingers. Putting his arm around Ella's shoulders, Singamu says, '*Aha!* The poor thing!'

Ella looks at him. The long, wet hair frames his head like a halo, below that a long, gaunt mask, two small eyes blinking in their hollow sockets. The wet mask glistens when light falls on it.

In a string of hot words, Singamu Reli vents, 'So many people were at the bathing ghat; wouldn't someone have held on to her? What a pity the poor thing drowned! There were so many people in the ghat and so many more walking around, it wasn't nighttime but eight o'clock in the morning, broad daylight, when the ghat's full of people. Yet no one came to her rescue! People are like that, re; they'll look on passively when someone's drowning. Look at the state she's in, poor dear! Aha!'

Neither mentions the gold that she supposedly had on her. It's almost as if the two of them have gathered on to themselves a bit of the pain of her last, tortured moments.

Their heads hang low.

The swollen river flows in the darkness, breaching the embankments on either side.

She has been left far behind.

There is the familiar hubbub, the throngs that are visible and distinguishable, and then the houses, the yards, the groves in the middle—to feel and experience.

Originally titled 'Kagaja Danga', 1941

Crows

Gosh, these crows are so aggravating! Irritated, Siba Shankar pushes aside the curtain, steps out of the room and stands on the veranda.

It is 9 a.m. The vast compound of the bungalow looks forsaken. Beyond the compound wall and over the rich canopy of dense trees flanking the road, large murders of crows circle, cawing raucously. They fly in and out, hover over the bungalow and continue with their pandemonium. Within the compound wall, a few of them perch on the isolated, densely foliaged trees, which are spaced far apart from one another, and continue their boisterous squawking.

'What's wrong with these damned creatures!' Siba Shankar despairs. 'Isn't there someone around to chase them away?' He glares at them in utter disgust when suddenly he realizes that the area is devoid of people! Every morning it was always teeming with people—people spilling over beyond the gate and on to the sides of the road, people milling around, parking their cars, scooters, rickshaws and bicycles; people who came and waited, to get an audience of a few moments with him. Today it is deserted!

His mind is besieged with a burning sense of sadness and disappointment, laced with anger and betrayal. It has been a scorcher for him since 5 p.m. yesterday when he got the bad news. So distraught was he that he couldn't sleep a wink the previous night. He had retired late to bed, but sleep eluded him; he got up several times and pottered about the house, then went back to bed and tried to snatch some sleep. But his disappointment had seeped into his mind. He could not sleep. He eventually left the bed early in the morning, ran through his daily chores and got back to his bedroom to sit glum and muted. He licked his wounds like a bruised animal. Suffused with grief and anger and a sense of offence, he did not wish to meet anyone. He knew that words of sympathy or curious inquiries would only add fuel to the smouldering fire within. So, he had taken the phone off its hook and had shut himself inside, sealing out all sound.

The crows carry on unrelentingly—their cawing harsh, sharp and sudden is an annoying irritant. Their cacophony has piqued him so overwhelmingly that he can't hold himself back any more and he is now out in the open. He feels that they are raucously and incessantly bruiting the sad news all around; the same woeful news that he had heard repeatedly last evening on the radio, much to his chagrin, and the news that would have been—or will be—read in this morning newspapers.

The list of candidates nominated by his party for the forthcoming election has been finalized, but his name does not figure in it.

Everyone will realize the significance of the news and the possible knock-on effects of his name's conspicuous absence.

There will be another election in a month's time. The party winning a majority of seats in each of the states in the country will form the next government and run the administration for the next five years. The winning candidates are the party's representatives in the State's legislative assembly. From them will be chosen the State's administrators for the ensuing five years—the ministers. It seems almost certain that his party's candidates will take most of the seats in the election and retain power for the next five-year term. But he, Siba Shankar, now stands no chance of being a minister. Neither will he be a member of the legislative assembly. Minister, huh! He will just be one of the hundreds of thousands of party workers. Just that.

He isn't that the only one to have been excluded. The names of a few current ministers and some sitting members, too, have been dropped from the list. New names have been nominated instead. A few names from the present list of ministers are retained, as also the names of a few from the current lot of members in the legislative assembly. Winning the election, they will once again become members of the assembly, and from that lot a few shall become the ministers. Alas, Siba Shankar will, for his part, not be one of them!

'They'll be, not I!' Siba Shankar was hurt, and he is ranting. 'They'll become ministers, but not me! Pray, what haven't I done for the party! What criticisms and insults haven't I faced! How much did I not sweat day and night! It was my untiring efforts and mental acumen that had won the party the spurs and put them right up front. Who doesn't know the stellar role I played? But look at the deception, this injustice, this ingratitude meted out to me! This treacherous world! As they say—once you're done with someone, just roll him over! Huh!'

He can't see anything else; this mix of his thoughts and images that simmers and scalds him, this indescribable hot wave of fury that spills over and spreads afar—how far?

The crows flap about and fly around, circling and proclaiming the tidings endlessly. Wide-eyed, Siba Shankar stands—entranced and transfixed—his shock of hair just as dishevelled as it had been when he had stormed out of the house in the morning. It lies in an unruly mop over his broad forehead, stark jet-black hair against his wheatish complexion. A round, fleshy face and a snub nose, his thick lips twisted in an infuriated sneer. He has on a vest on his well-built upper torso, he is in a lungi—his attitude conveys his customary nonchalance, strength and arrogance.

Before him, in the elegant garden of his official residence, miscellaneous flowers bloom in the manicured flower beds—some indigenous, some exotic—in multiform shapes and various hues. The array of bushes, creepers, trees are in many sizes and shapes, and spread all around. Their off-beat colours indicate a singularly classy, well-maintained garden, the plants brought in from various climes. He never really enjoyed the flower garden. Neither did he fancy reading the wide range of books stocked in his almirah. Nor did he enjoy the expensive decor or the objets d'art that catch the eye as one enters the house. They were merely to impress visitors—to convey to them that he is far above them in every possible way. That his tastes are exclusive and upper-class! He had personally made no conscious effort to create the garden; all he'd done was to direct the groundskeepers tending to it: 'See to it that it turns out to be a pretty and beautiful garden!' Just that.

'No one has a garden so wondrous!' Such words were music to the groundskeepers' ears and filled him with a sense of relief. 'Who else could have had such impeccable taste? Who else could have created such a delightful garden?' Siba Shankar felt very happy and fulfilled whenever he heard such lavish praise. He may not have had any particular fancy for it, but even so, whenever his eyes swept over the garden, he sensed his mind de-stressing and the clouds of workaday worries and concerns, dissipating. It indeed was a sight to cherish.

But as he stands there today, his eyes don't—*can't!*—see the garden. As if it didn't exist and were invisible. His mind is scarred with excruciating pain, his existence and the agony seemed to have conflated into an undifferentiated whole.

He's forty-five, and strong and healthy. Since his grandfather's time, or perhaps even before, his has been a rich farmer's family with plenty of farmland. His grandfather was also the village's main moneylender. His father, too, was a rich farmer and moneylender, who had built a house in the town. He had started a new business, the business had flourished, and he had grown into a well-known contractor in the village. Thereafter he had established a hotel and an industrial enterprise, and he had gone on to earn respect as a rich and famous businessman in the town. His family had grown, his business had expanded. Siba Shankar was brought up with love and in comfort; he didn't know any of life's miseries. He studied in school, then in college—not exactly out of any love of academia but for something more commonplace. It was like getting dressed to go out, much as others did, wearing clothes that everybody did, regardless of what it looked like on him or how it felt on the body—it was the garb and the imprimatur of civility and decency. He somehow managed to clear exam after exam without putting in any effort; in point of fact, being someone who didn't quite care for studies, he just went by the extant societal norms that placed a premium on ingenuity and innovativeness to get past the rush of examinations that confronted him in his path.

He was shrewd and astute and knew very well what it meant to achieve success in life, and how it had to be achieved. These attributes he had acquired from his family, from the examples set by the dissolute people of his class and from his rich peers—the world that corralled his being. His mind had been storing visions of life's possibilities ever since he was in the higher classes in school. He had learnt that success in academics did not necessarily translate into earning more and becoming rich, or acquiring fame and name, or a role in society that helped to arrogate to himself more power and pelf. His mind had recalibrated his life goals to his own personal know-how and experience. He had often marvelled at the desperation with which these studious souls had hunted for jobs; despite their endeavours, all they could do was to land jobs with meagre salaries at his father's or some such businessman's enterprises. Plus, he realized that even people in lofty perches in government earned such a paltry sum in a year that it didn't even add up to what the grocer in the bazaar earned in a month.

The more he thought along those lines, the more he'd understood that the bright students earned plaudits in the country, travelled abroad for higher studies to turn out to be highly regarded industrial scientists and engineers, before getting back home. Upon their return, they sought and got employment in large industrial firms on high salaries. But their remuneration has been just a fraction of the lakhs and crores of rupees of profit that the entrepreneurs churned out by leveraging the former's knowledge, wisdom and expertise in their day-to-day production and assembly lines. No matter how high a government servant's position, it was far from analogous to the respect that was accorded even to a ruling party's feckless local political leader. Ministers, doubtless, are the crown jewels that one must aspire to. And it didn't really take an exceptionally bright or honest person with great qualities of head and heart to become one anyway. Not being endowed with such qualities might be advantageous, too, he had concluded. Every exemplar who passed through his mind represented these home truths to him.

It was time for him to get real. See how the elders preach ethical values from the family pulpit and how they themselves fail to practise them! All the teachings of the shastras and dharma wrapped inside the books are best locked up and displayed in the almirah, much like the way pictures of the gods and enlightened souls encased in glass frames are hung on the walls in its most achingly humdrum manner. Over time, totems had become banal, merging into the everyday living of existence as a decorative part of the room's familiar aesthetic set pieces—no one looks up and stoops and bows in veneration, no work or behaviour or the foul transactions of quotidian living are disrupted by their presence and beneath their sublime gaze every known appalling activity goes on without an iota of qualm.

His ideas and beliefs had firmed up. He was convinced that to be successful in life was to get rich and powerful—that is where one success begets another; and from the commingling of these two shiny stars a man is recognized, admired, feted and blessed with multitudinous offerings. Ascending this ladder of success involves intelligence, tact, cunning, the horses-for-courses touch, the glib talk to inveigle people and, in turn, to enchant the world. Using whatever means thought to be most effective to satisfy selfish interests and goals is kosher. Family members must also step up and act appropriately. Lying, making false promises, misleading and battering people with lies and more lies, betraying them, being untrue, heartless and cruel, and even blurting out any cringe-worthy thoughts that come to mind—nothing is beyond reproach to achieve the objective. It's what they've been doing all along silently, as if they were the secret tittle-tattles from the restaurant's kitchen, which has a markedly different ambience to the glammed-up dining decor meant for public consumption.

These kitchen gossips sometimes do come out in the open in tiny whispers, but not from the mouths of family members. Their faces are instead adorned with generosity and happiness, their self-effacing attitude ablaze with the efflorescent fragrance of the flowers growing on the heap of composted faux idealism and high principles. But, ironically, these things are what one has to learn from them, too—the utterances, their demeanour, their attitude, their posture, their subtle usage of language.

He had heard of and read about Mahatma Gandhi's idealistic principles of life: how he made truth, non-violence and ethics the cornerstone of his life; how the Mahatma, imbued with these ideals, walked the righteous path eschewing arms, bloodshed and violence to successfully launch India's fight for independence from the foreign yoke; how the millions of people moved by the great man's ideals flocked to him, followed him, forgetting their many personal hardships and losses that came their way; the sundry people who sacrificed their lives at the altar of the freedom struggle; and how indeed the Gandhian way had illuminated a new path for humanity to emulate and live ennobled lives.

But for Siba Shankar they were mere hand-me-down words, precepts and clichés. He was seven when India attained independence. He wasn't old enough to appreciate Gandhian ideals. Mahatma Gandhi, too, had never taken over the reins of the government. He became a martyr soon after India gained freedom. As Siba Shankar grew up and became aware of the world, he didn't even get to see a Mahatma Gandhi around him. He didn't discern anything special in the behaviour and work ethics of the numerous people who chased eminent personalities that epitomized Gandhian principles and values. Nor did he discern the Mahatma's ideals imbued in them, notwithstanding the frequent allusions and incantations of the name and the values preached by the great soul. It wasn't that a few odd Gandhians, minuscule though in number, weren't around—of course they were, but they seemed to be living in a different world—sworn to asceticism and fasting or, alternatively they seemed like the ascetics of some order. The paths they chose did not let you earn a living or help you solve mundane issues. Nor did they let you attain material goals for the fulfilment of a worldly life.

So, he grew up instead following the zeitgeist of the times—not the Gandhian track. On the cusp of his life, he turned out to be a savvy businessman. His father even acknowledged that his son had the nous to be a wily businessman. He had even something more in him: courage, daring, the art to hoodwink people, a keen business sense, the craft to work out ways to slip off the legal dragnet while simultaneously hammering out clever ways through push and pull to get in and stay ahead of others.

As time went by, he saw that he wasn't one to be merely defined by his own business. Earlier the businessmen would indirectly help political parties, in exchange for some favours—a kind of quid pro quo, a you-scratch-my-back-I-scratch-yours trade-off that suited both sides; gradually the vision changed, the trajectory bumped ahead, and they got into active politics; if successful at the hustings they could reap redoubled benefits for their business—power in their grip, people around them to do their bidding, and the respect that flowed and followed them naturally, unasked for. From under the veil, the capitalist face could be worked upon and morphed—to present them as selfless public servants in the service of the nation. The vast acreage of politics was a wide fertile ground—open to people blessed with tact and ingenuity. So Siba Shankar stepped into politics—not he alone, but many others like him, too.

He thinks and mulls over all this now, as his mind zeroes in on himself, and he continues to commune with his past.

He grew, he prospered; others too enjoyed themselves, others too luxuriated; and what a stellar reputation he had earned for himself! He dared to dream! Everyone got to see his skill sets in the full panoply of public display in getting things done. He made good for himself, but he worked tenfold more and did enormous good for people. More than his own share of the booty, he let others have theirs too in ample measure—loads of filthy lucre. Do others ever do that? Nope, they gobble up everything and do precious little for others.

His mind flips back and he keeps thinking: look at these ingrates! How they'd once applauded him hoping to make a quick filthy buck, and how they've dismissed him from sight now—the past wiped off their radars! How their neglected regions had seen the dizzying pace of change and how overnight had turned into gold with his Midas touch—how they'd prospered and grown rich! But they've let him down now when he needs them the most! What does public memory entail? Well, this is a crucial lesson in human behaviour—a day had come when they had forgotten Madhu Babu, too!

And what about his so-called friends—the ones who took advantage of his 'doer' image and drew succour from his muscular presence to make good in life? Paradoxically, around the same time a stab of jealousy shot through them and they burned in envy, and they seemingly backstabbed him when he was most vulnerable. Workaholic he was, but he lacked the nous and the skill to placate and flatter people with sugary, syrupy words. His words were direct and pointed, delivered without nuance and pretence— they came out straight like a tracer bullet. Possibly, some ideas, somewhere, sometime, might have occurred to him and would've rolled off his tongue involuntarily, and these wretched blokes are now getting back at him, avenging those slights. Know this well—everyone is an opportunist . . . a base, ignoble, selfish creature! That's how some managed to retain their names on the nomination list one more time, while they conspired to push him off the cliff so that he literally had no chance to climb back up again.

His cogitations lead him to look inward: Why all these worries now? How did they really concern him? Was he the anointed one born with the responsibility to rescue this world? Should he, therefore, stay the course, and remain condemned to this cesspool of politics? Why do these anxieties and temptations of power haunt him still? He tries to buoy his spirit to justify an insight: people will one day put you high on a pedestal, and another fine day they'll disavow you and leave you high and dry.

Yet, in his mind this argument doesn't quite wash; it pales in no time and extinguishes itself and becomes invisible, leaving behind only the monotonous sound of his inner monologue. When he hadn't had the kind of experience he has now, this argument would've held up; but now that he has tasted the sweetness and opium of power, he knows in his veins that political power is everything—without it, nothing is ever going to taste as sweet and heady, and life will be so achingly humdrum. His mind, like a beast in the wild, unspools and roars with implacable resentment and jealousy.

The interminable squawking of the crows feels like merciless jibes piercing his aching body and mind, as if inciting and taunting him. He can do precious little about it, and strange as it may seem it is hard to ignore it, too. His face is twisted in rage, his eyes afire, his neck drooping, his visage contorted in pain and anguish. With pinched face, much like the Dussehra's image of the dead Mahishasura, buffalo demon!

> Caw, caw, caw—no respite from cawing,
> Word-of-mouth is what papers are doing.
> No respite on the news gathering front,
> The crows go on squawking upfront.

Originally titled 'Kau', 1956

Lustre

The sun is setting.

It's as if the boundless sky hasn't quite put on its wonted lustrous face, so full of hope, and looks sad instead with dark streaks streaming down its doleful demeanour. The aching brassy hue too hasn't touched it yet, neither the deathly pall of the silvery moonbeams. It's hard to say whether its colour can be identified—for example, the colour of any lifeless object: blue like Robin blue powder, or aquamarine like the colour of the steel almirah here in front of me, or it's this colour or that colour like the myriad tones of saris on display in the retail stores. It's hard to label the colours of the sky. It's harder still to assign disparate names to them—very unlike describing Rs 20,300.40 in arithmetic, or a two-storey structure of a reinforced-concrete building, which are distinct and can be measured in clear, unambiguous terms. At the most, one can say that the sky is a vignette, a collage of mottled colours—formless, but with no extant lexical choices to dredge and filter, analyse and sculpt, to define it.

Amid this minuscule consciousness, a tiny thought arises: 'This is the creator's handiwork: like the deep, fathomless oceans, the sky too is dressed in randomness; it mimics the oceans—vast, limitless, endless—this, the inscrutable sky, the deep void with its cosmic imponderables, this creation of the vast unknown, the eternal truth, *nitya sanatan!*'

'What else is it?'

It is—

Like the grasses, shrubs, mosses and lichens in the tundra spread across the Siberian prairie in the wake of the melting snow.

Or, as in the impenetrable depths of the dense forest of the dark African continent, where the giraffe stretches its long neck, or like the images of the icebergs floating in the Icelandic sea.

It's like the consciousness of their day-end dreams emanating from the hapless workers on the face of a cloud of dust kicked up when a thousand miners stick their pickaxes into the ground for the first time.

Notwithstanding the vivid images—the haze of dust; the spiralling smoke of bidi-cigarette-*pikka* or the dry wick or the rubble burn or the smoke billowing out of the kitchen fire— he still gropes clumsily to help paint the real picture.

That sky is now lustrous; a momentary life-spark that comes to commingle with the disparate elements, bringing back memories and then driving them away.

The sky is just like that, Sumanta realizes, when suddenly— it is as if his eyes are riveted on one end of a long, hollow, iron tube. He's looking through it just like one would examine a rifle emptied of bullets by resting it on his shoulder. It seems he is circling back to his own vivid past. One segment is quite clear, the rest, though not rusted, isn't quite distinct and lights up a topsy-turvy, searing collage. As the light flashes in his head, he can only see the vast emptiness at the other end of the rod. And as he looks up at the sky, he glimpses, through the long, hollow tube, a dark face cheerfully humming a tune, jasmine flowers tucked in her hair, the beauty of her face bursting forth. She's in a blue sari, a garland of flowers on her neck and her hands are wrapped in strings of flowers like so many corsages. She sways gracefully as she walks and tilts her head a little as she smiles, revealing her serried teeth which look like rows of jasmine buds; the look she flashes travels across the nettled fence, the rose garden, the edge of the *gangaseuli,* the coral jasmine tree, where a clutch of red chickens is pecking at the dirt, scrounging for nuggets, creating ripples.

Here sits the bald, rotund, broad-faced Patnaikilu, his grim, scholarly, bespectacled face for no earthly reason always furrowed in thought and, as that bewitching look floats in from the middle of the road and goes past Patnaikilu's Hitler-stached face and pierces Sumanta's eyes, the heart goes into a flutter, and he emits a deep sigh, much like the flower blossoming on the ends of a small and slender stalk of *sugandharaj,* the tuberose. That is the moment! The face wafts into vivid focus; the beauteous thing then ebbs away like a wave, close to the tile-roofed tea stall and the tin shed in front of it, where steel sheets are tamed into steel trunks—there the road winds, and there Lalita peels away into oblivion.

The sky's aglow with colour that can now be captured in words. Patnaikilu will glare fiercely at Sumanta, and then smile.

Maybe he'll say, 'Eyes like dark bumblebees, accompanied by wide-eyed, doe-eyed innocence! What a nose! What a face, what a figure, what a gait! When a dusky beauty is diamantine, it really is a work of art!'

'What a lover-boy you are, Bhai Ramananda!' Sumanta would say.

Patnaikilu would guffaw and say, 'You saw her, Lalita, didn't you? Every day she looks, smiles and moves away. You think she's merely giving you a passing look, don't you? However, her limbs, too, have eyes, they too can see. Her back is also watching you!'

'You or me?'

They go out on a walk.

But they don't run into Lalita on their walk, although they meet a bevy of women returning home from work. They too wear flowers in their hair, some of them are singing songs. Boisterous steps and giggles, some looks are wet and moist, some are gluey. Sumanta doesn't care to spare them a glance.

They discuss the state of the country, the state of the administration, politics, local news, and of human beings. The last one was the most interesting, also the most illuminating. The ways of people, hatching plans—scheming, strategizing and getting ready for action! Some people have fallen flat on their faces, some have leapt ahead. Someone exultant, someone sliding back down and some, biding time. So much injustice and oppression confronts the world; and households are beset with diseases, misery and problems.

The road ends and a cluster of buildings looms into view with the old, hoary mountain silhouetted in the background. At the base of the mountain is the Bhradeshwar Temple. Many paans have been chewed and many cigarettes smoked. Standing, arms akimbo, looking at the maroon sky overhead, Sumanta curiously asks Patnaikilu, 'Bhai, who's that girl—Lalita?'

The memory of that incident comes back to him like an answer to his question. Patnaikilu doesn't know who she is. Long ago, he'd heard her friend calling out 'Lalita' and she had responded—that was when he'd learnt her name. He understands that, but nothing more. Perhaps she, too, works as a coolie. And she loves flowers. Patnaikilu had seen her purchase three–four anna's worth of strings of flowers at one go in the flower market. Just that.

Another day passes. The two friends are back from their walk—Sumanta Misra, the electrical engineer, and V.L.N. Patnaikilu, the pest-control officer—the two workers who symbolize the country's resurgence. Only after they had discussed various other issues do they tell each other, 'Well, we're happy with our way of life, although we can neither bite nor scratch!'

Around sunset, whenever Sumanta is not travelling and is in town, his heart suddenly skips a beat. He senses it's time for her to arrive. If he doesn't see her there, his heart would sink in anguish. She invariably walks down that very road, as Sumanta, feigning lack of interest, is actually all agog, his neck craned to ogle at her. Lalita hovers into view, turns her face, casts an anxious, knowing look, smiles and then walks past.

One day, there was an incident when V.L.N. Patnaikilu was around. As soon as Lalita turned her face and smiled, Patnaikilu called out 'Lalita'. It was so sudden that Sumanta was taken by surprise.

Before they could say anything, Lalita had walked up to the gate and asked, 'Did you call, Babu?

Sumanta could feel the perspiration on his face. Lalita was standing there, her head bowed. She was wearing an orange-coloured sari. Her thick hair was coiffed, a jasmine wreath engirdling it, with the pointed end of the fragrant *kiya*, screw-pine flower, tucked into it. On her neck and arms were wreaths of yellow amla flowers. She was lithe and pretty, exuding youthful lustre, an exceptional sculptor's wondrous handiwork. Lalita raised her eyes and looked at Sumanta. Someone ahead called out, 'Lalita!' She quietly walked away, as though intuiting something importunate had happened. Patnaikilu was grave, his gaze lowered. Dazed, Sumanta kept staring at the road. Five minutes passed. It seemed like both men were paying tribute to the memory of the brief encounter. They weren't standing but sitting on chairs. On the table were two empty teacups, the tea long since drunk, and an empty paan platter, the paan long since chewed.

'Patnaikilu!' Sumanta said with a contrite face, 'It just wasn't right on our part!'

Patnaikilu disagreed. All set to contest the criticism of his actions, he muttered with a twisted smile, 'Oh, pooh!'

Sumanta had nothing to add, but Patnaikilu continued, trying to use the remnants of his courage to redeem himself, 'Oh, I just called out to her light-heartedly, so what's the big deal? In our eyes, she has always been a walking shadow. I thought the shadow could speak a few words before she vanishes. Now you know she does respond, and she does come over. She's like that!'

'This isn't poetry, sir,' Sumanta said. 'It's like killing a pest!'

'No, no, no,' Patnaikilu had said grandly, 'it's more like light illuminating a lifeless pole!'

'No, not at all,' Sumanta rebutted as quickly. 'What do you mean by "She's like that"? That most people have such proclivities—every person goes through the same daily grind, be they poets, ascetics, or even the most enlightened and exalted; everyone is human—can the soul detach from the bodily desires? That's why I say let her be the way she is. What difference does it make to you?'

'Okay, fine. Let's go out.'

Five to seven days go by. Lalita doesn't even cast a glance at the house when she passes by, almost as if the house didn't exist and there's just the road that stretches ahead.

Then a few days later, when she walks along that road, she seems to be looking for the house. But before Sumanta could emerge from the house, Lalita has already left. One day, maybe with some good fortune, they may run into each other again.

Lalita, who is she? Who is this Lalita? She's nobody to him. She has not shown him grace during his illness or difficulty, nor in his happiness. She has never been anywhere around him. Maybe she's just another traveller on the highway of life—not a person who might matter to him. She isn't one of those whose name is inscribed in the pages of the history book of his life. His is a separate world of happiness and grief. It enfolds his family, his wife and children, his relatives and friends, his responsibilities, his job, his friendships and his enmities. In his accomplishments and failures, in his meetings and isolations, his kinship and relationships are calculated and measured precisely in terms of dates, days, months, events and money.

There's no trace of Lalita in that parchment of life, not even a speck.

Life moves on inexorably. He's relocated to another town. He leaves behind Patnaikilu, much like he has left behind many such friends over the years in his life's journey. His experience here too will be added to his life's footnotes—connecting the many such transient dots of experiences spread across time and place; and over time will pale into the crusted dossier of the minutiae of his personal history.

In another part of the country, directly in front of him, close to a small railway station, is a small settlement. This place is about a hundred miles away from the earlier place and sits on a mound; on one-half of that area, a sub-station is in the process of being set up. The shanties nearby are crammed together, sitting cheek by jowl with one another.

'All the thefts of our tools and appliances are the handiwork of these scoundrels, *saar*,' a local official tells him. 'Two of them have been nabbed, but it has had no effect. These people are from many different places, they live like families, but no one is sure whether they actually are related or not. As dusk settles, there's always a party happening, every day. Drinking, gambling and all such activities. That shack you see there,' the man says, pointing to a hut in the distance, 'the one near the guava tree is the house of their leader, a veritable *shaitan*! These people don't move out of here, but they are at the root of every trouble. They have the support and approval of influential people, what can I say, saar? So, let them be!'

These were the motley group of local officials briefing him of their grievances. A woman comes out from beside the guava tree. A dusky, slim artistic image, like a slender iron rod, swathed in a faintly tinged, green nylon sari and blouse. Two plaits hang in front, over each shoulder. The bony face is caked with vanishing cream and powder, dark kohl graces her eyes and there is the hint of a fine moustache above her upper lip. She looks like a living corpse. The red lipstick on her is like a smear of fresh blood. She twists the palm of her right hand to shield her face as she tilts her head to look out. The nails are long and uncut, they too appear painted a fresh blood red.

'This is the shaitan, saar, the leader of the mafioso, the root of all evil,' whispers the local official. 'Everything about her is a sham; her hair is bought, the dentures too. She has three grown up girls with her—three of four different kinds! Look, here they come . . .'

Sumanta watches as the three women hover around their leader like three small cats purring around a big cat. One of them is tall and alabaster fair; one is short, dark and plump, her shoulder and head look conjoined; and the third is a thin, fair, flat-faced lipstick-smeared woman with a flat nose, slit eyes. She is draped in nylon and carries a vanity bag in her hand. Standing in a row, they are gaping back at them. Their inspection over, they leave one after the other.

The last to turn around and leave is the woman who seems sculpted from a slender, rusted, iron rod, a dusky, lissom woman in flimsy clothes. Watching her from behind as she walks away fills Sumanta with a sense of déjà vu and resurrects memories that waltz past the same long, hollow tube. His mind floats past kaleidoscopic pictures of a sculptor's amazing creation as he recalls the past, seemingly lost to him. A fulsome menu of memories scrolls across his consciousness. His subordinates have already turned away and are leaving the place. But Sumanta's inner thoughts ferment the past festering within him, and without any regard to the time or the place, he involuntarily says out loud, 'Lalita!'

The local officials turn around to look at him quizzically. The dusky, statuesque image carved out of rusted iron lets out a raucous scream. 'Who called?'

On the other side, the goods train is standing at the station. Like a somniloquist, the train engine mumbles, emits a shrill whistle and starts chugging out of the railway station.

Sumanta turns around quickly and abruptly moves towards his work site. His colleagues look askance at his face because their catalogue of plaintive grievances wasn't exhausted as yet. 'You saw them for yourself, saar, you saw them!' they say, a trifle befuddled. 'Yes, those ones!'

Over the babel of their voices, Sumanta speaks up, uncorking his rambling mind, 'Tell me, the latest news of the transfer? This equipment is being built for the first time in our country and we're receiving it for the first time. I think these are going to be better than the foreign stuff. What do you think?'

His timing to talk business is still a slightly off—what can they say in response?

He feels a bit befuddled and despite his proximity to his colleagues, he doesn't seem to have heard them. He seems to be in his own world, lost in the tantric tendrils of his memories and swathed in images within his own mind, he glimpses the twelve-year-old, still-luminous, still-lustrous images—fraction by tiny fraction, just beyond the distant, green hedge that served as a barrier—the momentarily fresh and beautiful face that had come into view. There is no rust there. His eyes are both pure and youthful, and cloaked in empathetic, warm compassion.

Suddenly Sumanta says, 'Why are you scared, saar? If you keep the door locked, no one can come in and no one can cause you any harm!'

It is the rattle—the knocking on the door—that's the rub!

He smiles, imagining V.L.N. Patnaikilu looming large over him—standing right in front—watching.

Originally titled 'Aabha', 1971

Town Bus

College Square. It is 4.30 p.m. The town bus has halted. A host of young men and women pour out of the main gate of the college and rush towards the bus. A *kadai,* wok, slung from one hand, Julu Ray follows them. He has to compete with these youngsters to get a seat on the bus. He huffs and puffs as he doubles his pace and runs. Through the corner of his eye, he sees that the young crowd has already surged far ahead.

A pang of jealousy stabs him. Embarrassed of his girth, he compares the narrow waists of these youngsters with his own. His waist measures 38 inches! And below it is a spherical expanse; the silk kurta that stretches tightly over it, emphasizes its shape. Flitting lightly across like so many dragonflies, the young men and women pack themselves tightly into the bus. The bus is already full and is on the verge of moving away. Hefting his bloated form, he waddles the short distance and reaches the door of the bus. He holds on to the rod at the entrance and heaves himself up. Jostling to find standing place amid the crammed passengers, he takes a deep breath. The bus lurches and moves.

He lifts the kadai slightly and looks at it. It is a sturdy utensil, heavy and wide. Exactly what he wanted. One look at the kadai and he thinks of his home. The person who makes the pithas, pancakes, and feeds all of them. All ten of them. The youngest boy, much petted and pampered, because he is the youngest. His face is swollen due to a cold and cough. The boy is disobedient and sneaks off to eat berries and drink water immediately after the meal. If only the eldest son had kept an eye on him. This youngest boy has repeated each class twice, roams around in long-sleeved shirts and at this young age, declares that he wants to get into business! The eldest girl too hasn't grown up to be like her mother. Three years ago, she dropped out of school and now hangs around at home. She is a good-for-nothing when it comes to household chores. She can't even snap a straw in two. All she does is some embroidery, some inane figures of cats and dogs in coloured thread. The rest are in school, each stacked one after the other.

And their Bou. How nice it would be if she were a touch slimmer and her tongue a tad less raspy! The stomping of footsteps pervades his mind; the harsh, heartless screech comes floating in—how he wishes Usha were a shade gentler! If you were to draw attention to this, the screech would transform into a scream: with no domestic help, I've worn myself out doing all the household chores and who has the time to learn to speak tenderly? It has been nineteen years since I came into this household. What joy have you given me that you demand so much? What a household, what a pittance you earn; were I not around you would've been on the streets long ago! Aren't you ashamed of yourself that you dare to talk like this?

He himself is a gentle, peace-loving, portly man. He knows that he's scared of her. But she's the mainstay of the household. The house wouldn't run without her. In this kadai she will make chakulis, pancakes. And in her characteristic style she'll put them in front of him. She will say, will you now shove them down your gullet or will you play with them like a child?

Maybe she'll smile a little when she sees the kadai. She would ask how much it cost, and she might smile a little more when she realizes that he got it cheap. But then, was man born to take care of the household and live a life committed to one's duty? Or was there something more to life—a place for tender, loving care, soothing words, some moments of lazy do-nothings?

Also, some space for a little wrongdoing! The moment he thinks of wrongdoings, he experiences fear and anguish. The house next door. The new tenant, Ragini Debi, lived alone with her children. Her husband was in a foreign land. Within a few days, he had bonded with her; he would visit her and spend time with her. She too voluntarily helped the family in many ways. She'd teach a child a tune or how to play the harmonium. She taught someone how to use her sewing machine and how to make a variety of homemade recipes. Things like that. Ragini Debi didn't shy away from him. She looked him in the eye and spoke to him freely, face to face. The intimacy that developed between them surprised him. It gradually became a habit to visit her after he returned from his tours. He would sit with her and inquire after her children, and discuss the philosophy of life with her over a cup of tea. His children would also troop in and walk away with their friends. Sometimes, other women from the neighbourhood also dropped by. No one had ever said a word. And *she* too would stomp in. She would glare at them like a wild cat. But Ragini Debi's mesmerizing warmth and enveloping affection would enchant and thaw her, and she would smile and stay. Ragini Debi would even playfully tease him in his wife's presence. His wife would also join in the banter and mercilessly pull his leg. They would joke about how forgetful and foolish he was. But he enjoyed it all.

One day he glanced into the depths of his mind, at a time when all other thoughts had paused like still water in a tower of glass. This is the moment when one can see the sand at the bottom. He sees the magic of fluttering eyelashes, the way they dance and then half lower—like tiny red leaves on wilted trees—and his consciousness is suffused by a fresh wave of creation. Behind locked doors and closed windows, he closets himself from the outside world and opens the treasure trove of his chimerical dreams. He indulges in his many fantasies and that makes him happy. A new swiftness, a fresh enthusiasm fills him, the pace of his life quickens and the drudgery of old routines appears light and easy. He can do a lot more work, he looks more agile and the weight of living that he carries on his shoulders feels lighter. His love for the children and the attention he gives them and his household perceptibly increases.

His association with Ragini Debi has significantly increased his self-confidence. He pulled his chair a little closer to her when he spoke to her. And even though he never knew her husband, one day he found himself addressing her as Bhauja. From that day on, he found himself indulging in light-hearted teasing and bantering with her.

And then *that* evening.

He had returned from his travels and was at home for barely five minutes before he rushed over to her house. There was a reason for this hasty visit. He had hardly set foot at home when he heard that Ragini Debi had been unwell with a fever for the last couple of days. When he reached her house, he sensed that Ragini Debi had been anticipating his visit. The untied hair hung loose around her narrow, pretty face. Her hot, flushed face glowed. As he looked at her, he felt a warm excitement inside him. The limp body of the woman, sitting at the edge of the cot, mindlessly swinging her legs and slurring her words tinged with longing was like the surface heat of the cracked, parched earth, whose intense desire could move the heavens to shower silent blessings. And he found himself beside her, within her magnetic pull. His eyes were riveted. He had gradually drawn up the chair by the bed and was bending towards her as he continued with the conversation. He was blissfully unaware of what either of them was saying. He only sensed his consciousness dwindling at the firm tug of his heartstrings. His senses pulled away inexorably by the ebb of the tide; there was a sense of excitement here, also a sense of liberation—as if this were exactly what he wanted and what he had long awaited.

Around nine thirty in the night. He doesn't remember hearing the thud of stomping feet and the raucous voice that normally preceded it. No one did. He was suddenly jolted to his senses and quickly straightened himself. Ragini Debi too jumped up, startled. The wife stood before them, her face contorted with horrific expressions, hurling endless abuses, spewing unspeakably vulgar and vitriolic words. Then, lifting one heavy foot, she landed him a stout kick. 'Shame on you!' she screamed. She then turned around and walked away like a typhoon. He followed her out meekly, without a backward glance. He didn't even attempt to console the tearful and humiliated Ragini Debi nor did he apologize to her. He had never broken societal norms, but he had never had the courage to stand up for himself. Instead, he believed that he had erred, had been at fault and had been unfair. The fear of scandal overtook his consciousness.

In the dreadful days that followed, each moment was filled with excruciating pain. Life became a nightmare. He couldn't say how the shame and sorrow dissipated, how the scar eventually healed, and how the old life came back. Time was the great healer. The balm of forgetting eased all pain. The old leaves fell.

With that, the old relationship was also severed. Within three months, Ragini Debi not only left the house, she also moved out of the city. Years passed. He had even had three more children since then.

In an attempt to be one with this crowd of burgeoning young people, he had stirred up his past and rediscovered Ragini Debi. If not in body, in spirit he was still young. Nothing untoward had happened that night, but the mere hint of a scandal as an imagined possibility had vindicated his youth.

The bus continues to move. Many get off, many more get on. When he emerges from his thoughts, he realizes that he is looking at the back of a woman. At the expanse of skin between the two shoulders, skimpily covered with a strip of purple cloth and a gold chain strung across it. Perhaps it was that tiny sliver of cloth on which his eyes had unconsciously alighted which had triggered a memory.

He shifts the kadai to the other hand. He dismisses these random thoughts and thinks about the kadai, pitha and his home. It is a materialistic world he lives in, and he is beset with many problems and worries. Here, only success is lauded; there is no sympathy for anything else.

'Who's this? Is it Julu Babu?' someone shouts from the other end of the bus. The veterinarian, Gopal Babu, continues. 'When did you return from Sukinda? Are you done with the audit there?' A tall, muscular man, he wears a hat even inside the bus. 'Since you were there to take care of things, I left. What's happening there anyway? And what brings you here? How much did the kadai cost? And when do you travel again? Do you live around here?' A volley of unrelated questions. Not for him the answers. For him only the pleasure of talking to someone familiar after standing quietly among strangers for so long. 'We spent a nice day together at the dak bungalow. Our doctor didn't know you. I admonished him. "What do you mean? Don't you know Julu Ray, the auditor?"' the motormouth continued.

Cuttack Chandi Square. The town bus halts. The shoulders in front of him quiver. The woman turns around. Startled, Julu Ray gapes at her. Is this Ragini Debi? No, not she! But isn't the face gradually lighting up in recognition? But it couldn't be her! No!

Before he can make up his mind, he is pushed by the crowd and unsteadily gets off the bus. The bus has moved on. He wipes away the past with a gusty sigh and inserts a paan into his mouth.

As he walks towards his house, he again assesses the weight of the kadai. She may scowl at the purchase, but it is a heavy kadai, so it would last a long time.

His wife would smile, Julu Ray imagines, as he trudges back home.

Originally titled 'Town Bus', 1988

The Heir

Sura's shoulders shook, his back heaved, he stooped even further.

'Stop!' His Bou, Suna Dei, intervened. 'You've chastised him enough. Come, come for dinner now. Let me get done with my chores.'

'No! I won't! Where is truth, honesty, integrity, godliness, dedication to duty? Or will my son be . . .'

Suna Dei screamed in anger, 'W-e-l-l! Then shred him to pieces and devour him! Kill me too! Strangle the children! Burn down the house! Or all of you stay here and I'll walk out!'

Sura lifted his head, but didn't turn around. Hara Babu walked away, seething and fuming.

Stroking Sura's back, Suna Dei said, 'Arey Sura, come, come to have dinner.'

Sura didn't reply.

'Come! Go and change. Come!'

'No!' Sura intoned. 'No . . .'

'Arey, don't sulk over what Bapa says, Sura! He says whatever comes to his mind when he's angry and he forgets it shortly thereafter. He rarely pays attention to what is happening in the household, then one fine day he steps in and rants. Maybe something went wrong in the office today and he is upset, who knows? Come, come!'

Sura straightened up and looked at his mother. His dishevelled, long hair framed his flushed, fleshy face. His eyes, reddish-white, held a wild expression like that of a lunatic. He was solely focused on himself and seemed unaware of anything that was happening around him. He still wore the clothes that he had worn to college in the morning and later in the evening, when he had stepped out with his friends—a pair of narrow trousers and a shirt. Sura was a tall, well-built young man. Suna Dei looked at him and thought he looked just like his father had done twenty-five years ago.

While hurriedly walking away, Sura said, 'I don't want to eat anything. I'm going to bed.'

Suna Dei turned to her husband, her face pale.

Sura lay on the bed in the darkness of his room. He hadn't bothered to switch on the fan, the mosquitoes swarmed around him. His troubled mind tormented him. He felt exploited and insulted and decided he couldn't take it any more. When and how had he ever harmed anyone? Was his mere existence a crime? No one seemed to acknowledge that he existed—it was almost as though he were invisible or a mere shred of paper drifting about in the wind. It didn't matter whether he was alive or dead.

He existed, and therefore the world could think of him as a scrap of wastepaper, could blame him for everything that went wrong, could take him to task—and Bapa represented this world.

What, then, remained in this life? Why should he continue to live? Whom should he trust? What happiness was here? What hope? Who was good? Who was true?

The experiences he had gathered in the eighteen years of his existence seemed of scant consequence, dissipated as they were—everything he valued looked trite, meaningless, vapid. It would be better if he were dead—this life was just not worth living!

Despair buzzed in his head. He could hear his mother telling his father, 'You stubbornly cling to your opinions. You don't understand or ever listen to me. Don't tell me later that I didn't warn you.'

'What's there for me to understand?'

'You berated the boy for no fault of his. In the heat of the moment, you say whatever you like. You infect a fresh flower with worms. Your anger blinds you. All children like to enjoy themselves; he isn't the only one. He isn't a child any more. He'll soon be a graduate; don't you think he deserves some dignity? Doesn't he know what is right and what is wrong? Isn't he aware of his responsibilities? Won't he take care of himself? Doesn't he apply himself to his studies?'

Sura strained to eavesdrop.

'Humph! As if mere studying is all there is! If he failed an examination, where would he be?'

'Whatever is destined for him will happen. Hundreds of students graduate every year but are forced to stare unemployment in the face. You and I can't write his destiny for him. You use such harsh words to chastise him. Will those words help him in any way?'

'Character . . .'

'Stop talking loftily about moulding character. Don't children have eyes and ears to perceive the world around them? How many people do they see who are worthy of respect? You yourself say so.'

'Do I say so?'

'Then do I? You talk in much detail about the world outside, and we all listen to your narratives. You've told us so many tales about the evil deeds of people whom we have looked up to. And today you talk of character! *Ma lo!* You tell us that it's impossible to live without telling lies or without graft or without indulging in evil deeds. And people like you, who always tread the path of truth, are targeted and tormented. Be that as it may, this is our destiny. This is *kaliyug!*'

'Are you saying that I should just stand by and watch passively as my Sura goes to the dogs?'

'Why don't you understand? In what way is he a bad boy? Compared to his peers, I believe he is a lot more commendable. He's young, he craves excitement. As he gets older, he'll mend his ways on his own. He'll change and wise up as he moves along in life.'

'But I want to know why he isn't interested in his studies.'

'If he wasn't interested in his studies, why would he sit with his books?'

'Huh! Is this any learning? When we were young . . .'

'Your salad days are long over!' Suna Dei interrupts. 'You graduated; you got a job. As you yourself have often said, gone are those days. Those who have done well in life, those who have made tons of money, are they all educated? Does their education help them to garner more wealth?'

'Dacoits! Shaitans! Fraudsters!'

'*Uff*! Some of them are your teachers, some, your lords and masters and some, your moneylenders. If required, you'll prostrate yourself at their feet and with craven, ingratiating smiles.'

'Who? Me?'

'Well, that's nothing to be ashamed of,' Sura Dei softened her words. 'You turn to them to ask for favours. To reverse a relocation, to seek a promotion, to ask for a loan. You do reach out to them and you will continue to do so. Who are they? You've always raked the muck around their names. All of them are sinners; their wealth, ill-gotten; their only capability is a sin, their riches too! Everything is impure! And yet you go to them with your most ingratiating smile. We all live in an age where they're the overlords. You take it amiss if I don't visit them in their homes. You don't understand that I hail from a village. Will I be able to talk to them or do I like visiting them? I'm not defending my shortcoming; I realize this is my own inadequacy. I know I can't socialize with them as an equal.'

'So, you want Sura to take the path of dishonesty, to earn a living using dishonest means and to fend for himself and support us that way?'

'Why would I want something that is so wrong? But I do know that the Lord who brought him into this world has already decided how he will make a livelihood. When the time comes, he'll follow his chosen path.'

His Bou's words were music to Sura's ears. What she said was exactly what he thought. Bapa would never win the battle of words—his lies and intimidation would never triumph.

The rage he harboured against his father slowly turned into hatred.

He recollected so many things.

Character, morality, generosity—his father had always extolled these virtues, yes. When he spoke about it, his face would light up and his eyes moisten and glow with passion. But he himself had overheard the doctor, Priya Babu, warning, 'Careful, Hara Babu! Your wife's health is fast deteriorating. She has borne seven children, she's extremely anaemic and she has to do all the household chores without any help. It's difficult to say what will happen to her if she conceives again.'

Sura, Nila, Moti, Rukuni, Pira, Babu, Budha—they were seven. Many a time Sura had woken up in the middle of the night to the sound of strange shuffling noises over which he had heard his father's voice muttering passionately, 'Suna! Suna!'

Sura would shed silent tears. In fear. And then he heard that his Bou was pregnant. Again! And how his father transformed after that! Not a trace of happiness on his face. He chanted fervent prayers to invoke the blessings of the gods twice a day—every morning and every evening. He sat brooding in the evenings when he returned from the office. He visited the doctor frequently. He argued constantly with Bou, then the bubble of arguments burst and he fell silent. He was reduced to a veritable timid mouse. A tall, fair-complexioned man with a long face. Now the face has turned bony and the forehead furrowed. Sura's heart overflows with pity for him. Eventually, Kuna came into the world, and Bou survived. Hers is a resilient life. So, she has lived. It had nothing to do with Bapa.

Certain things needn't be articulated to be understood. But doesn't he get the drift of these things?

Truth, piety, *honourable* conduct.

Where were these evident?

Truth be told, these virtues weren't apparent in his father.

Ever since his childhood, Sura had seen his father bring home paper and pencils from the office. He would carefully instruct them about which end of the pencil needed to be sharpened. He would ensure that whatever was imprinted on it was carefully shaved away. Sura eventually realized that this stationery wasn't something his father had paid for. Some items may have been purchased, but not the whole lot. What happened to integrity, honour and truth?

He remembered asking his father, 'Bapa, you bring all this back, won't you be questioned?'

'Arey, no! All this is what I am entitled to, therefore it is yours!' Sura isn't convinced. But his father tries to disabuse his mind. 'Arey, everyone claims them, these are such insignificant things; if you attach too much importance to these things, how're you going to get ahead in life?'

But Sura's suspicions remained. He mulled over them.

Then there was the incident of using the office car. They sometimes drove out in the official jeep at night. In spite of that, Bapa would be irritated with the driver. He would say unpleasant things about him—not to his face, of course, but at home, behind his back. He would say, 'The man is so ungrateful, such a wretch! He himself steals petrol from the jeep and indulges in many underhand activities. If I were to expose him, he would go to jail. I accommodate him, provide him with cover and make sure his pilfering isn't brought to light. But, when I ask him to bring the vehicle around at night, so that the children can go out, he lies to me and says that the vehicle is unavailable. Don't I want the vehicle? Let other people use the vehicle for shopping, for socializing, let him not bring it for me! Let's see!'

Was this piety? Honesty?

These were petty things and there was plenty more along the same lines. People would visit. If Sura was at home, he would be sent to fetch tea, paan or a glass of water.

After they left, Bapa would go back into the house with a broad grin on his face. Bou would open and shut her box.

'What is it, Bou?' he would ask.

'Go away! Mind your own business! This isn't for children.' Sura would understand but wouldn't say anything. His mother would start complaining. 'What a time we live in! Everything is so dear, and we have to buy all that we need. What do I feed my children to keep them nourished?'

His father would preach every day, 'We will be satisfied with what God gives us. We walk on the path of honesty. That will protect us.'

Sura learnt that a man of the world may do as he pleased, but *must* speak in clichés like these. His father spoke vehemently about dishonesty, misappropriation and the malpractices of others, some of whom were friends and relatives, some strangers—but the conclusion was the same—in this day and age, truth was dead.

Students in college discussed this issue as well. They highlighted their discussions with multiple examples. Dishonest people ruled the roost in all spheres of society—in politics, in business, in careers. They concluded that, in this era, in these times, one rarely glimpsed honesty and piety. The faults of public figures, who otherwise ought to command love and respect from students for their idealism, were discussed the most. Students said that for their own gains, in their own self-interest, people in power could indulge in all kinds of sin and nefarious activities: irregularity, fraud, injustice and many such unbecoming acts. They could make the deserving undeserving and the undeserving deserving; they could pass one failed student and do quite the reverse with another; they could even change their views and their loyalties a hundred times. Everything was conceivable if only one had the gall to do it.

All this wasn't mere hearsay; they spoke from their own experiences, too.

It wasn't that Sura was particularly drawn towards injustice and corruption. He presumed that, in the world he lived in, it was futile and ridiculous to try to win accolades for justice, morality and good behaviour. One shouldn't regret being unable to get them, and if one did manage to get them, it wouldn't always feel good. He himself abhorred falsehood, lies and cheating, for no other reason but that it would diminish his self-respect. He had no idea what he would do after he graduated, but he wasn't worried about that. Deep down he sensed that he wouldn't really amount to much in life, nor would he be able to achieve anything remarkable. The more he thought about it the more he wondered whether he would be able to match his father's financial status. He also wondered whether he would be able to lead a normal family life.

He understood that life had little to offer him, hence there was no need to be too serious or reserved. Life was better lived cheerfully in the company of friends indulging in fun and laughter.

'Sura re, won't you get up? Won't you have something to eat?'

It was his mother calling.

He wanted to shake himself free of these disturbing thoughts and to get on with life. Again, the same indecisiveness in his mind. No, he would not eat.

He turned over to the other side in bed and closed his eyes.

He wasn't really hungry. He had snacked heavily in the evening.

He was the first to get up in the morning. He sat cross-legged on the bed for a while, with his eyes shut like he was meditating. He opened his eyes and saw two pictures on the wall in front of him. One was of Mahatma Gandhi; the other was a calendar with the picture of a half-naked girl. He rarely looked at these pictures on the wall, but that morning he scrutinized the pictures with some degree of curiosity. He derived new meaning from the pictures—both transient. Mahatmaji had been deified. His name appeared only in his writings and speeches and he was briefly emulated, but was quickly forgotten after the grandiose celebrations marking his birth centenary. His teachings were like the preaching of the shastras and the Puranas, they sanctified the ear when one heard it. But that was all. And this half-naked nymph—that too was an all too familiar sight—the eyes tired of it and it ceased to titillate.

What else remained?

A mechanical life—close your senses: eyes and ears, and don't let your mind think. Live a life in which you are unconscious but the limbs move; and when you become conscious, all that you experience is turmoil and tumult.

His eyes sparkled suddenly as if he had discovered a profound truth. He looked at the blank wall and addressed his invisible audience: 'Death is the only truth. Pain is truth.

Turmoil is truth. Everything else is a lie. These are the axiomatic truths of life—pain-turmoil-death. *Swayambhu!*'

As he got ready for the day, his mother served him his breakfast of rice flakes, curd and sugar. Putting a morsel into his mouth, he said to his mother, 'pain-turmoil-death.'

'Why do you say such inauspicious things early in the morning, Sura?' his mother asked.

'It's not inauspicious! This is the truth. Everything else is a lie!'

'Come, come! Eat! Shall I give you some more?'

'You're afraid to speak out against the truth of this age. But you live in this age and follow all its norms.'

'What's this that you say? Have you lost your mind?'

'Whatever one may do, no one will live. The atom bomb will destroy everything. Until then, one man will kill the other, he, in turn, will be killed by someone else, and so it will carry on. No one's riches will remain. One man will grab another's riches, his riches too will be stolen by someone else and yet another will snatch someone else's. And so it'll go on, interminably. You too know this; that is why you say Laxmi, the goddess of wealth, is fickle.'

'What is wrong with you?'

'I have received enlightenment—the supreme knowledge. What I require now is Bhalluka and Tapussa. You are my Bhalluka.'

'Yes, yes, I am your *bhallu*, a bear, what else!'

Bou was broad, short and dark; she pottered around. But did he mean that she was a bear?

'I didn't say a bear, I said Bhalluka. One of Buddha's first two disciples. His own experience of life. Just like yours. Your life has been one of pain and turmoil. And then, in the end, you'll experience the final truth. Death!' Suna Dei stared at her son. His face was expressionless. He was surely sulking after last night's incident. 'Listen, Bou, tell Bapa that I'm no longer a black sheep. I have attained enlightenment.'

Without another word, he sat down with his books.

But then he thought, 'Why should I study? The cycle of pain-turmoil-death cannot be erased.'

And to what end was this education? At the end of his studies, he would be gifted with a toy—that paper which would say he had passed an examination. Who would guarantee that the evaluator of his answer script hadn't assigned marks without bothering to read beyond the first page? You heard rumours of students threatening evaluators and extorting marks at knife point. The society that believed that the gods could grant boons and answer one's prayers if you offered oblations had long since authenticated a world in which injustice, corruption and negligence thrived. So, what was so novel about this?

Dharma-artha-kama-moha. Which of these would education grant? How much education did any of the people who became ministers, leaders, industrialists, businessmen and moneylenders have? All the people whose paths were carpeted with money—those who made thousands of people dance to their tune because they wielded power and authority, those who indulged in buying and selling and traded people like horses—how many of them had received any education?

He closed his books. He hadn't realized that he had been sitting at his table for so long. He looked at the clock and shouted, 'Bou! Quick, give me some food! If not, I'm off! It's getting late!'

'Arey! Come sit! I'll serve you immediately!'

As he ate, he kept muttering, 'Enlightenment—*trisatya*—pain-turmoil-death!'

'Stop pecking at your food like a bird! Eat properly!'

'What would you understand? This is enlightenment.'

He quietly mounted his bicycle and rode away.

Hara Babu was pleased with himself. He laughed as he said to his wife, 'So, did you notice the change? I reprimanded him last night. The medicine has worked. Sura was at his books early this morning, no indiscipline today. He sat silently at his desk for three whole hours, engrossed in his studies. Earlier, he would get up from his desk in a little while and do the rounds of the locality. It's very necessary for children to be chided every once in a while. It changes the course of their life. You can take it from me that he will fare very well in his examinations. Then I'll see what I can do to get him a good job. I have so many contacts; I'll have to exploit them.'

'Ha!'

'Why do you scoff? You have to discipline children once in a while, otherwise they go astray. You err in taking his side. You pamper him.'

'Well, will you eat now?'

There was a congregation of students in the atrium of the college. A brawl had started at the other end. A lot of students were crowding the college office and a clerk had raised his voice at a student, and had said sharply, 'Get out!' That had led to a lot of shouting and hurling of invectives. The student and the clerk found themselves in the atrium. The ruckus attracted more students and some faculty, too.

'Apologize first!'

'Prostrate yourself before him!'

'Apologize!'

The faculty that was there tried to pacify the students, but their 'Wait, wait, listen!' was drowned in the din. The students raised allegations against them. They had a lot to say, and their demands, suppressed for so long, burst forth.

'We don't have a common room to sit in!'

'We don't have a playground!'

'We don't have books in the library!'

'We have to park our cycles in the sun!'

'We don't have sufficient washrooms.'

'We don't have equipment in the laboratory!'

'Apologize!'

No one knows what happened next. There was a lot of scuffling and shouting. And then Sura shouted, 'Meet all our demands!'

And then all the voices rose in unison, 'Meet all our demands!'

Sura shouted, 'Long live the revolution!'

The crowd shouted, 'Long live the revolution!'

'Take them captive!'

'Take them captive!'

'We will have an answer!'

'We will have an answer!'

'Break—burn!'

'Break—burn!'

'Come! Burn the library!'

'Come! Come!'

'One group, go smash the library!'

'Away! Away!'

The president of the students' union, Bhimeswar Pahad Singh, addressed the students, trying to placate them, 'Brothers, what are you doing? What is this leading to? The guilty will be taken to task. Why this indiscipline? Why this uprising?'

'He has been bought!'

'He has deep pockets!'

'Pimp!'

'Thief!'

'Assault him!'

'Break-burn!'

'*Inquilab* zindabad!'

'Kill! Kill!'

'Brothers, stop this base trickery! Some students want to discredit the students' union by indulging in violence. Their acts will ruin all of us!'

'Assault the smooth talker! Kill! Kill!'

There was a scuffle between the two groups of students. Stone-pelting ensued. Fumes belched out from the library. In half an hour the ruckus had subsided. The students had dispersed and had gone home.

Pahad Singh put Sura in a rickshaw and held him close as they made their way to a doctor. He bled from a wound in the head and his shirt was torn and blood-stained. Pahad Singh was holding Sura tightly, so Pahad Singh's shirt was also soaked in blood. There was no enmity between them; there never had been.

Pahad Singh asked, 'How do you feel?'

Sura tried to laugh and said, 'Not too bad!'

'What just happened?'

Sura said, 'Who knows?'

Originally titled 'Bansadhara', 1988

Festival Day

The tall, slim, dark man stands out because of the clothes he wears: a pair of maroon shorts and a half-sleeved, pink bush-shirt. People in this locality wear short, dirty clothes; some of them wear either a brown or a red *gamuchha*, a small coarse towel, that blends with the colour of the earth, draped over the shoulder; their tousled hair either fluffs in the breeze or is slickly brushed back and tied in a knot at the lower end. The young man's sartorial elegance underlines the difference—he also wears a watch with a white dial on his left wrist and two fountain pens, one red and the other white, are clipped on to his breast pocket. He wears a pair of slippers, carries an umbrella and a filthy black pouch is slung across his shoulder. His oily hair, slickly parted on the left, shines bright and barring the pencil moustache, the rest of his face is clean shaven. His features are largely indistinguishable from the local people.

It is 8 a.m. The day is getting warmer; the dust-free sky looks azure although banks of fluffy, white-grey and blackish clouds are visible in the distant skyline. It is hard to say whether they will move forward or withdraw from the horizon. The young man walks past the empty, barren fields with long strides. He climbs the slight incline and stops in front of a solitary, tiled house which is a short distance away. He extracts a gamuchha from the pouch, wipes the sweat from his brow and looks around—not a soul anywhere! The tamarind and mango trees are to his right a few paces ahead, and beyond the trees, he can see a section of the Bijaputa village settlement. There is no activity in sight.

Some stray goats and cattle are grazing about. The cattle are all skin and bone; with the bones sticking out from under their skin they resemble four-legged walking skeletons. *Shravana* is almost over. A few intermittent light showers have caused a sprinkling of grass to sprout here and there, and the hungry cattle are nibbling at these freshly sprouted offerings. The young man is thinking to himself. 'We are in for a really bad time, two consecutive years of drought: Goddess Laxmi seems to have forsaken this place!' The enthusiasm that had accompanied him on the four-mile walk from Tuchhahandi village to this place has quickly dissipated.

The house in front is the primary school of Bijaputa village. He has been teaching here for the last two years. His name is Shyamaghana Bagha. Helped along by the government grants offered to Harijans, he had been able to pursue his education in government schools and pass the matriculation examination. Thereafter, he was appointed as a primary-school teacher and came to this village. In the early days, he lived on the veranda of a person of his caste in nearby Kendumundi village, while securing his personal belongings inside the house. After his marriage to Saraswati, the only child of Kuladhara Ganda, a year and a half ago, he has been living at his in-law's home.

The village is about four miles away, and it takes him almost two hours to walk the distance to the school. Almost a year ago, he bought himself an old bicycle with his father-in-law's money and rides it to school. There's a small inconvenience, however. He has to either drag or carry the old bicycle over short stretches on his way to school. The bicycle has broken down today, and it is a holiday.

His has been an easy life, spent mostly in the shade, under the roof of schools and classrooms. Unlike his father, brothers and other family members, his body hasn't been seasoned in the sun and rain. Neither his mind nor his body is conditioned to undertake any strenuous physical labour; he isn't inclined to do it either—carrying the bicycle for a mile was a very strenuous task. But today, he enthusiastically trudged the entire distance to the school without a murmur because it's 15 August—it's the day of India's independence. He has rushed over to hoist the national flag in the school. He recalls all that used to happen on this day in the town where he lived as a child. He had seen the flag being hoisted twice in the city as well, he had heard of the joyous celebrations on the radio, he had also read about it in the newspapers and all things put together, he had also dreamt many an outsized dream in his mind: the festival rush and the wide array of celebrations—music, procession, parade, flag-hoisting, speeches, hope, courage, liberation, fearlessness, joy and enthusiasm. *Jana gana mana adhinayaka jaya hei* ringing across the country from the Himalayas to Kanyakumari! The world's largest independent republic! Seventy crore Indians! We celebrate India's Independence Day—independence from the foreign yoke!

The reality is he himself hasn't experienced British rule; that had ended fourteen years before he was born in one of the native states of Orissa. He hasn't experienced monarchy either. He has never been the subject of a king. But he has heard many stories about this and that—did it actually happen or were they figments of someone's imagination? Let alone the seventy crore, he hasn't yet seen a gathering of even a lakh of people. He has seen the district office, but he has never stepped out of his district. True, he has heard and read about the outside world. He knows that on this very day, years and decades ago, an era had changed and a new age had been ushered in, and under a single flag stood a huge independent nation.

In his mind, he was looking for an open space in front of his primary school where he could unfurl the national flag on a bamboo pole. And below the flag, he would stand as the representative of a large independent republic! He, their teacher, Shyamaghana Bagha. The children would stand in rows in front of him. People would watch as they emerge, united in their determination to build an independent India. They would salute the flag and pray to God for the wellbeing of the nation. He has, therefore, rushed over to the school with great enthusiasm and joy. But on arrival, he finds no one around here. Where's the toran of mango leaves? And where's the bamboo pole to hoist the flag?

He steps up to the school veranda, unlocks the door and flings open the doors and windows. On all the other days, the children would already be gathered here by now, huddled together on the veranda and around it in front, his eight, chirpy lot as he was wont to tell everyone, anxiously awaiting his arrival. They would sweep the floor of the veranda and the room. They would stand together and sing and pray. He makes them sing, teaches them their lessons and makes them play games; he never raises his hand to hit them or rebukes them; he prefers to patiently explain things to them and make them learn through stories and games. They all love him.

When he first came to teach here, there were about twenty-five to thirty children in the school. But over time, the number dwindled. The number of children coming from areas badly affected by drought and poverty steadily shrank. He knew why this was happening. He would go from village to village to motivate parents to send their children to school. But the ground reality he came upon was stark, and he was hardly left with any wiggle room to urge and motivate them. The parents went out to forage for food. When the elders went out looking for food, the older children had to stay at home to care for the infants. Sometimes they would send the children to gather food: some spinach and leaves, a fruit plucked here, or a tuber dug out there . . . whatever. Who can go to school to study when the stomach is on fire? Bijaput, Chandili and Bhalukhola are the three neighbouring villages from which the children came to study in this school. Most of the people are poor and landless. Some others are small-time farmers, sharecroppers or daily-wage earners. Almost all of them are either Harijans or adivasis. Only a few of them own some land, five or six families are toddy-tappers and moneylenders and of rich, feudal pedigree, and only a few families are farmers. Seven or eight children came from those families and were quite regular in attending school.

Today is a festival day. He had particularly told them and had also reminded the eight students who had attended school yesterday about the significance of the day. He had asked them to spread the word among other children in the villages. Earlier, he had himself visited the villages and told the villagers about the importance of the day.

'The flag will be hoisted in the school that day. Do come. We'll celebrate the festival together. We're living in difficult times now and have lived through many such famines in the past. It is all God's will. Hunger and starvation grip the state. But does it mean that we forget our mother? Forget our country?

'Hoisting the flag is our way of offering respect to the mother, our worship to the mother-nation! The worship of our independence! Today we have an identity as citizens because we live in an independent country. Earlier we were immersed in darkness; the Englishmen ruled us and we were subject to the whims of local rajas, maharajas, zamindars and the moneyed people. They oppressed us, treated us like goats and cattle, sucked our lifeblood and looted us. Independence brought us so much good; more such good will come about soon enough, plenty more. The nation is ours; we vote in elections; our vote decides the government and all these rights and privileges have come our way because of that flag of Independence. What else do you think has made all of this possible for us?'

'*Hoi!* Hoi! Very true!' Some people had cheered, but their affirmation was weak and lacked the vim that he was wanting to hear.

'This school that has been established here dignifies us and buoys our spirits. If you don't study you don't get smart, you don't become aware of the world around you. Education will open your eyes to the world, it will help you prosper in life and your children too will have better lives. We had nothing to begin with, but over time, things have changed and continue to change, and now some people have started reaping the benefits. They'll get more and more enlightened, more and more prosperous.'

'Hoi! Hoi! Very true!' they had agreed. 'But, guru, the reality is we somehow managed to survive before. But now, there's nothing to eat at home. The kitchen pot is completely empty. Many people haven't eaten anything for days on end. Work is hard to find. People are no more in a position to give us any help; we'll soon wilt and die of starvation. Many have left this place already.' This is what some people had said in response to his fervent appeal to attend the Independence Day ceremony. So, they didn't turn up; but that not a soul should show up here! That was surprising!

It was as though the festival is only for him to celebrate! Not for others, no one else! He feels immensely hurt.

There's a broom in a corner of the room. He picks it up and sweeps both the room and the veranda. He takes out the small flag from the wooden box. He reverentially brings the flag up and touches it with his forehead and, holding it in his hand, stands in front of the school and starts singing '*Jana gana mana adhinayaka jaya hei*' as he looks straight ahead. Then he puts the flag down and prostrates himself before it. But that isn't enough to satisfy him. He wants to pay his homage to the nation and wants children and people around him as he triumphantly hoists the flag. It is a moment of glory, of satisfaction, of pride! But around him, he finds that he has no bamboo to hew into a flagpole, no implement to dig the earth to plant the pole. He puts the flag back in the box in disappointment, locks the door and starts walking back to Bijaput village.

From the far end of the village, he could hear the pathetic wail of a woman. The bamboo-mat doors of all the houses he passes are shut, no one's around. There are three or four old women and an old man in front of a house. The wailing is emanating from inside the house. 'What has happened, Mausa?'

'What else could happen here? His son, Pienbudi, died this morning. Yesterday afternoon he had blood diarrhoea, and today it's all over.'

'You mean Siba's son, Pienbudi?' he says, in great remorse. 'He was in my school. Yes, he hadn't been attending school for the last few days. I had sent for him several times, but the children came back and told me that they weren't able to meet him. I tried, but couldn't even find his father. And now Pienbudi has died! Alas!'

'Exactly, Babu! See where this cursed famine has taken us! Not a morsel of food anywhere. No employment is available for us to toil and earn money to buy food. Every waking moment is spent foraging for food—leaves, tubers, fruit, whatever. Children too have to join the search. Look at this: the boy's father has been away for five days scouting for food and the boy Pienbudi roamed around, hunger gnawing at him. He came across a group of people huddled together, boiling *biluakanda.* It's hard to get the poison out of biluakanda, Babu. Eating it without cooking it right can cause blood diarrhoea. But all the edible *kandas,* tubers, have long been eaten. The child had a big helping of boiled biluakanda. Soon afterwards, he had blood diarrhoea. Just two days, and it was all over.'

The old man is bent, skeletal. The three women are also portraits of skin and bone. There are no words in their mouths; they are merely gawking at him with ignorant, lifeless eyes.

The old man pauses and says, 'Do you have anything that you could give us to eat, guru? I haven't had any food for the last two days. Just drinking water doesn't sustain this life. I have no strength left in me either. Otherwise I, too, would have gone away somewhere.' Helpless emanations of deathly despair!

Shyamaghana exhales a deep sigh. 'I've brought nothing with me, old man,' he says, with a hangdog look, a look of defeat, and quietly leaves the place. The face of the boy who had died that morning rises in front of his eyes and behind him is the piteous cry of the boy's mother. A pall of gloom clouds his mind channelling grey thoughts. He's troubled with a deep sense of remorse, shame and fear as if he has committed a grave crime. He no longer entertains fancy notions of calling people over to dig a hole to plant the flagpole and hoist the flag. He starts walking back to the school. He feels as though he's being frogmarched by the scruff of his neck and driven out by a spirit of fatigue, defeat and hopelessness. For him the optimism of the morning has turned into a solitary, suffocating, stifling *jaistha* afternoon.

He shuts the windows and doors of the school. He has tenderly replaced the flag back in its box. He looks at his watch, it is 12.30 p.m. He realizes that the parade would be over by now, the flag of independent India would be fluttering in all parts of the country and celebrations would be going on everywhere.

He steps off the school veranda.

His father-in-law's place in Tuchhahandi village is four miles away, and he'll go back there. He remembers that, as on all other days, his father-in-law, Kuladhara Ganda, won't be at home. He has four acres of land and a pair of bullocks. His cultivation has been on hold this year in the wake of the drought, but he has another profession to fall back on—collecting the hides of dead cattle, carrying them away, and selling them at the godowns of businessmen. With the ongoing drought getting more severe with every passing day, more and more cattle are dying from hunger and starvation and there's an uptick in his trade. His mother-in-law and Saraswati will be at home. Saraswati is in the family way. He'll soon become a father. He has his secure job, and he also has Kuladhara's property. He has his own refuge.

As he navigates the stretch down the incline from the school, he sees in his mind the picture of children coming to school to study and leading them is a cheerful Pienbudi, bounding with a spring in his step. Shyamaghana quickens his pace to get back home.

Originally titled 'Utsava Dina', 1985

Just around This Bend

God hasn't blessed her with children.

Mamata, silent for a long time releases a sigh, short but sharp.

Startled, Jeetendra asks, 'What's it, Momi?'

The rickshaw creaks in her shuffling.

'No, it's nothing,' Mamata answers.

'But you sigh so deeply!'

'Oh, that!' Mamata stretches herself some more and yawns this time. 'Feeling bizarre and on top of that you've got a hand-pulled rickshaw that keeps rocking interminably.'

'Count yourself lucky that I didn't get a cycle rickshaw,' Jeetendra laughs. 'The number of vegetables that you're carting away from the fair wouldn't have found space in that vehicle. The many offspring that you've picked up—the elongated bottle gourd, radish, elephantine sweet potato and pumpkin—wouldn't have sat still on the floor of the rickshaw; they would've battled for space and then jumped out to free themselves and frolic on the road!' Jeetendra laughs dramatically. 'So, you'd have had to clutch them tightly on to your lap, softly crooning to them all the way back home to get them to behave themselves and sit still!'

Jeetendra is a great big hulk of a man and his enormous paunch bounces about involuntarily as the rickshaw moves. The rickshaw puller glances back at them one more time and prepares to haul the rickshaw up the steep incline. Motor cars, lorries, bullock carts and bicycles approach from the opposite direction. In the bustling traffic of vehicles, big and small, the creaky rattle of the rickshaw and the *tring-trings* of the handbell are distinct sounds.

The rickshaw puller is a tall, frail man, with an old, crumpled sola hat on his head and a tattered, worn-out, striped shirt plastering his back in blotches of sweat and covering the hitched-up clothes girding his loins. A misshapen pair of shoes grip the feet at the end of his narrow, sinewy legs. Everything about him seems crushed and deformed with intense labour; his moustache, too, droops—in testimony to the dust, sweat and pain. Yet, despite a harrowing everyday life, he is full of pluck and enthusiasm—determined to live his life. He braves it cheerfully and refuses to slow down; and to all the vehicles—cars or bullock carts—passing by, he hurls his imprecations and runs along nonchalantly.

Death can't silence him; even in his death he'll not die; he'll live on in his four children—the world will always know them as Kapil Jena's sons. That's so edifying, such an ennobling thought! He's working hard for their sakes, what else can he do? A seer of rice costs almost a rupee and people have started downsizing the pomp of weddings and reducing the expenditure on live bands and fireworks. He had himself eked out a living for fifteen years as a drummer in a band. Every step of the way, as he pulls his rickshaw, he sees the faces of his children in his mind's eye. He's spoken about his children to everyone: the corrupt men, the rich men, even the ones who take to the streets to vociferously protest against price rises shouting slogans and marching to the refrain of 'Zindabad, Zindabad'. Their mother's dead; his sister, the children's *peesi*, is raising them. So many tales about them! Mamata has heard them all.

God's will is truly inscrutable: those with money and wealth to spare aren't blessed with offspring, while those who are poor are bounteously endowed. The destitute children will grow up, form groups and torch the world to quench the fire of hunger burning in their stomachs. What else can they do to douse the blaze? That, in a strange, ironical way, explains why the poor rickshaw puller has children and she doesn't.

Who's to blame for this? Jeetendra tells his friends, 'She has some issues, she has this infirmity; she's always been like this. Ever since she left her natal home. I've taken her to many doctors, given her multiple medicines, but to no effect—it's been such a colossal waste of money. My father and mother are insisting that I take another wife. They keep saying, who's going to light the lamp in this hearth? Who's going to give us a little water in our last days? Who's going to inherit the property of our ancestors that we will leave behind? It's only natural for my parents to be anxious, fifteen years is a long time! But is that the right way to go about it? Another marriage—only because I'm not blessed with a son! Huh?'

How magnanimous, how chivalrous, how gallant—these words! They circle back and reach Mamata's ears. She feels torn, even singed; but laughing sarcastically, she'd say to Jeetendra, 'Promise me, swear by me that you'll remarry. You'll indeed be blessed with children; you indeed shall be! You must remarry.'

Generosity indeed!

No sense of shame, is there? He's after all a man, so he can go around telling people that the wife is the cause of their plight, while she, a woman, can't quite do that. She can't tell the world that it's the husband himself who's the cause of their barren state, not she. Is it really her fault? So close together physically, they're locked in the rickshaw, yet so far apart! Enigma! Life itself is a bundled-up enigma!

She simmers in rage whenever she thinks about this. The torturous thoughts arising in the unfulfilled recesses of her mind cloud her consciousness and in a delusion, the hidden part of her soul quizzes her—*Who the hell is this man? I don't know him! No, I don't! Why, of all the people on earth, was this man chosen to keep me unfulfilled? Unfulfilled! Yes. Why?*

That is when a furious Mamata gives Jeetendra a fierce, scalding look—a look dripping with her regret and anger. Her mind wanders about, afar; her entire personality pulls itself apart from him and turns away to a faraway world where he isn't around. Yet she's still close to him in body and day-to-day living; she commits no solecism in her marital behaviour and responsibilities, she violates no societal norms of decency. Friends who visit them join Jeetendra in animated conversation while Mamata plays the unstinting hostess, plying them with cups of tea and platters of savouries. They return to their homes gushing over this remarkable couple.

And with a tinge of jealousy in their voices, they say, 'Jeetu and his wife are the epitome of the ideal couple. They're the happiest pair in the world; they enjoy every minute of their lives together. How warm and affectionate they are, what sweet exchanges! Fifteen years into their marriage, yet how wrapped up they are in each other! As if only yesterday was their bridal night! And look at his wife, how well she has preserved herself; even today how vivacious and nubile she looks! True, they don't have children, that's the sad missing piece in life's puzzle, but it does take enormous effort to stay young, bubbly and healthy.'

Ironically, Mamata's well-toned, youthful body is the cause of her unhappiness. Jeetendra, in the fullness of middle age, is no match for her. Like the billowing centre of the earth, in tune with the common trend, he too has bloated at the midriff and looks like a small drum.

The two are wrestling for space. With Jeetendra's ample girth filling the rickshaw, Mamata is forced to pile herself on him, with the husband wrapping his arm around her shoulders. A taste of the better half—two deadweights in the rickshaw and the poor rickshaw puller is desperately towing them to their destination! *Two bitter halves!*

Two youngsters in bicycles sporting thin, dark moustaches, Hawaiian shirts and Kabuli shoes hover around them, inching closer and then pulling away. Nothing out of the normal—the usual idle curiosity that makes people ogle at couples.

Many such have come and gone. Many!

Mamata's mind is silently pierced by the desire and flirtation of the unknown passers-by. She quietly experiences a sense of hubris enveloped in fantasy.

She has looked after herself all these years despite the responsibility of running the household. Jeetendra too had always wanted it that way. So today she's wearing a faux silk, printed sari; around her neck is a faux diamond necklace studded with bright, faux stones and in her hair is a string of plastic jasmine flowers needing no moisture to keep them fresh. The kohl on her eyes, too, is ersatz and in her face spreads the peaceful shadow of manufactured happiness. She honours all norms of society—the vermillion in the parting of her hair as a badge to proudly proclaim her marital status. Strange, oftentimes she feels that too is fake. And caught up in the whirlpool of her sham persona is the clutch of transient admirers swirling around her in close proximity, sometimes close and sometimes a tad away, but orbiting around her—a lit cigarette clamped between their lips to emphasize their immense personas but ironically turning out to be a soundless raising of their faux relevance.

These shadowy admirers have accepted Mamata's shadow. And she theirs—admiration! Who wouldn't?

Unbeknownst to her, she is piqued with Jeetendra. Not out of line. Bizarro world!

Jeetendra's mind is distracted with spiralling thoughts of his own. He, too, has seen people at the fruit and vegetable fair. As they moved along, he has plucked out and discarded many memories, yet some remain. Many of his unfulfilled desires have morphed into images and are passing by in his mind's eye, and he has not yet found an argument to squelch them. Silently, in his mind, he is living them over and over again. Age holds no bar, and neither does his present lot.

S he rides ahead in a cycle rickshaw. She is sculpted like a slender figure in gold; she is no more than seventeen or eighteen. It was like this then as well—twenty years ago. Jeetendra's sharp gaze was riveted, but Jeetendrajit wasn't as yet the hero or the Prince Charming, but an itinerant beggar. He would keep staring from a distance, withstand the crush of people milling around him, and take in the rough rides of fast-moving vehicles and court danger. Maybe closer to home he will be prompted to sing a song on a moonlit night and diminish himself to an inconsequential, even infinitesimal being, dream the dreams—and live the dreams in his fertile mind. But before he succeeds in fulfilling his wishes, he will be pushed back into the melee.

Jeetendra was running on the untrodden path.

Mamata was running, but in the other direction. In the mad scramble, she had settled on one. As though a familiar soul from the world beyond had come to life and was walking in front of her. No one else around. Unknown the path, so undulating. He was here some time ago but had disappeared; now she has found him again. She'll not tear herself away from him this time around. Even so, she won't let life's calculus and society's intolerance separate her from him this time. Her desire for womanhood must be met and fulfilled.

How quickly the years have melted away and the luminous sun has set!

In the murky light of the setting sun, she sees a temple on a mound and near it—a pond full of blooming lotuses. In Mamata's imagination the man is striding up ahead to that upraised ground and she's following him.

In Jeetendra's dream is the pond's edge. His dream. Below him is the lotus forest, and beneath the steps, nothing. He will rest there.

Will she let him find her this time?

The rickshaw puller is running in the middle of the road. The rickshaw turns the bend.

Unconsciously, Mamata encircles Jeetendra's lower back with a reflexive, tremulous arm. It was as if Jeetendra's deadweight of the whole quintal had shuffled forward, pressing on her the weight of his upper torso. Momentarily, the rickshaw jerks and tips as it rocks unsteadily.

'How far is it, babu?' the rickshaw puller asks.

A touch self-consciously, both of them blurt out, almost in unison, 'Just around this bend. We're almost there.'

Originally titled 'Khali Gotae Banka', 1967

Despair

Rajendra Babu didn't say a word. He kept looking at his son. Silently.

Chewing a paan, Babloo too stood quietly waiting for his reply. It was a made-to-order paan, bought from a paan shop, but its strong fragrance barely disguised the putrid offence of alcohol on his breath. A tinge of pink glazed his eyes.

He had cannily chosen this propitious time. His father came home for lunch around 1.30 in the afternoon. All through the day and throughout the evening he worked at a chemist's, dispensing medicines. Babloo had said that he and his friends would take a train to embark on an excursion that very evening. Most of the expenses would be borne by the college. But he needed to have at least a hundred rupees with him. His Bou didn't have any money to spare, she had told him to ask his father. There was no option but to incur this expense; this was an unavoidable expenditure and this excursion was a part of his study course; and more than any other, it was imperative that he travelled, especially for the sake of his reputation. If he didn't go, he would lose face in front of his friends and teachers.

He had already put forth his justifications; now it was Rajendra Babu who had to battle the logic in his head. No, this isn't an illusion, Rajendra Babu thought to himself. He had indeed caught the whiff of alcohol on Babloo's breath. The stench, those ponderous eyes, the dazed look, the flushed face, could they ever be masked?

He can feel the anger engulf him, from the top of his head to the soles of his feet. He wants to roar at Babloo, pound him and break his bones, even flay him alive. His head reels and he sees Babloo, his only child, the apple of his eye, the mainstay of his sense of security and the hope of his future; once his tiny tot, his loving son and, notwithstanding his poor academic credentials today, an undergraduate student in the final year of an arts course. He has made every possible sacrifice for his sake and met his every want and need, but that was for the Babloo of his mind. This was an image created out of his own hopes and dreams. But who is this person who stands before him? Is he *his* Babloo?

At forty-five, Rajendra Babu looks like an old man of fifty-five. His shoulders stoop; the look on his face conveys many things: sadness, tiredness, despair, the compounded apprehensions and nightmares of a man struggling to make a decent living. He had started many enterprises on his own, and every time he'd done so there was the hope of success. However, every time it had petered away and become a sheer waste of money and labour. Friends had turned into ingrates and were keen to grift and skim him. Finally, after so many failures, he found refuge in this insignificant job and is somehow managing to make ends meet. The job saps his energy and vitality. But despite the string of setbacks and hardships, he had pinned his hope and aspirations on his son,

Babloo. This dream, incubated within him for years as a refuge for his soul, has remained undimmed. But where's the Babloo of his dreams?

This twenty-year-old man, standing before him is a whole other person. While Rajendra Babu is five feet five inches tall, Babloo is taller by a full five inches, at five feet ten inches. He has a large head, a broad chest and a narrow waist. His arms and legs are muscular and well-built; he has the youthful vim about him. If he so wants, he can grasp his father, shake him up and pin him to the ground. When angry, the boy can turn into a veritable Bhima. His overall demeanour speaks of a nonchalant, reckless attitude. He seems to convey insouciantly: Look, I'm an independent and autonomous unit; I'm used to living on my own terms; I have the rationality and intelligence to make my own decisions; and unless convinced I can't be forced to accept other people's opinions.

If he hears anything unpalatable about himself, the words might play on his mind and he might be incensed—and who knows what his reactions would be?

Rajendra Babu's anger dissipates; he shuts off his mind in a haze of confusion and sits down, looking stupidly at Babloo.

'What do you say, Bapa?' Babloo breaks the pall of silence that had descended on them. 'I'll be able to go only if you give me the money! I have so much to do before I leave.'

Rajendra Babu feels that the young man in front of him is a stranger—a stranger who is making an urgent claim on him. But he quickly senses that this isn't a random stranger asking for a donation; he's a young man merely placing his demand before him, a demand that he has to fulfil immediately. If he doesn't, it'll be hard for him to extricate himself later from what this tricky situation could escalate into. He has no choice

but to give in to his wilful demand—it was as if he owed the
boy money and he could reclaim it as a matter of right!

He has the urge to tell him: Don't hide facts from me, don't
lie to me, today you're drunk, admit it! Is this the first time
you've had liquor, or have you been drinking for some time
now? From where do you get the money? Do you hoodwink
your Bou and take it from her or are there other sources? Is
it just liquor or are there other deviations too? What kind of
life is this? What are your habits? How're you going to make a
living, and what's the path you've chosen to follow in life and
to take care of both of us? Do you want to squander away your
life and ruin both of us?

But these thoughts merely play in his mind. In reality he's
speechless; he can't utter a word. Soon the futile anger turns
into cold remorse, and his eyes fill with tears that are about to
spill. The mind can hear the repeated intonements from within:
Careful! Be careful! A single wrong or an awkward sentence
said in anger now could mean a lifetime of regret and remorse.
There's no imagining what youngsters can do in such situations.
Someone commits suicide, someone runs off, yet someone else
deliberately repeats the same offence thereby increasing the
animosity and another consciously besmirches himself and the
family; everything in life thereafter is complete perdition. No,
he won't say anything that will lead to any of that.

Looking at him piteously, Rajendra Babu decides to make
his appeal. 'You know the situation of the family, my dear
Babloo, you've seen everything with your own eyes. It's not
easy living in a townhouse in times of rising prices and having
to incur daily costs right from the moment one wakes up to
whatever one does. The paltry salary I get after putting in
such arduous work is hardly enough! Yet I haven't shied away

from sending you to college for your education and ensuring that you dress well enough to match your peers. It has left me without any succour and now all of a sudden, you're asking for a hundred rupees! Tell me, what do I do?'

Babloo gives his father an encouraging smile and says, 'Bapa, I understand everything. I wouldn't have asked you, but I'm helpless. I would've somehow managed on my own. Are you really able to fulfil all my needs or am I forever in need? This is an absolutely essential trip that I can't afford to miss. Please do give me the money from your budgeted household expenditure now, then you can make the adjustments later.' He is silent for a moment, making some calculations in his head silently. 'Fine, give me just seventy rupees,' he deigns to say, 'and the rest I'll try to find elsewhere.'

Rajendra Babu actually walks over to the chest, takes out seventy rupees from the money set aside for household expenditure and hands it to his son. He exhales a deep sigh. His eyes are brimming with tears and his face is as downcast as it always is. He wants to say: Look, Babloo, never ever touch alcohol again, don't be friends with the wrong people and remember the values I have taught you since your childhood. You are our Babloo for all time and all places. You alone are responsible for yourself. But he doesn't utter a single word. No, let him not realize that I know he has started drinking; let the mask he's wearing shield his face, let not my hand tear it away and reveal that his self-pride and self-confidence are a sham, with no earthly consequence.

Babloo senses that it does hurt his father to part with the money as it reminds him acutely of their needs and his own helplessness. He thinks of providing some warmth and as if to provide consolation to his father, he says: 'Bapa, you're worrying too much. So many years have passed; the night is getting over; are you sorry that the proverbial tiger is taking this away in the early dawn? I'll graduate in a year, and you won't have to pay for my studies any more. I should also have been able to find my own feet by then. I'm eagerly waiting to get my bachelor's degree. Is it really possible to find a sure-fire way to earn a decent income with a bachelor's or a master's degree? Look, you have a master's degree. What has come of it? There's such a big difference between your time and now! There're sundry ways today to eke out a good living. Innumerable avenues are available, yet there's so much unemployment—maybe that's because people aren't street-smart or they don't have the cleverness and cunning required to make it in life, or maybe they don't like those ways and hence shun them. If so, how will human beings survive today? One has to move with the times and learn to fit in. Bedevilling problems and violence plague us; people today live by a new set of morals; they're clever and crafty and Machiavellian and will go to any lengths to get what they want. They would indulge in all kinds of cruelty and violence, commit the most heinous crimes and use unprincipled means and oppression. How can the old, principled ways, the ethics of yore apply to this changing world?'

Babloo continues with his peroration. 'You trod the straight path, but the old order changed right before your eyes. You were cheated, but you consoled yourself with the thought that you've remained true to your principles. So whatever happiness others got in plenitude was denied to you. Your values, ethics and principles were inculcated in me, and I too persevered, but then fate interjected, and I was greatly influenced by the time and circumstances of our lives. From topping the class in the lower classes in school, I passed the school-leaving examination with a second division; then you wanted me to enrol in the intermediate science course and become a doctor or an engineer, but I failed in the very first year itself. Thereafter, when I entered the intermediate arts course, I had that bout of illness that laid me low for two months before the exam, and I passed with a third division. Now I am in the final year of this bachelor's course.

'But I have earned my spurs in various sports and wrestling events; and more than that, I have earned vast experience in diverse fields and directions; and, of course in cleverness. I'm not being presumptuous in saying all this, but I do know a whole lot of people in various fields; I have innumerable friends; in their eyes, I'm a doer and they depend on me for various activities, they fête and pamper me. That's a testament to my future success. I will surely go forward on my path, far ahead of all others. Just wait and see! Piggyback on one and stand on someone else's shoulder—these are the kinds of ingenuities you need to go up the totem pole of life and prosper, and I've learnt them well enough. You don't have to worry about me, Bapa. It'll be a cinch for me. Just wait and see.'

Babloo left after delivering his eloquent speech, with the money in his pocket.

Rajendra Babu sits back, dumbfounded. How he wishes he could have said, 'My child Babloo, my dear, my wealth, what's come over you! Why don't you rest and sleep awhile?' But he didn't say a word. Still, in a daze, he's thinking of all that Babloo had blurted out. Why all this? Was he loquacious under the influence of alcohol? But he also felt the comforting warmth of the voice with which he had spelt out his own mind—in words that were so simple and cogent! Which path has he chosen? Whose mind has he tapped into? Who has given him strength and confidence? He didn't find any answer. Then a question arose in his mind and kept on pinging: Who's that young man? Whose voice was it? Was he really his Babloo?

Could it be someone else, created and nurtured by the spirit of the age, the open sky, the fierce breeze, as well as by the newly paved paths and enlightened ways of the town? Who knows? Maybe both are real. 'But how well do I actually know Babloo? When did I ever get the time to get to know him? I was always caught up in my own worries and my daily grind. When he was a little boy, he depended on his mother or on me, a boy so small that he was with us all the time—but he is no more that little one!'

Rajendra Babu's head whirls as he sits in a stupor. He suddenly hears a rustling sound and looks up to see his wife leaning against the wall by the door. She is quietly standing there, her face filled with gloom and despair. He doesn't know for how long she has been standing there. Perhaps she too has heard Babloo's spiel, who knows?

'Should I tell you something?' his wife asks, hesitantly. 'And you're not going to fume at me! The truth is, we have always been hounded by our wants. You tried to give your all at all times, and you are still doing it now. However, if you keep harping about it all the time, especially in front of the child, a fear enters his heart, a sense of insecurity creeps in, his confidence is shattered, and he feels lost. You keep fretting at me, but I have told you so, so many times.'

'But what did I do now?'

'Well . . .'

'He asked for money, and didn't I give it to him?'

'True, you did,' she fumbled for words, trying to stitch them carefully, appropriately. 'I also know where this unplanned expenditure has landed you now! Still, do carry within you your own efforts and your own burdens. Does the incessant parroting of your destitution benefit either you or him?'

He wants to ask, even roar, 'Didn't you smell the stench on his breath? Didn't you notice his eyes? Did you not hear all that he said? You're a mother, have you kept a tab on him?' But those thoughts too don't dare detonate on his lips.

He thinks instead, what's the point of asking these questions? His own mind is already on fire, why ignite the fire in her head as well? It will only create an inferno in the house. No, let it be. So be it.

'Why do you keep sitting here?' his wife asked him. 'It's getting late. Come have your meal.'

Originally titled 'Tumbi', 1986

Rebirth

Twelve hundred years ago.

That day too, the earth was like this—generous and expansive—the lush, green grass covered its surface, and the vast sky spread like a canopy overhead.

That day, too, stood here this huge banyan tree with its aerial prop roots twisted and knotted as a living memorial to the passing of time.

That evening, too, the moonlit night underscored the essence of life. Life, suffused with the fragrance of hope, seemed full of verve and enthusiasm.

That evening, too, a boy from a far-off land had bared his heart to the girl he was half-familiar with, and with much trepidation had said, 'Tell me, Chintadevi, are you going to let me live or let me die! I'm no more able to contain the secrets of my heart! Love has overpowered me; it has made me mad. I love you!'

He had stood before her with bated breath. A little away from the banyan tree, on a flat stone platform, sat an exquisitely beautiful young girl. Her face was turned towards the moon. Through the interstices of two unruly prop roots, the moonlight cast a wavy black shadow on her. The scalloped edge of her sari was iridescent with multiple hues. In the serene evening, far from the teeming crowd, the boy stood transfixed after announcing those words—his heart refusing to beat any further, and time seemingly stalling in thrall. He was focused only on the void, awaiting the answer to his question. That would determine the path of *his* life.

Evening—and then a new world would emerge from the void. What shape would it take?

Time ticked by. The young woman sat casually on the platform, one foot dangling loosely and the other crossed and tucked under her. Her beautiful face rested lightly on her left hand. Her exquisite beauty appeared to have made the moon self-conscious as it repeatedly hid behind the crinkled veil of the clouds, peeping out only occasionally to furtively look at her. The young man looked at her closely, his face aglow in anticipation, his heart fluttering with anxiety. Trembling with nervousness, his eyes were riveted on the softly parted lips that held the hint of a smile. There, too, was the same casual expression—but not even a trace of an answer.

That was twelve hundred years ago. A thousand years had passed since Gautam Buddha had attained nirvana. Then, too, the triumphant Buddhist religion was spreading across the world; but instead of Gautam Buddha's Mahayana sect, it was the Vajrayana sect that was in vogue. Kalinga was the rising kingdom—Oddiyana—the name Odra (later named Orissa) was still embryonic. Its region extended from Ganga to Kaveri, but its intellectual and spiritual influence embraced Sri Lanka, Malaysia, Vietnam and the numerous archipelagos of the

Indian Ocean. Its capital Dantapura was on the coast, lapped by the eternal waves of the sea. Close to it was the famous centre of learning—Odantapur Vihar. So renowned was it that its replica was built and established in a small township in Tibet by the Kalinga prince Guru Padmasambhava.

Odantapur Vihar was the research centre of industry, literature, art, science and every other branch of knowledge. The philosophy of ennobled living was its language, and cosmic were its thoughts. It was the product of the sadhana of thousands and thousands of scholars and researchers and radiated—like the sun in the solar system—knowledge and wisdom. Many scholars from far-off countries came here to glean the fruits of knowledge and take them back with them to benefit their countries—so too students, both boys and girls, with their loads of scholarship. From beyond the seas came people in Kalinga's boats. Also, from across the land, traversing miles over rivers and forests, people travelled for years from Kabul and Khotan and Tibet to this peaceful and cerebral centre of learning—Odantapur.

Chintadevi is a young teacher of philosophy, pursuing her quest for knowledge at the university of Odantapur. Although the youngest at the university, her knowledge of philosophy is profound and unparalleled.

Dusk shrouds Odantapur. The clouds have cleared. The moon over Kalinga is glowing bright like an embellished, iridescent *kalingi* canopy. It glitters like a giant sparkler in the sky. Down below, in the moonlight, splattered in the amazing multi-hued colour of the painter's brush, like a painting in the Ajanta caves, spreads out the coruscating canvas of the multi-storey building of Odantapur University. In the distance, from the harbour of Dantapura, the sound of the distant sea resonates as though playing with the metre of a song.

'Chinta, do you hear me?'

Chintadevi laughs. Wordlessly, she looks up at the moon. The youth's heart skips a beat. Agitatedly, he pleads, 'Tell me, Chinta! I've placed my entire life at your feet—my life spark and my consciousness, everything. Ever since I saw you, I've wholeheartedly offered myself to you. I've nothing more left; I am only your shadow now.'

Chintadevi turns around. In a trembling voice that's as mesmerizing as the all-encompassing melody of a veena, she says, 'I know that, prince!'

He's startled. All that he can manage is a weak monosyllable, 'Prince?'

Chintadevi smiles. 'Aren't you the prince?' she asks. 'Deny it and you'll break your vow; you'll be accused of . . . of . . . lying. I know you're indeed the Prince of Magadh—Dombi Heruka. Not just the prince, you're the heir to the throne of Magadh. Who else would've been so impudent as to offer his love to his acolyte, Chinta, here on this altar of Kalinga's Odantapur?'

'Pardon me, Devi!' he sighs and then begins to cry piteously. 'Yes, the prince! But what's in that—does it really amount to anything? I've given up the kingdom, today I'm just a hapless mendicant. I had thought—well, let it go, it matters little. Yes, I've been impudent, forgive me, Devi! The shadow of Dombi Heruka will no more besmirch this earth. As a last supplication to you, I fervently plead your forgiveness. And I beseech you to permit me to take your leave.'

Disconsolate and in immense despondency and gloom, Dombi Heruka bends over to pay his respects to her. Chintadevi breaks into a peal of laughter. Gracefully alighting from her perch, she touches Heruka's arm gently as he stands in front of her with a bowed head. 'I bless you, Dombi Heruka, be the Siddha Yogi, the enlightened ascetic!'

Chintadevi's touch sets every pore of his being on fire. The bowed head is raised. He trembles. Broken and sunk in despair, in a voice heavy with wounded pride, he asks plaintively, 'Who wants blessings? What will I do with enlightenment? I seek none of that; I only seek your pardon! With your forgiveness, I shall be able to snap my relationship with you forever. Dombi Heruka will not be anywhere around, nor will he express his thoughts before you.'

Chintadevi clamps her teeth over her lips to suppress a laugh. 'You want forgiveness?' she asks. 'And you're seeking my pardon, right? If that's so, go over to the banyan tree and seek . . .'

'You're mocking me, Devi . . .'

'Mocking you, Dombi Heruka! No, no, I'm not—that could never be! Although if anyone in this world sees your present state, they might be able to see it. Imagine what the other students would say! They'll say that the uppermost bough of the jamun tree has snapped and fallen off. What will your friends make of it? Do have pity for this poor Heruka, pity him, he direly deserves your pity! And if chairman Darikapa gets to witness this sight: the silent night, the gentle breeze wafting in the stillness of this night . . . and just the two of us together—a young man and a young woman—so far from the university—imagine the consternation it'll cause!'

In despair, Dombi Heruka covers his face in the palms of his hands and sinks to the ground, his head hung low. He mutters incoherently, 'Oh, Chinta! Chinta!'

'You're right, ascetic,' Chintadevi responds. 'I'm neither Mercy nor Pardon, I'm just that—Troubled-thoughts.' Her heart melts with ennobled piety for him. She sits on the ground, close beside him and putting her hand in his, she asks in compassion, 'Heruka, you're extremely anguished, aren't you?'

Heruka is quiet, he is speechless. Tongue-tied.

In his consciousness, memories of his life float past him. He has abdicated royalty and left Magadh questing for knowledge; he has renounced worldly life and pleasures—what determination and what effort has it taken him to morph into geriatric ways when in the prime of youth! He has travelled to many lands, across many countries, and after many such travels, he has arrived at Odantapur. This is the centre of scholastic excellence, where erudite and knowledgeable scholars become pupils seeking insight and sagacity. He has been a student here for the past four years. A young girl from an obscure village had recently joined one of the senior batches. She's a fount of knowledge and wisdom; chairman Darikapa is hugely impressed with the young woman's unbelievable acuity, sensitivity and display of maturity far beyond her age; she's signed on as the philosophy teacher in Odantapur. Heruka's life, too, seems to have changed. Hope blossoms within him again like colourful blooms. Alas, that wondrous life has proved far too short-lived for him. The hopes and determination have been dashed and stand extirpated today and, with that, his present life, too, appears to have come to an end.

'Who shall pardon you, Heruka! What is your fault? And why are you so upset?' Chintadevi asks with slow deliberation. 'The truth is, you are a refuge of your own inner consciousness. This consciousness has given birth to this world, this consciousness has conferred myriad offerings of life and this consciousness is also the source of all sorrow. Desire is born out of this consciousness, no matter what its form—pure or impure. Who, then, in this world has the power of forgiveness? This is the truth and the reality. And so much of this is for the absolution of your own soul, Heruka! Stay calm, stay serene.'

Her touch and her proximity seem to have a magical effect on Dombi Heruka. His eyes close and he feels happy. He senses the night is slowly coming to an end and morning is nigh; in the various water bodies around the university, thousands of lotuses bloom, and the gentle morning breeze will soon waft in their sweet fragrance.

As one in a dream, he mumbles, 'You mean I'll pardon myself! But why must I? That would mean tearing down and throwing away the lotus that shines inside me like a diamond. This is the lotus that I have stashed away in the core of my heart! Why must I do that? So what if Chinta is not mine; so what if she doesn't reciprocate my feelings. Would I, then, tamp down my memory of her and deny my own existence? Where will I be able to hide then?'

'You're right, whatever you have said is very true,' she says calmly. 'Your right is only your own—yours alone! Who has the power to snatch it from you? The *thought* of Chinta too is entirely yours, entirely yours . . .'

Happiness fills Dombi Heruka. He raises his face. Love is manifest in his expressive eyes. The moon, high up in the sky, has moved ahead on its arc; it's a clear moonlit night, and the happiness it exudes spreads across his bashful face. He says, 'Chinta—is Chinta mine?'

The young woman again looks at him serenely. She locks her eyes with his. A silence reigns over them. She says softly,

'If your consciousness so wills and so desires, then Chinta is indeed yours—of course, she is yours . . .'

Desire suffuses Heruka's face. His voice trembles as he whispers, 'Chinta . . .'

'No! Not that way! Your voice is still laced with immense excitement and ecstasy,' her tone is benign, equanimous. 'But it's weak in its determination to explore the ephemeral meaning of life and existence; it's suffused with transient pleasures and physical desire, it's sullied and diseased, even bloodied—it's admittedly a call of the flesh and blood. You'll simply not be able to achieve the Great Happiness with this outlook, Dombi Heruka!'

The 'Oh!' that escapes Dombi Heruka's lips says it all.

Like a deflated balloon, Heruka's face falls and he looks down. Unperturbed, Chinta gently caresses Heruka's shoulders with her dainty fingers that look like the petals of a champa flower. 'Why this tone of defeat and capitulation, Heruka? Why? Your consciousness has created this desire for a woman, it's entirely your own creation; but what kind of love do you pine for? What are you going to do with that? Have you ever given it a thought?'

She continues. 'The warm person you crave will only consign you to the inexorable whirligig of the cycle of life, old age, death and rebirth. The years will pass by, one after another and yet another—and you'll be left counting the numbers on your fingers. Is that the Great Happiness that you seek? How long will you be able to preserve Chinta's youth and beauty, how long is the fullness of Chinta's pulchritude? These are mere deviations framed in your consciousness—the reflected images of your consciousness. If you came all the way from Magadh to Dantapura with all your sadhana focused on a woman's body, then take it. You came seeking the elixir of lofty ideals, not the banality of everyday living—but choose the banal if you want to. Tell me, Heruka, the future king of Magadh, will you be happy if you take Chinta with you and anoint her as the queen of Magadh?'

Heruka is parched, but he isn't in a state of mind to slake his thirst. He finds himself getting more restive, feeling more stifled in his thoughts. He trembles in agitation, his vision clouds over and his eyes now are leaking tears.

Innocent Yogini Chinta withdraws her soft touch from Heruka. 'You're weeping, Heruka!' she says, her voice seeming to float in from elsewhere, a world far away. 'This certainly isn't the Great Happiness you seek. Even now you are tied to me in memory. It's your consciousness that is responsible for this. Consciousness operates on multiple levels. It tortures animate beings and manifests its ingenious forms everywhere. Illusion stays within—lurking deep inside you—and spreads its tentacles and holds you captive.'

Heruka feels crushed. 'I'm indeed the fallen one!' he says hapless and tearful. 'Help me, Devi! I'm the slave of your slaves; I beseech you—please guide me! Be my guru and lead me on!'

Chinta's voice sounds remote, much as it did before, and it seems to drift in from afar—from up and beyond the abyss. 'You're indeed my disciple, young man! Have no doubt about it, have no fear and have no regrets. You cannot hold on to anything that is destined to leave you; so, do graciously let it be. Don't hold yourself responsible for the preternatural ways of your consciousness. You're not to be blamed. Experience the emptiness, the void, the *sunyata* of the world, and stay away from falling into the tempting ways of imaging worldly designs that sprout bizarre thoughts in the mind. A time will come—it surely will—when you shall unravel Buddhatwa with ease. Focus on wisdom and the means to obtain it. And you shall indeed be the possessor of Great Happiness.'

Dombi Heruka closes his eyes and sits down in meditation. He senses a calmness he had never experienced before. After a while, he raises his head and looks around. He experiences quietude and solitude. The moonlight bathes everything in a gentle glow, and there isn't a soul around. His consciousness imagines a resplendent woman's image—she's the shining star in the void, the epitome of perfection, the fount of wisdom, it's the image of Chintadevi. But this Chintadevi in the consciousness of her own transcendence appears brighter, shinier and all-pervading. Meditation comes easy to him now. Uncertainties are dispelled and as he offers his obeisance times without number to the effulgent light that shimmers before his eyes, he drifts back to his asana to continue his meditation, presently deepening with each passing moment of the early dawn. The guru has whispered the mantra, shown him the many ways of the path, and from now on, it is only sadhana that shall hold him in thrall.

Slowly the body stills and gives a quietus to his inner consciousness. The mind has surrendered itself to the guru's feet. The *samskara,* genetic memory of many past lives, refined and choreographed, circles back to his mind.

That guru, the legendary Chinta, was a little-known Kalinga girl. In history, she became famous as Maha Siddha Darikapa's disciple, 'the innocent Yogini Chinta'— the author of *Baikta Bhabanugata Tatwasidhi*, the treatise that articulates the innermost thoughts of mind and elements—the Devout Yogini.

Oh, spirituality seeker, prince of Magath, Siddha Yogi Dombi Heruka's guru, Chintadevi!

That was twelve hundred years ago.

Originally titled 'Punarjanma', 1951

Chakrapani

Who didn't eat biscuits? Everyone did. If people didn't eat them, why would biscuit manufacturers put in so much effort into making them, packing and sealing them in tin boxes with attractive pictures pasted on them before dispatching the boxes to far-off places? But the day Chakrapani Mohapatra, the seventy-year-old grandee of the village, playfully snatched a biscuit from his seven-year-old grandson, Dandapani, and started nibbling on it, that made headlines. This startling news was not just confined to Chakrapani's village but spread far and wide—to the seven adjoining blocks. Such was the furore that people talked about it whenever they ran into one another on the street or at the village fairs, telling each other in a curious daze, 'Have you heard? Chakrapani Mohapatra has started eating biscuits!'

Chakrapani was an esteemed personage in the area. Not merely because he was a rich zamindar or because, as Dr Kambupani's father, he embodied the honour of being the doctor's revered sire; he was an eminent Sanskrit scholar and astrologer in his own right. While people compared him with the revered Hari Brahma for his erudition in Sanskrit, he was considered the coequal of Shri Bhojraj Udgata Shastri for his knowledge of astrology. Both Brahma and Udgata Shastri were dead, so, Chakrapani was now the only scholar of eminence who remained and was considered the credentialled repository of all knowledge.

It was fifteen years since his wife's passing. He had always lived a pious and devout life, sustaining himself with *prasad* from the temple, and spending his waking hours sitting on the raised veranda of the front yard, beside the *chaura*, the potted tulsi plant, telling beads all day and looking out at the daily goings and comings. And there, in front of the veranda, life was a hive of activity, playing out in moving images: people setting off to the field with their ploughs; people driving their herds of cattle to and fro; children padding along to school with their satchels; loads of gifts sent out to a daughter's house; people dolled up in their finery setting out to the town; and the postman's quotidian visit with his bag of letters. The uniformed chowkidar, too, took this path to report for duty at the police station. The shadows of the trees lengthened and shrank; the newborn arrived in the world and grew up, while the old and decrepit disappeared. But Chakrapani sat stock-still on his perch all day, chanting, 'Krishna! Krishna! Krishna!'

It seemed as if the only purpose of his life was to chant the name of Krishna and, with a beatific smile of acknowledgement, nod his head to bless those offering their respects to him as they passed by.

Whenever it was time to hold a *sathi* puja to bless a newborn child with a long life by knotting a cord and invoking the names of people who have lived long, Chakrapani's was the first name that came to everyone's lips. For the simple, bucolic folks steeped in local dharmic norms, he was indeed a living god. Not just that—whenever people undertook a tough assignment, they first sought his blessings. And he showered it on them, graciously, unstintingly, as he kept chanting, 'Krishna! Krishna! Krishna!'

For all their reverence, although, no biscuit-chomping human had ever entered their calculus: biscuits were meant only for those who knew English, went to the theatre, feasted often . . . in short, people with *bon vivant*—the kind of lifestyle that the unpretentious village people always abjured. Theirs was a humdrum life, lived on high ethics, worship and an unending cycle of rites and rituals—a tuft of hair at the back of their tonsured heads, a string of wooden beads around their necks and the name of Krishna inscribed in sandalwood paste all over their bodies. The revered old man's immobile form and ubiquitous hallowed presence was a still, small voice of calm for these innocent souls when they confronted disease, grief, doubts, danger. So, when they heard about his eating biscuits, it was like the proverbial stone thrown at a beehive, the news spreading far and wide, 'Chakrapani Mohapatra has started eating biscuits!'

The ideals built with such grace and effort had now come crashing down—ideals that had granted them solace and filled them with faith, conveying in no uncertain terms Chakrapani's core message to them, the common village people:

There are, of course human embodiers of the Almighty, and not everyone is weak. With sadhana, even ordinary, worldly men can attain this goal. As much as these are the signposts of societal development, such rare beings, appearing once a while across ages—regardless of what people say—are the true signifiers of the advancement of humanity's civilizational mind.

People quickly spread the news across villages and towns; some raised their eyebrows and expressed surprise, before sighing deeply. 'Well, everything happens in these besetting times,' they mourned, their despairing words laced with their invocation of human forms. 'Gods, after all, are mere stone idols, so what can one say of human beings?' A few of them, upon hearing the news, merely groaned in hopelessness.

But the one whose acts had spawned these doleful thoughts in people's minds was unfazed and unflustered. He couldn't imagine what changes would be wrought on his putative seventy-year-old persona to give people a different opinion about him. After all, isn't God the creator of everything— even biscuits? Doesn't He instil cravings in people from time to time? Sometimes He fulfils them. But the common man's desires are seemingly endless and interminably tortured by cravings and temptations. An enlightened soul sees God in everything, even the temptations that come his way, and accepts them as prasad. He, Chakrapani Mohapatra, was just like the enlightened soul, so what difference did it make?

Casting his mind back to his past made Chakrapani smirk sometimes—how he had loved nibbling on unripe guavas as a child. How lost he would become at the sight of his wife's face during the first few years of marriage. How he then became obsessed with the idea of enhancing his fame and capabilities. How all that eventually led to chanting Krishna's name in a mantra. If truth be told, this indeed was life, what else?

He was amazed at how the idea of living had changed over the course of his lifetime. While boisterousness had been his hallmark of recognition during childhood, telling beads had become the hallmark in the dusk of his life. Many incidents had occurred on this journey as he moved from one level to the other: some happy, some sad—like his wife's death—before he transcended to another level. But time is the true healer and, with the passage of time, man learns to bear all. People around him today sang old tunes the old-fashioned way, and how strange and outlandish they sounded, yet how evocative they were! Everything was, after all, God's wish, so why worry too much about it?

This was the way in which the ruminating Chakrapani Mohapatra tried to veil his past and forget the excitement of happiness. He had pivoted away; now it was just the seat on the front veranda, the puja room and himself, the chant of Krishna! Krishna! on his lips.

So, one afternoon, he sat on the veranda chanting the name of Krishna and gazing at the world outside. In his yellowing eyes were the shadows cast by the flaming krushnachuda—Krishna's Crown, the gulmohar—heavy with bloom, the banana orchard and a few small, thatched houses. The sparrows hopped and a young, black heifer tethered to the stake looked about expectantly, flapping her ears and exhaling deeply. She kept thrusting her neck from side to side and lowed in a gravelly voice.

On a platform, before him, cow dung fuel cakes—flat and round—were drying. Old Netai Ma, the sweeper woman, with cow dung running down her elbow, was patting down new cakes, grumbling to herself, 'They've tethered this heifer right here. Why couldn't they have let her out? She's in heat—and refuses to even touch the straw. She'll butt people if anyone gets close to her. Soon enough she'll break free and run away like one possessed. Why do people deliberately invite trouble into this busy area, already bustling with activities with the constant to-ings and fro-ings of villagers? Water will douse a fire, but what's with this goddamned thing they've done in tethering the heifer?'

'Krishna-Krishna-Krishna-Krishna—'

Outside in the open, the game of light and shadows played out endlessly, changing rapidly, shrinking and imprinting itself in the dark pupils of his two, sunken, tawny eyes. Krishna-Krishna-Krishna—this is the essence of living, no matter how much one aged, it's inconceivable to tire of living: the eyes saw these images, the breeze wafted in and caressed the body as it whispered in one's ears and the enunciation of people's words were so much like the favourite song one loves to hear! This was the handiwork of the eternal Almighty: it descended in heaps; the new leaves, the new buds, the newborn babies and the blooming flowers, much like water squirted by an elephant in the month of *Ashadha*—with the myriad forms and hues it took on these days. Textbook knowledge was hardly of consequence. It merely touched the dried outer bark, barely penetrating the tree's innards. What penetrated was the belief: in faith that you found Krishna—the one skittering away afar!

The words of Netai Ma penetrated his consciousness and overwhelmed him. Chakrapani looked at her now with eager eyes. In his puritanical mind, he seemed to have witnessed the sun rise and then traverse its path before slowly descending to set, quickly dipping into the horizon. It seemed like just yesterday when Sapan's wife had come to the village as a bride. She was a buxom girl with a full, round face and bright, alert eyes. Encircling her wrists were thick, heavy, brass bangles and around her ankles, thin, twisted brass anklets. A short distance away from this mound, beyond the bamboo forest, was their house. She walked all this distance every day because she worked in many houses in this area and also in the fields and the groves. She hadn't looked like one born into a poor sweeper's family, someone who ate snails and slugs and did menial chores. Her face hadn't looked so pinched or harsh and brutal; her skin hadn't seemed like it was distilled from frog-hide to encase her bones and innards; her voice at the time was soft and tender and nowhere like this croak. Sapan's wife, though born into a sweeper's family, had imbibed the versatile values of health and education of any well-bred girl; she lit the fire in the hearth, she filled the waterpots, she harvested the yield and looked after the home—the complete homemaker, nurturing peace and tranquillity.

His eyes were riveted on her.

The dense krushnachuda tree was a riot of colours.

A soft breeze wafted from the many weed-filled ponds and blew into his face.

Suddenly, old Chakrapani's thoughts drifted back to her. 'Where's Sapan's wife? Who's she—this doddering old woman—when did Sapan's wife age so?'

So many have been carried away on a bier hefted on four shoulders—that was an all too familiar journey. The grave, mournful intonation of *Ram naam satya hei*, the dirge of the musical instrument, the *baidi*, and in the funeral procession a flame flickering like a slice of Hanuman's burning tail. Following them were the piercing, heartbroken, disconsolate laments. People realized that someone from the village had died. Many such village folk had left the world—seventy years was a long lifetime. Once in every two or three years, an epidemic struck. Sometimes it was cholera, at other times, smallpox and yet other times, dengue and even malaria, both of which had now developed into a regular scourge. These afflictions took their toll and then death disappeared for a while. Newborn babies grew up, but to what end? They all circled back, there was no permanence in living; the youngsters had left the village, what remained today were the dregs of the living—only the goats and the sheep.

The deaths of the people to whom the living paid their respects were the deaths that mattered. But what of the deaths that went unnoticed and unmourned? These people still stood there as others called them by their names, but they had ceased to be human beings—in appearance, in mind, in temperament. In what way was their living any better than death?

So many people lived in this death-in-life state; the Baurisahi boys decamped. When jackals barged into the village there were only the skinny, pathetic dogs to keep them at bay and just a bunch of women to chase them away. The handful of frightened, pitiful children clung to their mothers' legs. Living too was Sapan's wife, but she wasn't really alive—she wasn't this haggard old woman. And Chakrapani broke into chants of Krishna! Krishna! Krishna! to assuage his mind.

Suddenly it came to his mind that death was a lie—a complete lie. Only the times had changed: the father had built the house, now it was the son; the mother-in-law, a young woman then, had sat on the inner veranda, with her legs stretched out in front of her—combing her hair and looking at her smiling face in the mirror, her hands restless, a kiya, screw pine flower, beside her; he could visualize her tucking the flower into her bun with the hairpins. The daughter-in-law did exactly that now.

Out in the open, on this scorching afternoon, at the door stood Noka, the yogi, in his *khadam*, wooden clogs, glass bangles on his wrists and eyes lined with kohl and the dainty young woman placed a handful of rice in his begging bowl. He lived on . . . would he ever accept death? No way!

'Netai Ma, how's your daughter-in-law?'

'Well, that effing bitch! That scorching firehole!' Netai Ma muttered and went on with her litany of complaints. 'Saantay, she is such a drama queen!—she'll feed her stomach and shine her body with that dirty, filthy fire-ash that we never ever got to see. Now they smear their faces and bodies with it and then flaunt themselves around the village. If I tell her, she bristles; she's gone rogue. "What's that to you?" she'll demand. "How does it concern you?" Her hectoring is billowing by the day, Saantay. She's now the bull in the house and I the poor goat—just one stomach to feed and I boil a separate pot of rice! I said to her, you all-devourer, you shame me by staying here. The son has died; you're young; why shame yourself by living here, you vile, evil devil? Why don't you find yourself a man and move out of this house and in with him? In turn, she skewers me. "Why should I move away? I didn't come to your house on my own. Your son died—not I! I'm still around, and who's going to snatch away my share when I'm still alive?" Oh, is this why God had given you a life—to squat on my chest, pull out my tongue and suck the blood and flesh from me? What a home I had and what a home it has become! Where has all the generational culture gone? The values and heritage of our sweeper community!

'Day and night, whenever you look around, you see people assembling like a pack of dogs: if one is under the eaves, the other is stretching his legs out on the veranda and smoking a pikka and yet another sits there, faking a cough, ably shrouded by the kiya bushes; there's still another tittering and another dog-whistling. Who do you stop? When I ask them, they'll say, "Well, this is on the way to the fields; is this path barred for us? Tell me, Saantay, do all the paths of this region run past my door? When I ask why they have to sit on a sweeper's veranda, why not under the trees? they promptly retort, "What's wrong if it's a sweeper's? Those days are long gone; these days there are no such inhibitions or distinctions—everyone is equal, where's the question of any discrimination? Any hot scorching day or when you're tired and exhausted, you naturally tend to sit down and rest on any veranda. Will your veranda lose its sheen if we sit on it?" And all the while she'll be giggling inside the house. Tell me, Saantay, when there are so many paths, is mine the only path to traverse—to congregate in and sit on? Is my veranda the only place? Sometimes you have the urge to pee, sometimes to poop and you do all that beside the fence! Gone are the days when your words held relevance in this village, Saantay.'

Her agitated voice rose. 'During your heyday, you were the only towering presence in this area; but ever since you turned to spirituality, chaos has reigned. Today, everyone thinks he's the leader—these upstarts! Neither do they have any respect nor any honour for anyone; who heeds another person and who accepts the other person's words? Everything will turn to ashes . . .'

Netai Ma's *bohu* was indeed a problem and everyone in the village knew it, but there was nothing that they could say or do—much like the weed-infested, peat-bogged pond in the middle of the village that everyone abhorred. If these duckweeds and infestations weren't there, the village would be a healthier place, but no one was prepared to pull them out. Much advice had been proffered, but when it came to the crunch—nothing gets done.

Netai Ma kept muttering, 'Death doesn't take me away, neither does cholera afflict her! The life force of so many cherished people burst like a water bubble. They melt away and disappear, but for the unloved, unwanted people, there is no death by drowning or from cholera or from drought!'

Oh, this imagination! The body only tried grappling with earthly worries and got more and more mired, more and more miserable. What else was there to it? *Jibana—se sundara, se kamya*—life truly is beautiful, life truly is dutiful. People flouted dharma and vilified life and knew nothing about how to live and enjoy themselves. *Nachi na jani taala ra dosha*— blame the ungainly dancing, not the beat!

Netai Ma too doesn't know.

Her last few words had brought to his mind a strong sense of contradiction. 'No! No!' he had murmured under his breath. 'The life force is not like a water bubble!'

But Chakrapani reacted very differently to what she had said earlier. Listening to her complaints, he felt goosebumps all over, as though someone had lightly tapped at some hidden nerve centres in the brain and awakened long-forgotten sensations in him. In his mind he grappled with restrictions imposed by social reformers, while his senses came alive with the half-forgotten memory of an irresponsible life, something that could've led him astray. He felt happy.

Chakrapani sighed deeply as Netai Ma continued with her harangue. His sighs evaporated. His thoughts dissipated, his Krishna-chanting mouth had fallen silent and his eyes stayed focused on the far distance. How the riotously blooming krushnachuda swayed in the breeze, bursting in glorious colour, its familiar colours expressing age-old thoughts!

A simple, unremarkable incident had happened at this very place when Dandapani, his grandson, had walked out of the house eating a biscuit and holding two more in his left hand. He had been wearing shorts and a half-sleeved shirt, a satchel slung over his shoulder. In the satchel was a slate, some books and notebooks. He had been ready to leave for school. Teasingly he had said, 'Jeje, I'm eating a biscuit. Would you like to have one?'

'Yes, give me, give me one!'

'But can you bite into it with your teeth?' he teased his grandfather.

'Give me, give me!' Chakrapani commanded.

'It has egg in it—and water that the sahibs have touched, you know this, don't you?'

'Oh, give me, give me!'

Chakrapani Mohapatra had put his arm around Dandapani's shoulders very lovingly and had extracted the biscuit from his hand. Dandapani was surprised. In his short span of worldly experience, he had noticed that his Jeje never touched any of these things; perhaps Jeje believed that touching them would pollute him. Bou too had said that 'If you touch any non-vegetarian food or biscuit or egg, don't go anywhere near Jeje—beware he's a spiritual soul!'

'What's this—spiritual?'

'Those people who don't touch any of these things and are engaged in continuous worship of the gods all the time—they are the ones on the spiritual path.'

Getting over his surprise, he had said, 'Jeje, you're a spiritual person, aren't you?' But by then, Jeje had broken the biscuit into two small pieces and had stuffed them into his mouth, masticating them. His toothless gums acted like a grinding machine and crushed the biscuit to pieces. Jeje's face had betrayed no signs of surprise—it was a mundane incident like the cow chewing the cud—what else?

Dandapani stood there, gaping. Suddenly he became aware of his loss, the immense loss of two biscuits and flew like a kite into the bowels of the house. 'Have you heard this, Bou? Have you heard, Bou?'

With a tuft of hair in the centre of his tonsured head, his body adorned with the symbol of Krishna in sacred ash and the beads in his hands, the man who epitomized a pillar of society in the village remained on his seat. The tip of his tongue licked the lips, slowly, repeatedly, first this way and then that.

He called Netai Ma over and spoke. 'Why is it that your bohu doesn't come here? Only if she meets and interacts with respectable people will she learn good things and change her ways. What will she learn if she stays at home? Tell her to come here. I'll speak with her.'

'I'll tell her, Saantay, I will,' Netai Ma replied. 'But will the blighter listen?'

Dandapani's mother heard her son's tale but found it hard to believe.

However, that very evening, when Dandapani's mother came out with his usual meal, a bowl of boiled milk and a mix of soft *khai*, de-husked and puffed paddy, along with two bananas on a plate, Chakrapani smiled and said, 'This isn't enough, Bohu; give me four biscuits, they taste really good!'

The bohu was stunned and gaped at him.

'Yes, get me four biscuits. From now on, we'll have biscuits with tea.'

'You want me to get biscuits for you?'

'Yes, yes! Why don't you get them for me, Bohu?' Chakrapani asked, hearing the incredulity in her voice. 'All of you are eating them, aren't you? So, what's wrong?'

Quietly, Kambupani's wife walked back into the house, a tepid smile on her face. A sudden fear gripped her as she wondered, 'Is father-in-law on his way out of this world?' Mournfully she assumed that this was an omen of an imminent farewell, the tragic arc leading to the inevitable end. All these days his statuesque, venerable presence had graced the household; people respected him because of his cachet and the house shone brightly on the coattails of his fame. 'My He', her husband, was merely an itinerant and busy employee; he hardly had the time to even shave. Would he ever be able to look after the village home and manage the property? As they say, people generally indulged in uncharacteristic quirks before death; they developed all kinds of eccentricities and ate naughty foods, and it was very likely that this was what was happening to her father-in-law.

She sensed death approaching their home; the darkness outside had now taken on a new meaning and acquired a new form; she looked up at the coconut trees corralling the house and felt something ominous lurking in the crevices of the dense, dark fronds; she couldn't bear to look at the serried peepul tree and the sahada, sandpaper tree, the spectre of an unnamed fear haunted them as well. A shiver ran down her spine. Small *chemeli,* sun birds, fluttered below the bamboo grove; fortunately, they weren't the evil-presaging owls! The feeling was surreal. She was convinced that death inched ever closer, here—it has almost arrived! The very next day she wrote a letter to her husband and posted it.

But the changes that came over Chakrapani that night after tea and biscuits seemed furthest from the state of dying. The *Bhagabata* opened only perfunctorily. He desired to go out and sit in the dark for a while. In the breeze, he sensed the soft mellow caress of the 'lost hands'; he longed to rest his body on the earth and let his mind fly into the star-spangled sky, above, just as children let their kites soar. Today, when he summoned a prayer and started chanting the name of God, his many desires became stridently eloquent.

Krishna! Krishna! He closed his eyes and muttered the name of Krishna mechanically for a while. First, the darkness, then the light, then a bluish hue, then the image of God Krishna in recognizable form and around it written in Oriya script a white, glowing 'Om'; and from it, like soft light emanating from the starry vault, the rays spreading across the blue sky. He had loved looking at such ethereal pictures. Today, after he had changed the samskara of his seventy years to partake of tea and biscuits, when he sat with closed eyes as was his wont, he wasn't able to see anything clearly. He sensed that the *deepa*'s haze was on his eyelids and the darkness was all-pervasive and growing. When he tried to retract his eyelids to shut out the glare, he glimpsed the many faces from the past and instantly felt the urge to open his eyes and dial back to those faces—and think. He had closed the *Bhagabata* and opened his eyes. Suddenly he was infused with an arcane suspicion: God did not appear today, is he annoyed with me?

But his suspicion was quickly dispelled in the arguments of the shastras: Chakrapani himself was not snared in worldly attachments, so why would God be angry with him? Had he caused any harm to anyone? He was having a dialogue in his mind. Why had the new desire descended on him if He hadn't had a hand in it? He and He alone had shown him the path of abstinence for several years, now here too He was showing him the path of desire; and he recalled the *Bhagabata*, 'Satiating the atman is to go the way, so why ask now the pathway,' or something akin to this.

His suspicion evanesced. He accepted it rather blithely that his wishes were indeed God's wishes! Both were inseparable.

Looking inward, he rationalized the battle of thoughts raging within him—we haven't gotten our fair share! In the temple of the gods and in the land of dharma he could see a crowd of hungry beggars flanking the pathways, screaming out loud: what's going to happen to us? What's going to befall us? With so many of his longings unrealized, was it possible for a man to go to heaven when he died? He kept thinking, his mind in a turmoil.

It was as if the noble soul, who had begun all these activities, had suddenly fallen asleep; and then the time had passed and the situation had undergone changes. By the time he had woken up, a lot of chores had piled up, but he had neither the means nor the strength to do them. At long last, after intense introspection, he had come face to face with his own old age—the howling winds swirling within an empty pitcher and setting off whirligigs that keep intoning: 'There's no time left; just no more time left!'

He was gathering his thoughts around him and assessing his own past, but with a logic that was new. There, in times past, even when the appetites raged, they had to be reined in; no sacrifice was large enough on the altar of fame. Dressed in the severe, saffron robes of spirituality and sacrifice, his had been an endless quest to ferret out knowledge hidden in books and manuscripts and imbibe that subliminal wisdom. Everything seemed diminished now; in him now lurked many a pique and in the distance, he could hear the roar of the sea. All that he had accomplished—duty, responsibility and determination— appeared narrow, illogical and irrelevant today; all those efforts hadn't been able to end sorrow, disease and death; everything had faded and wilted and alas, would not come back.

When he turned in at night, his mind hearkened back to the memory of the events of the sunset hours, the krushnachuda tree, the racy eagerness of the black heifer, Netai Ma's past and her daughter-in-law's present zany state. Fair enough, there was a need to see Netai Ma's bohu. Hopefully she would come and listen to his homilies. He fell asleep.

The next morning, Chakrapani summoned his bohu and revealed his new idea. 'I think I'll have to have fish and meat. Nutritious food is required to sustain this body. Many people believe eating non-vegetarian food is a sin. That's a wrong assumption. What if we don't eat it? Others are having it anyway, it'll be cooked for them; will it make any difference whether we have it or not, or will our partaking add to the number of animals slaughtered. Will our abstinence help stop it? It's just a matter of one's taste; I didn't take it because I didn't feel like it; now that I feel like having it, I'd like to have it. You've collected a lot of new recipes from your friends in the village. Try out some of those. Let today be the beginning.'

Dandapani's Bou took pity on him and thought to herself, 'Poor old man! Let him have whatever he feels like having.'

But, troubled to the core, she wrote out this tale in a missive to her husband.

> Do come home quickly. I feel very awkward and nervous; were anything to happen I'm afraid I won't be able to handle the situation. It's not in any woman's remit to handle such a scenario.

She tried not to publicize her father-in-law's change in food habits, but Dandapani was a school-going boy and on his way to school and back, the boy broadcasted his new-found knowledge, 'My Jeje has started eating non-vegetarian food, so Bou says we're going to have meat and fish every day.'

The village folk visited his house just to see the change— first in trickles, then the tide of disbelievers increased. People weren't prepared to believe that, just as the river could change its course, human beings too could change their habits; that huge trees could be uprooted in the wind; and those places where people live today could turn into swamps and ditches where crocodiles nest. The elderly people believed that Chakrapani Mohapatra had lost his marbles and he was clearly nearing his end; the wise old man sitting on his veranda like a ripe mango would not be there for long and another exceptional soul from the village would be lost forever. So, they came to him, to take a long look at him and bask in his presence. The village youngsters, too, came to watch the fun. The old man had lost his mind, maybe he would veer off course soon, maybe he would even cavort around for a short while and it would be naïve to miss this high entertainment. So, they came and waited, standing there quietly. They too had lost their respect for him after hearing what they had heard, and many forgot to pay their usual respects to him. Some of them had deep sympathy for him, while others looked at him with heartless scorn. But the fact was, their veneration for him had undeniably faded.

The changes were conspicuous. Earlier he was a holy man and, no matter what people said, he continued with his chant of Krishna! Krishna! and continued nodding his head in apparent blessings. But today he was loquacious; he had smiles and chuckles for everyone and even a few words. As if after days of incarceration, he had come out into the open, everyone was his well-wisher and loving friend, and they had come to welcome him back. And in this proximity with people, his personality had broken free—and had unfurled.

'Come and sit here,' he summoned and welcomed the throngs of people. 'Can someone get some paan? Aren't there tender coconuts up on the trees? Let someone climb up and pluck them. These people have been in the hot sun. Can tender coconuts do them any harm? Do sit down. What was I saying? Please wait a while, I'll continue.

'You, son Swain, I hope your farming goes on well, you don't have any worries, your business remains under your control and you don't ever have to depend on anyone else.'

The words would soon change course as they merged with his lifelong dharmic instincts and sermonettes. 'And you, Beherai, how's your work going on? Shouldn't you be telling your friends: water added to milk doesn't add to your money and fame! If you want to make more money, you'd do better to add quality to your herd of cattle; they'll produce more milk; what fame do you earn if you add pitchers of water to dilute the milk, what's the meaning of that kind of money?

'Hey, Satapathyie, your father was in the habit of teaching Sanskrit to many people, now the study has hollowed out—it has become a practice to hoodwink people with a show of Sanskrit knowledge; will this practice go on or is there any move to change its pedagogical paradigm? It's so nice that you all came here.'

He felt cavalier about life. 'I want to share so many things about this village, but I'm unable to recall everything. Bear with me; it'll slowly come back.' He would pause, collect his thoughts and start again with a laser instinct for the culinary details. 'Yes, why are these youngsters becoming so listless? You've seen how, in the earlier days, there were people who could wolf down a three-quarter seer of *chuda,* flattened rice, in the morning and digest it in no time. Then, in the afternoon, a half-kilo of Cuttacki parboiled rice and a half-seer of urad dal served in bronze bowls, with a big chunk of dried and salted fish. That kind of food is not served any more, neither are there such people to gorge on them, nor are the ingredients available now. And the size of the pithas, snacks— some steamed, some fried—and the pancakes—such magnum sizes! The girls and bohus of today have even forgotten how to prepare those dishes.'

He paused again to catch his breath. He was living out a dream of those purported pithas. The people had started exchanging glances and nodding acknowledgements—the poor old man was craving for pithas! The women in the family would run post-haste to the kitchen to prepare the pithas— yes, why shouldn't he eat to his fullest? The pitha would soon be forthcoming!

Yet every word that he uttered triggered different ideas among the people assembled there: some finding one meaning, someone else another—had he gone bonkers? And yet someone else, driven by his nimbus of fame, believed that this indeed was the core of universal truth. However, one thing was clear: there was nothing in this speech relating to spirituality and canonical discourses; everything centred on the mundane. Everything uttered by this enlightened soul was focused on this earthly living, not a word of the astral. Many old people sitting around him sighed deeply in despair: in Chakrapani's spigots of peroration they saw the hellish scene of destruction—what was the endpoint of his years of spiritual journey if there wasn't a word of spiritual advice from the lips of this wizened old man? No, these were the edicts of Kaliyug, that pure developed souls would renounce their habits, that ascetics would convert to material living, that everything would turn upside down; everything would crumble and break.

The old man had started to speak again after resting a while.

'What's relevant is the strength in your bones and muscles, the number of years you've lived and of course, a disease-free body. If that's not there, everything is lost. What's the meaning of the suit of knowledge and wisdom without all that? No one can gift you your life and strength! It's all a matter of the vital life force within the body.'

He looked from one face to the other as though he had lost the thread of his exposition. Then he spat out bits of spittle and resumed his pitch, 'Everywhere you get to hear the same thing—love, love, love! It seems these youngsters have nothing else in life! Even if I am sitting here in radio silence, I haven't turned stone deaf. Your songs are full of it, which is why you have such a fascination for drama and theatre. Go ahead, who's stopping you. You've hardly any strength in the loins, so I ask what's the worth of your love!' Chakrapani broke into loud guffaws and added with great enthusiasm, 'Eat what you love to, first strengthen your body, yes this is what I wanted to say but I kept forgetting—build a wrestling *akhada*, platform, in the village; collect funds to engage someone like a Shamsher Pathan as your guru—be disciplined, learn to play the game of pirouetting sticks, do push-ups, do whatever it takes to be strong and muscular.'

One of the youngsters, blasé in his behaviour, asked him, 'Will you come if we set up the wrestling ring?'

'Why won't we go there?' Chakrapani's reply was pat. 'Aren't we human, too? We may not be able to wrestle, but is there a ban on spectators?'

'Is that why you've started on a non-vegetarian diet? To rebuild your body?' Another youngster tried to needle him.

'That's the whole thing, you took the words out of my mouth!' Chakrapani's eyes alighted on him. 'I kept mulling over so many things, then it occurred to me to ask myself, what have I done for my body? Death is inexorable, it's inevitable; I'm getting on in years, and who on earth can help it? But whatever time is left, why don't we live like human beings?'

'And fish and meat will be followed by Hari-naam!'

'Hari-naam will not stop—ever. Tell me, isn't Hari everywhere! He's not visible; it's just a matter of realizing him and this realization will be through the body and the mind. If the body is no longer a body, how can one realize Hari? If you're afflicted with a cold or have a bout of fever, will the breeze feel like a breeze and the water taste like water? Remember, first comes the body and everything else feeds into it and enwraps it.'

'If that's the case, why did you abjure these things for so many years?' The youngsters were ping-ponging with him now.

'The body had no complaints whatsoever; the mind just didn't have the urge to have it. If the body doesn't need it, there will be no desire for it. There is a need now, so I feel—what's wrong with that? The shastras say you can do anything as long as you do it without attachment and then, like a crab, you can scuttle back into your shell. We are worldly people, but there are so many ascetics around. There's nothing there in it, there's nothing in anything, and if we've survived, it's a tribute to one's father!'

So, on it went with questions of various kinds, with the old man answering to the full extent of his ability. As soon as the village folk had learnt the art of catechizing, they enjoyed the fun and frolic, as though someone from a foreign land had descended and was holding a crowded press conference, where journalists were relentless with their volley of questions. The answers, too, were in sync with his behaviour; those who heard the replies spread the news far and wide, and that was inevitably followed by criticism.

'Hey, an unhinged man, a fake saint! How people give their nutty reflections a high-gloss spin! "He doesn't eat fish, he doesn't eat critters; he realizes Hari through his body, and when he gets past one Hari the other Hari looms into view—the speaking Hari, the disappearing Hari, the chasing Hari and the Hari entering him!" He's lost his head and that's why he keeps rattling on without making any sense.'

But Chakrapani looked content. At last, he had been able to publicize his message of the truth. It would spread its roots and do a lot of good to society. As soon as he started speaking, it was as if he had been bitten by the communiqué bug—people milled around him and feeding off their energy, he kept up a continuous stream of chatter. At times he looked sick and demented, his voice quivered; and at times he stammered, yet he invited people over to him and bade them sit with him, and he carried on relentlessly with his oratory.

When the one-eyed oilman passed by with a load of oil on his head one afternoon, he shouted out to him, 'Listen, Achyuta, come here, wipe the sweat from your brow and rest in this shade. You keep working day in and day out. I hope you're eating well enough. I know you won't be doing justice to yourself: every time it'll be "my son, my grandson, my wife, my bohu"—how are they relevant? It's just avarice—pure maya!'

Achyuta nodded in agreement—what else was this if it wasn't maya! But the torrent of the speech continued anyway, 'He's the maker of everything; can we undo anything when we run this rat race? If you were to take my advice, you should have had a bellyful of *pakhala,* fermented water rice, and spiced, roasted pond-fish and then slept quietly in the shade, with your feet up on your wife's lap, telling her to massage them and pay her respects to her husband. Did you ever enjoy that kind of bliss and happiness? What kind of happiness did you get in life? Every day it's the same old tale: hunger in the stomach and an inhibition that holds you back from asking; the hunger, after incessant roaring, dies there in the pit of your stomach. You can't even look people in the eye; and then, when you age, you'll not have an appetite and then you'll lament, "Why didn't I feed myself when I had the appetite? People who knew how, enjoyed themselves, while I kept picking up the empty shells!" Achyuta, do listen to me when I say the truth—this is life's well-kept secret!'

Helplessly Achyuta, the one-eyed oilman, looked around to all sides with a pinched face, then winced as he rubbed his hand over his stomach, 'Ah! There's a thief in my stomach; he's calling out!' He got up with his load of oil and broke into a run.

The bohu stood demurely before him with lowered eyes, and said in a low voice, 'Too much talk will cause harm to the body, do partake of the meal and sleep for a while . . .'

'Well, well, listen to these few words while we are alive, when else are you going to hear them? I have a tongue, so why will I *not* speak?'

He sensed a stab of hurt; people seemed to be misunderstanding him. Consumed in his thoughts, he smiled and told himself, 'What's strange about it? The mahatmas and the enlightened souls, too, were misunderstood; all of them. People, these people! The less you speak about them the better! Ignore what people say—you can't take the kink out of the dog's tail no matter how hard you try! What can you do about it? Yet one has to perform one's duty. That is the only way to spread the message of piety and righteousness. People will run away from you, saying that they don't like to listen to your words. But you'll have to run after them, nonetheless, pouring your dharmic truth into their ears. That's the only way to inject a sense of righteousness into them. If you throw in the towel, you'll be like all others—what then is the difference, how are your efforts any better?'

When he sat down to eat, he told the bohu, 'You can prepare chicken and chicken eggs for me, too. If I do have non-vegetarian meals, let me go the whole hog, why only this halfway mark?'

To the bohu's ears, his words were baffling. Pressing the end of her sari over her mouth, the bohu affirmed, *'Hau!'*

As he lovingly caressed the fishtail and extracted the meat, he suddenly remembered his dead wife. 'I would eat seventeen morsels before baulking at the food and turning my face away,' Chakrapani began, a dazzling smile lighting up his face. 'She would keep urging me to have some more, but I would refuse. I remember all that. So now have you got what you wanted?' He said it in such a matter-of-fact manner, as if talking face-to-face with his wife, that the bohu thought her mother-in-law was actually standing behind her. She instinctively looked over her shoulder and pulling the sari tightly over her head, spat thrice to dismiss the spectre.

The old man's rambling thoughts appeared surreal, 'You were coercing me, and I refused, but now I am giving in to you, so you'd better watch out for me—the next meal will be eggs for dinner. Hee! Hee! Hee!'

The bohu turned crimson, her ears burning, while a nameless fear gripped her. Trembling all over, she looked around with apprehension, as despair crept into her mind and she grunted to herself, 'Why doesn't he come home soon? Why all these importunities on a mere woman like me?' She hadn't been satisfied with writing letters to her husband; she had also run a messenger across to him. But there was no need for her to tell him. This unnatural development had already spread far and wide in the village and people champed at the bit to blazon the news abroad. Kambupani wasn't too far off, only sixteen miles away. If only he could come home. As a doctor he would be in a better position to handle the situation.

Kambupani's wife saw terror all around her.

Today Dandapani was mollycoddled and heaped with love and affection. He demanded he be allowed to skip school. 'Don't go, my darling, my wealth. Go, have your lunch and then go to sleep.'

The sun beat down eerily. When a raven started cawing on the rooftop, it felt as if it were telegraphing ill tidings; the right eyelid twitched. She couldn't bring herself to look at the picture of the divine pair hung on the wall of the small puja room. She couldn't look at the sandalwood-paste-smeared holy books that she worshipped either. Today, dread and fear seemed to lurk behind everything in the room. She prayed to the gods and goddesses to help her tide over all that was inauspicious.

Chakrapani stepped out and sat in the open. In the scorching heat of the sun, how cool the shade was! Ah! There is comfort here. Slowly his consciousness drifted back to places where he saw the connectedness—in the earth, the sky, the trees, the roof, birth, people; everywhere the mind longed to merge with them; how could he let go of this attachment? He saw new meaning in his thinking: that happiness in real life was better than all these imaginings; that shastras and samskara and values were lofty ideals held in store only for those who were non-achievers. Those who were denied sweets must learn that eating sweets could cause worms in the stomach. How simple was this statement! He was reminded of many such truisms. This is original knowledge, the new meaning of life, the new instruments to view this new philosophy. Had anyone seen it like this before? No, no one; he alone had been able to realize this, but it had come rather late in his life.

The krushnachuda tree was resplendent with flowers, but today it didn't remind him of Krishna. The limitless beauty of the world suffused his mind, the beauty that was within his grasp, but which he could never fully appreciate. The tree would continue to stand there and on the other side, the *kadamba,* burflower tree; there would remain the green tendrils of the potato vine on the fence, the dense foliage backed up all the way like a green trellis; ahead where the road curved under the rows of coconut trees, the ever-cool thatched houses haughtily stood, wherein was tucked the mystery of creation—where the light and the breeze shall always be felt. It would all remain but, unfortunately, he would not enjoy it. As if all the hidden, enticing memories were strewn before his eyes like vibrant flashbacks, the past leaped into view in the form of a string of *Not Achieved's* in multicoloured splinters of glass. Although broken, the shards were tough and smooth; the small, even the tiny granules, were luminous in their beauty, and in his look, the unfulfilled desires grew—and grew even bigger—to loom around vividly.

He could hear a bustle in the village. An aircraft was flying overhead, flying fairly low and the roar was distinct across the clear blue sky. All the people of the village—men, women and children—came out into the open, agog, craning their necks and looking up at the sky. The aircraft flew past and the people were lost, hidden in the hubbub of momentary excitement.

Chakrapani experienced helpless remorse. He shivered. He sensed his attachment to the people milling around him; one day, that too would snap and melt away. He wouldn't be able to see these faces; all these familiar faces, every one of them, would stay behind here. The solitary aircraft's roar sounded almost like it was the expression of the pain wrenching its entrails; the roar seemed to drip down from its heights to the earth, far, far below. People say life flies by in a flash: was it like this? Images of his inchoate ideas sprang to mind and fuzzily played around his consciousness in rapid succession: the chicken's egg, the tall coconut trees, the beautiful face of his loving wife on their wedding night that he so pined for now—and unbeknownst, it dawned on him that from here on he would have to wear a pair of trousers. Well, his son wore them, so that was no big deal.

His one lasting regret: Netai Ma's bohu hadn't turned up to see him and seek his advice. His breath troubled him. It seemed to have stopped momentarily as though he were trying to hold it back. Then he sensed a sort of tautness of a bowstring being pulled; his inner self jerked and rattled, he seemed to teeter at the edge, life ebbing away—and then it felt like it was there no more. No more there!

When the doctor arrived, he was still seated in the same position, leaning against the wall. His eyes were open. The news had set up a scramble; a crowd had collected and was swelling by the minute.

When his body was taken out in a procession, people exclaimed and marvelled at the enlightened soul he had been.

Originally titled 'Chakrapani', 1956

The Foreigner

D entist.
'Open your mouth. Just a minute or two little longer!'
Posters of various kinds of dentures screamed down from the walls. Cupboards full of teeth. And outside, inviting the passers-by a picture of two full sets of dentures, and his nameplate.

Peering through the curtains one saw a gentleman sitting amid all the teeth—a yellowish complexion, a flat nose and slanting eyes. His posture radiated an unusual calmness, and the face seemed forever tranquil. In the large country that is India, amidst its teeming multitudes in its various towns and cities and their diverse appearances, his appearance fits in, too. The slight variation, barely discernible, had been handed down to him by his forefathers.

The nameplate on the front announced 'Soong Wong, Dentist'. The people of the locality knew that he was Chinese—of Chinese extraction, but neither they nor the dentist himself had ever been to China. He has lived in this city for many years now. No one was curious to know anything more about him. He had established himself as a good dentist. Patients flocked to him; he worked hard and earned a lot of money. Although frugal in his expenditure, he wasn't miserly. He was involved in all the functions held in the community. He didn't owe anyone anything. He didn't have any enemies, nor did he belong to any group or sect—he largely kept to himself. This was, by and large, the impression that people of the locality harboured about him.

The Sino–India war had started. Soong Wong was as distressed as everyone else. He too contributed generously to the war fund. Normally, he didn't talk too much with others about anything but his work; and the war was no exception.

When war broke out, it impaired the equilibrium. He had felt anxious. Why was the number of his patients decreasing? Why were so many people curious about him all of a sudden? What was his connection with the country that had attacked India? He didn't understand Chinese, although he knows that his ancestors were Chinese and had lived in China; but that was long, long ago! The language that he used to speak with his wife and friends wasn't Chinese. He knew Hindi, Oriya, Bangla and English. He had studied in the English medium and could write English, sometimes not so correctly. He belonged to this country. Who has attacked India? They were such vile people! They flouted civilized norms and committed atrocities. Just like any other fellow citizen, he had nothing to do with them, not even remotely. Yet his looks drove a wedge between him and the rest; his face, for no fault of his, carried the legacy of his forebears, and people were now suddenly wary of him. His face and facial features had suddenly become the petard for him to be hoisted on!

He lived in the hope that the suspicion would fade with time and after a few days, his customers would come back. In fact, this turned out to be true; after a few days, they did come back. The war too had ended. Yet, at the bottom of Soong Wong's mind, there still lurked the dregs of anxiety. His heart at times skipped a beat. Did something ugly happen somewhere?

Soong Chung was his son. His friends teased him and called him Su-su, Chung-Chung. Except for his name, there was nothing Chinese about him. Neither his complexion nor his features looked Chinese and he blended in with the general populace. He was born in this city and grew up with the flock here. His behaviour, the clothes he wore, the food he ate and the language he spoke were all like the people he grew up with. He too spoke Oriya and read both Oriya and English. At home, he sometimes talked to his parents in their language. Sometimes he spoke in Oriya. Both languages were spoken at home.

He was very popular with his friends. A pleasant, fun-loving person, he excelled in both studies and sport. He wasn't haughty. He was never unwilling to extend a helping hand to those in need. His friends accepted him as one of them—they didn't hold his Chinese ancestry against him.

Soong Wong had two older daughters. Both were married and lived in Calcutta. The elder son-in-law owned a shoe store. The younger one had a machine shop. In this city lived Soong Wong, his wife and son, Soong Chung. Soong Wong himself had never gone to school or college. He wanted his son to study, become a doctor and specialize in dental care. This business that had been handed down for generations, beginning with his grandfather, would then grow effulgent, distinguishing him. He would be respected all the more. The boy did well in school and passed the matriculation and the pre-university examinations in the first class. In college, too, a first-class grade in the pre-professional examination. Thereupon, he applied to a college in another city to study medicine. Soong Wong had chalked out his son's future carefully and didn't want anything to go wrong.

Soong Chung's spirits were high when he went to spend his vacation in Calcutta with his friends and relatives. His elder sister jokingly called him Dr Chung! He laughed it away. The other sister, who was always keen to visit her parents, said a little sulkily, 'Yes, you'll become a doctor. Bapa didn't think of sending me to college! I too wanted to be a doctor!' She had four children. They jumped up and down in excitement and shouted, 'Doctor! Doctor!'

When the two of them were alone together after dinner, the younger sister's husband, Phu-Teh, said to him, 'Let's sit here and talk for a while. So, tell me, what's happening in your city?' There was a hint of covertness in his voice. It sounded odd.

Chung felt awkward and said, 'I've been talking the entire evening giving you all the news. What other news are you asking for?'

'Er . . . you've been talking about general things that people on the street talk about. That's not what I need. I want to know about specific things—about the relationships of our people with the others, the Sino-India relationship, how are things for you over there? What arrangements are you making for yourself?'

Soong Chung looked askance, 'Aren't we Indians too?'
he asked, his face sombre.

Phu-Teh scoffs. 'I can't comment on that, maybe you can!
It doesn't matter whether one is Indian or not. *Hindi Chini
Bhai Bhai!*'

Soong Chung's face flushed at this ironic remark. He said,
'No one thinks like that in my city. We're just like the others.
We don't have communal riots there either. It's not like here
where people are just looking for an excuse to go for the
jugular and indulge in arson and vandalism. And pelt stones
from under cover. We've never allowed our Chinese-ness to
otherize us!'

This time Phu-Teh's tone was sarcastic, 'That's deep-
seated patriotism indeed!' He laughed again. 'You may not
look upon yourself as a Chinese, but the people of this country
will still consider you as one! You may not be able to see your
own face, but others surely can!'

Soong Chung gulped a couple of times before asking, 'So
what're you implying?'

'The Chinese, too, have a country,' Phu-Teh said calmly,
'and that country isn't India.'

Soong Chung replied, 'Have you seen that country? Have
you ever gone there?'

'No.'

'Your father?'

'No.'

'Do you want to visit that country?'

'Why should I? Why are you asking me all these questions?
Who has seen the future? Who can say what tomorrow holds?
I may not have been to China, my grandfather may not have

been there either. Even then, China is the land of my forebears, and shall always remain so.'

'Do you know how the government functions there? Have you heard about what is happening there? Do you support all that is taking place there?'

'How can I comment on what is happening so far away without ever having seen it with my own eyes?' Phu-Teh replied. 'If you want to know more about that, come with me. I'll introduce you to someone who will fill you in with all the details. And then we can talk.'

Soong Chung's apprehension increased. In an attempt to evade his brother-in-law's invitation, he said, 'I'll have to leave for the station in a while. Neither I nor anyone in my family is curious about all these subversive details. It would be appropriate if you too didn't dabble in these matters. We have lived in this country for generations. We have nourished ourselves with food grown in this country. We have quenched our thirst with water from her rivers. Come what may—this is our homeland, our home! China is not our homeland; we do not belong there!'

Phu-Teh laughed, a jeering laugh. 'Well said!' His tone was equally sarcastic. 'Keep saying that to anyone who will care to listen! But what I'm saying is that you're an educated young man, not benighted like us. When you look beyond, you'll realize that the young don't merely bury themselves in their books but also pay attention to what is happening around them and chart out their paths accordingly. Visit us again and we'll continue this discussion.'

'I'm not interested in these inconsequential things,' Soong Chung riposted. 'I'm asking you too to not bother yourself with all this. Bapa will be very upset if he hears about your interest in these matters. You'd be meeting all kinds of people.

I've heard that there are many people who've been recruited by the Chinese government to work towards instigating people on the sly against India. The police, too, work secretly to round up such people. These matters are played out covertly by the citizens as well as the police.'

'Aha! So, you have heard of these things!' Phu-Teh exclaimed. 'But from the way you talk, you can be mistaken for an absolute greenhorn.'

Soong Chung was bristling. He had lost his temper and retorted, 'We seem to be talking at cross purposes. I know that this land, this country, this India, is mine. I'm an Indian. An enemy of this country is also my enemy. You may believe and think otherwise. But I'm ready to take a stand against an enemy and, if required, will not hesitate to turn him over to the police.'

'Good! You've been very well indoctrinated!' Phu-Teh's tone was acerbic.

Soong Chung continued, 'If anyone thinks differently, he should openly declare his loyalties; he should inform the government that he wants to migrate to China. Living here, like a snake in the grass is sheer cowardice. No, Phu-Teh, I refuse to be a snake.'

Phu-Teh's was conciliatory now. 'Brother, neither am I! But what do I do with this face of mine? When Indians start looking at all Chinese with suspicion, where will I hide? Therefore, I must be prepared beforehand. We cannot accomplish anything if we are not united. When I meet Bapa, I will convince him.'

'You know my father; it's better not to tell him any such thing. He is above all this. He believes that work is worship. Come what may, he won't budge from his ideals. You too should embrace those ideals, Phu-Teh, otherwise . . .'

Phu-Teh couldn't help cutting in. 'Otherwise what?'

Soong Chung calmed down. 'Nothing! Do whatever you think is right. You are ten years older than me. What advice can I give you?'

There was no further discussion on this that evening. But Soong Chung sensed that he and Phu-Teh stood on either side of a geo-cultural divide, and a Chinese wall had suddenly sprung up between them. Phu-Teh had revealed a lot about himself without using too many words. His behaviour, his body language, his derisive guffaws, his veiled hints—all of it together made sentences that swirled around. And defined who Phu-Teh was.

How much did his sister know? No, he wouldn't ask her; he would have to wait and watch. Better still, he would take his sister and his nieces and nephews back home with him. And then let things take their course.

Phu-Teh didn't object. They left with him. Phu-Teh stayed back.

Happiness and laughter filled Soong Chung's household. The daughter was visiting after a long time. Soon, the son would begin studying medicine. There would be a preliminary screening. They didn't have any apprehensions about Soong Chung getting past that. He was an extremely bright student. He had a first-class to boot. The few years he had to spend in medical college would pass in the blink of an eye—and then Soong Chung would be a doctor.

A list of all those who were selected to join medical college was published in the newspapers. Soong Chung's name was missing.

The father and son left no stone unturned to find out if there had been a mistake. Soong Chung insisted, 'There must be a mistake, or the application may have been misplaced. Look, so many of my friends are on the list. If they could qualify, how on earth could I not?'

After making umpteen inquiries, they discovered that neither had there been a mistake nor had Soong Chung's application been misplaced; but when the final list was prepared, his name which *was* on the list had been scored out. There was no way to find out why that had happened. But there must have been a valid reason, they thought— maybe some criteria that he hadn't fulfilled. There could be no other reason—certainly no injustice or partiality in the selection process.

Soong Wong came home and prostrated himself on the bed. A fever racked his body. He said, 'I can guess the reason, son. We are . . . no, no! I won't say it out loud! I will sleep.'

Soong Chung sat as if he had been turned to stone. His mother and sister were gently caressing his father as he slept. Phu-Teh's face danced before his eyes—his derisive, mocking laughter echoed in his ears.

From his bed, old Soong Wong shouted deliriously, while the fever ravaged him, 'Storm! A big storm is brewing! Is everybody safe?'

Originally titled 'Bideshi', 1963

Acknowledgements

We are grateful to Dr Bijay Ketan Patnaik, Dr Binodini Das, Shashikant Oak and Shrusti Mohanty (Sudeshna's daughter) for their timely and unstinting help whenever we asked them for it. Their efforts made it possible to deconstruct intricate Oriya words and thoughts, and helped us translate the stories into English.

At PRH, we are immensely grateful to Saloni Mital, our editor. She not only saw merit in the book but steered it through to publication every step of the way with her incisive suggestions. Without her assistance, this book wouldn't have been what it is now. We are also grateful to Vineet Gill, senior copy editor, for his editorial guidance and quick processing and printing. If the cover design of the book captures the essence of the title story, credit for the same rests with Ahlawat Gunjan, not us. Our long telecons and emails, battling the fog of ambiguity to grasp each other's perspectives, found a happy ending in this captivating cover.

Thank you all, thank you.

Sudeshna Mohanty
Sudhansu Mohanty

·